WINDSWEPT

Visit us at www.boldstrokesbooks.com

By the Author

McCall

London

Last First Kiss

Innis Harbor

Wild Wales

Laying of Hands

Return to McCall

Windswept

WINDSWEPT

by

Patricia Evans

2023

WINDSWEPT

ISBN 13: 978-1-63679-382-5

THIS TRADE PAPERBACK ORIGINAL IS PUBLISHED BY
BOLD STROKES BOOKS, INC.
P.O. BOX 249
VALLEY FALLS, NY 12185

FIRST EDITION: OCTOBER 2023

CREDITS
EDITOR: SHELLEY THRASHER
PRODUCTION DESIGN: SUSAN RAMUNDO
COVER DESIGN BY TAMMY SEIDICK

Acknowledgments

A huge thank you to my editor, Shelley Thrasher, who sanded the edges of my words until they fell silently together like a forgotten pool of silk and brought the story to life. This book is richer and more vivid because of your talent, and I'm so grateful.

And I owe the people of the Scottish Highlands a debt of gratitude. Thank you for always treating me as one of your own, saving me the red velvet chair by the fire, and finally sharing the secret of why all the beauty in Scotland is savage.

Dedication

This book is dedicated to you, my readers.

In a world increasingly filled with flashing screens
and endless media scrolling, you've chosen to retreat
from the chaos and sink into the book I've written
with you in mind. I'm endlessly grateful for the
time you spend with me, and I never forget
that we create these stories together.

The alchemy of my words and your unique
imagination sculpt an entire world out of
nothing at all, and that's just…magic.

I can't wait to see what we do next.

CHAPTER ONE

The air was heavy and eerily still for New Orleans. The early November haze of fading warmth shimmered as Sabine walked up the steps of The Immaculate Conception Church on Baronne Street, the click of her heels echoing against the stone floor in the nearly empty foyer. She checked her watch again, her other hand poised on the door handle to the sanctuary. The soft organ music halted as she opened the doors, and heads pivoted in her direction like a flock of owls as Sabine hurried up the aisle, sliding into the empty space beside her sister.

"Here." Colette handed her a program and returned her gaze to the platinum-toned casket at the front of the sanctuary, the top half open for viewing, the bottom section draped with ornate sprays of pink and ivory roses that nearly touched the floor. "You're late."

"And you're wearing a red velvet dress." Sabine kept her eyes on the podium as the priest started to ascend the steps. "To a funeral." She felt her sister's eyes on her. "And it's not even December."

Colette sighed and rubbed her temples with the pads of her fingers. "What do you want me to do?" She hissed, dropping her voice to a whisper when she heard the echo. "One of the boys knocked a bowl of oatmeal into my lap this morning, and I only have one black dress. It was either that or this Christmas dress."

"Well, at least take off that ridiculous mistletoe pin on the shoulder." Sabine shook her head as she reached over and unpinned the enameled holiday pin from Colette's dress and slipped it into her pocket. "That's a dead giveaway."

The priest began speaking as soft organ music started again in the background, and Sabine slowly let go of the breath she'd been holding onto like a secret. As if on cue, the heavy length of hair she'd pinned into a slick twist loosened and slid slowly down her back, the two warped pins she'd managed to find on the way out the door that morning reluctantly conceding defeat, hitting the floor behind her with a metallic ping.

"Fuck it," Sabine whispered as she reached back to pull her waist-length hair over her shoulder. Her aunt Thea wouldn't care if she didn't look perfect. Three years ago, they'd been strolling in Lafayette cemetery after church, the heat so dense it undulated in translucent waves over the crypts, when Thea had reached out and run her hand over the edge of a headstone. Sabine knew her aunt had something to say, and it was only a moment before she said it. Apparently, it worried her that Sabine's hair was always in such a tight knot. Sabine knew what she meant, but nothing was going to change, and they both knew it.

The priest's monotone voice faded into the background, and Sabine closed her eyes tight against the memory of Thea sitting on a wooden stool backstage at the theater last Christmas, straight pins dangling from the corner of her mouth.

Thea folded and smoothed the costume on the actress standing in front of her as if she were merely a dress form, and then Thea glanced over at Sabine painting a bronze railing detail on one of the set backdrops. Sabine felt her glance and put her brush down before she looked back at her over her shoulder. She knew when Thea had something to say.

"Sabine, you have that beautiful copper hair like a medieval heroine, and no one ever sees it. It's a damn shame."

Colette whispered in her direction as the priest paused to shuffle his papers, the words jerking Sabine back to the present like a swiftly turned page. "So how did it go this morning with the grande dame?"

She leaned into Colette's shoulder, tempering her volume for the mourners behind them clearly trying to catch every word. "Celestine was dramatic, as usual. I was late getting downstairs this morning, so by the time I finally made it, it was past time to leave."

"And she was showered, dressed, and ready to go?"

Sabine rolled her eyes, mentally pushing back the headache starting to throb behind her temples. "She'd wrapped herself in Thea's dressing gown and had just finished last night's bottle of vodka. She said she was 'just having a mimosa or two, darling,' but I'm pretty sure those aren't made with a rocks glass of straight Smirnoff and a mist of orange juice from that damn spray bottle over the top."

"Shit. I'm sorry." Colette shook her head and turned to look toward her. "I knew I should have been there. Of course, she'd make today all about her."

"Oh well." Sabine slipped her arm into her sister's. "Same shit…"

Colette smiled. "Different day."

They both returned their attention to the podium. Sabine's head pounded softly in time with her heart as she looked around at the pictures of Thea on wooden easels surrounding the casket. Backstage at Les Misérables with a seam ripper in one hand and a glass of chardonnay in the other, then on stage at a cast party in the eighties with the actors and crew, tossing a handful of glitter into the air that sparkled like diamond dust in the stage lights. There were even a series of photos from Manhattan when she was just beginning her career in theater as an apprentice costumer. Sabine smiled, grateful that her sister had chosen those particular photos to take center stage. Those were Thea's favorite memories.

Sudden sharp voices from behind the foyer doors ricocheted around the stone walls of the sanctuary, and every single head turned to look, with the marked exception of Sabine and Colette. The doors swung open abruptly, as if they'd been kicked, and Colette laid a cold hand over Sabine's and squeezed. A latecomer was stumbling down the aisle as if she were on her way to collect a Tony award, slurring greetings that were equal parts hushed and deafening as she followed a tilting floor to the front of the church. Silence fell around them as the priest accepted quiet defeat and closed his bible.

Tinted sunlight streamed through the stained-glass windows and illuminated her faded blond hair, rooted with steel gray, as she dragged the back of her hand over her mouth and smeared her lipstick across her left cheek. Her black dress was loose, half unzipped, her long string of dramatic pearls caught on the button closure and draped haphazardly down her back. She'd made her way to the front and up the two steps to where the casket was placed when she tripped suddenly and knocked over two of the easels holding Thea's photographs. She shot slurred apologies over her shoulder at the packed, silent pews as she leaned on the side of the casket with both hands to steady herself. Rose petals drifted to the stone floor of the church as she brushed the arrangement to one side, clearly to get a better look into the casket.

"Holy Mary, Mother of God…" Colette dropped her head into her hands and whispered through her fingers. "What is she *doing*?

Sabine just shook her head, her gaze locked on the woman rummaging through the casket as she reached through the satin curtain and tugged on Thea's arm. She turned around suddenly, as if crushed by the weight of the stares behind her, and shouted, her voice shrill and uncontrolled, the words flying from her mouth and clattering one by one across the stone floor.

"It's *mine!*" She said it again, as if the shocked silence she'd encountered was direct opposition, then turned back to the casket, finally freeing Thea's arm and holding it up in front of her. "It's mine, and she stole it when she dropped dead."

"Oh, God." Sabine grabbed the back of the pew in front of her and locked eyes with her sister. "It's the ring. She's after the ring."

❖

It was after dark when Sabine's mother, Celestine, finally passed out on the couch, both arms dripping over the side like spilled mercury. Sabine usually tried to police her nightly drinking, but after what had happened at the funeral, she was too exhausted to care. She finally managed to lead her to bed sometime after ten, still in the twisted, half-zipped dress she'd refused to take off. Sabine slid the trash can over to the side of her bed next to her and switched out the lights, pulling the door closed softly behind her.

On the way back to the kitchen, Sabine pried out a bottle of pinot grigio she kept hidden from her mother for emergencies and filled a glass pitcher of ice. She wandered out to the back porch of the house that would swallow two people and sank down alone onto one of the porch swings overlooking the shared courtyard. She ran her hand over the peeling white paint on the graying wood railing, the edges thin and sharp under her fingertips. Even in early November, the scent of damp grass still holding the warmth of the late afternoon sun drifted across the porch as she unbuttoned her shirt and let it slip down her back, leaving only the black silk camisole she'd worn underneath. The humidity settled onto her shoulders, finally attracting a breeze so light it felt like breath across her skin.

"Thought I'd find you out here."

The screen door creaked dramatically as Colette stepped out onto the porch, letting it slap shut behind her, her feet bare against the weathered porch boards. Sabine simply nodded and kicked off her own shoes, pushing them to the side of the swing. The boards were still warm from the heat of the day, and they bent slightly with a lingering creak as her sister sat in the slick enamel chair across from the swing.

Colette had thick, glossy, chestnut hair that their mother had always wanted her to dye blond. Sabine was the only redhead in the family, which had seemed to irritate their mother, although her sister had always been jealous. Once when they were teenagers lying on the porch roof, Colette had hissed that Sabine's hair always looked "shot through with sunlight, like the damn sun follows you around or something," which was ironic considering it was exactly nothing compared to Colette's presence. Her sister was taller than she was, with broad hips that made her look like one of those pioneer women that could mount a running horse without a saddle. She'd always appeared to be the leading lady; Sabine usually felt like she disappeared into the same backdrops she painted in the theater.

Colette nodded at the bottle in a silent question and reached over to pour the pale gold wine into the glass she'd brought outside with her. She settled back in the chair and tucked her hair behind her ear, and Sabine noticed that the tiny lines around her eyes were deeper tonight. Colette looked over at her with tired eyes. "Why the ice bucket?"

"Because I had to hide the bottle in the floorboards. It's roughly the temperature of bathwater."

"Lovely." Colette shook her head and dropped three cubes of ice into her glass. "I thought as much. How is she?"

Sabine didn't smile, the weariness finally settling silent and heavy onto her shoulders. She flicked a jagged flake of paint off the railing with her thumbnail and watched it float down onto the grass below before she answered. "Can you believe she asked me to make her a martini when we got home from the funeral?"

"She's out of control." Colette's words had jagged edges, as if they'd just been pried from the face of a cliff. She shook her head. "I mean, I expected her to spiral for a while after the accident, but it's been three damn years."

"I still can't believe Dad's been gone that long." Exhausted tears burned behind Sabine's eyelids, and she leaned back in the porch swing to catch more of the breeze coming in from the courtyard. "But losing him in that accident was always going to be too much for her to handle. We knew that."

"Bullshit." Colette's words were louder than her voice as she looked over at Sabine. "He's dead because she drove them home from the theater drunk that night. She should have used it as a wake-up call to get her shit together. It's the least she owed him. And us."

"I know." Sabine finally clinked a handful of ice into her forgotten glass and poured. She leaned back in the seat and pulled at a fraying thread on the faded blue-and-white-striped seat cushion, winding it around her thumb. "Thea would have hated that I'm still here. I moved back in only to make sure she didn't drown herself in vodka during the first few weeks after the accident. But every time I talk about traveling or getting a place of my own again, she has a meltdown." She paused, watching the bats weave a pattern over the courtyard before disappearing under the graying eaves of the Victorian mansion across the street. "I don't know what I'm supposed to do." She drew in a breath and held it. "I can't make her be okay with it, and I can't leave if she's like that."

"She's a grown woman, Sabine." Colette waved away a lightning bug as she spoke. "And we live next door, for fuck's sake. James is always asking me if she needs something done." She paused, her voice settling slowly into softness. "She's still acting like she's the same pampered actress she's always been, except now she's using you to avoid reality since Dad isn't here to help her do it. And you know he and Thea would hate that."

"But now she's just lost her sister, for fuck's sake." Sabine clinked the melting cubes against the thin crystal sides of her glass, tilting it to capture the shards of gold light from the courtyard lanterns. "I mean, I can't leave right now." Her fingertips were tense and white against the stem of the wineglass. "What kind of a person does that?"

"Sabine, you've been wanting to take a break from the theater to travel for ages now, and you and Thea were always talking about going to Scotland. I don't want you to have to stop living because Mom did." She paused. "I know how you are at work. You're a take-charge, badass artist. But somehow Mom just manages to take advantage of you. I hate it. And so did Thea."

Colette started to say something else but thought better of it and looked up at the stars dusted across the sky like blown ash. Children's laughter tinkled in the distance, and the faint scent of grilling steak still lingered in the air from down the block. "I guess I'd better get home before James puts the kids up for sale." She shot Sabine a smile and settled her wineglass on the side table. Colette had two sons, ages two and ten, that Sabine happened to know she adored. "Not that I'd blame him."

Colette stood and hugged her, then turned back once she reached the door. "I almost forgot." She reached into the pocket of her jeans and walked back to Sabine. I have something that belongs to you."

She took the black velvet box from Colette and turned it over in her hand. She followed a streak of dust along the edge with her finger and didn't look up as she spoke. "But this isn't mine."

"Yes, it is." All the emotion they should have had the chance to feel at the funeral shimmered between them in the darkness. "She adored you. You know that."

Her answer caught in her throat as she opened the box and saw the antique diamond-and-sapphire band set in white gold. It was simple, but brilliant even in the darkness, and exquisitely made. Thea had worn it for as long as Sabine could remember, and for some reason, her mother had always been obsessed with it.

"Thea wanted you to have it. She gave it to me a few weeks ago when the cancer-treatment center sent her to hospice. She didn't want it at the house for Celestine to find."

She nodded, and the cooling night air seemed to warm as she slipped it on her finger. She looked up at Colette. "Thank you for this."

Colette looked out into the courtyard as she opened the door, tracing a jagged hole in the screen with her finger. "She also said to remind you that"—she paused, as if to line up each word in her head—"only love is real."

"What the hell does that mean?"

Colette smiled. "I have no idea, and she wouldn't tell me. Just made me promise I'd pass along her message."

Colette's phone pinged with a text from her husband that said simply *SOS*. She looked up, already rolling her eyes. "Well, clearly something's on fire, so I'd better find a better place to hide. You want to go to brunch tomorrow?"

"I can't. I have an appointment in town. She glanced down at the ring on her finger, turning it slowly to watch the stones catch the light. "I don't know how'll long I'll be."

The screen door squeaked as Colette blew her a kiss and disappeared, already on the phone with her husband.

She listened for the front door to close and let out an exhausted sigh that disappeared slowly into the darkness.

As if it had never even existed.

CHAPTER TWO

S abine overslept the next day and barely had time to make it downtown into the French Quarter to keep her appointment, twisting her hair into a hurried bun as she walked. Café du Monde flew by on her right as she hurried over the cobblestone streets and dodged a horse-drawn tourist carriage. She had to remind herself twice that even the idea of ditching a meeting with her aunt's lawyer in favor of the hot, melting deliciousness that was Café du Monde beignets was wholly inappropriate. Still, the rich, darkly roasted scent of coffee drifted across the road and followed closely as a reminder of what she could have if she could muster up the stones to blow off her meeting.

But whatever something like that took, Sabine didn't have it. She wasn't a risk taker, and she didn't like surprises—maybe because her dramatic mother had always provided her plenty of risks and surprises, even as a child, but in any case, it stuck. Sabine was the lead set dresser at The Orpheum Theatre, which her family had owned since it opened its doors for Vaudeville Acts in 1921, and her staff knew to bring any potential problems to her attention immediately so zero surprises occurred on opening nights. She was the boss on every one of her sets, chose every brushstroke of every backdrop, and had been called a control freak more than once, but over the last few years, her life had shrunk around her until it consisted of just the theater and her mother. No one could control the chaos that was Celestine, so any other deviation, especially romantic entanglements, had become too much to even think about.

The Rowan family had also owned two additional theaters for most of Sabine's life; her father Jacques Rowan had the Orpheum and the Marigny Opera House, but the latter had been sold to a restoration company after Hurricane Katrina nearly decimated the interior. Thea had also purchased the historic and very opulent Joy Theater in the nineties but had quietly sold it for an undisclosed sum the previous year when she was diagnosed with cancer.

Sabine used to secretly dream of getting the hell out of the theater, but over the years she'd grown to love creating sets; she was the first to read the scripts and spent weeks visualizing how she wanted the stages to look. The backdrops for every scene and set change were all hand painted, the stage flowers fresh, and the stage furniture sourced and perfected down to the smallest detail. Sabine even worked with a local perfumier to pipe in scents that drifted over the audience at the perfect moment, like an acrid waft of diesel for a scene set in Manhattan, or a crisp pop of frying bacon for a home kitchen, which dissipated quickly and drifted silently up to the open three-story, gilded ceilings.

Sabine made a sharp turn down a quiet brick alley so narrow she could touch both walls with her arms outstretched. Freshly watered ferns and hot-pink azaleas from the overhead balconies dripped humid moisture down the crumbling stucco walls, and the copper railings were heavy with slivery green patina. The brick buildings on both sides blocked the glare of the morning sun, and she paused to dig the address out of her leather backpack. The strap slid off her shoulder as she watched a waiter at her favorite café roll up its awnings, shaking the dew from the red-and-white-striped fabric. Henri's.

I could totally still blow this off.

Truthfully, she had no idea what this meeting was about, but she assumed it was something to do with settling her aunt's estate. Her mother was counting the days until the reading of her sister's will and had said so several times as she was escorted out of Thea's funeral. Sabine glanced down at the sapphire-and-diamond band on her left hand. She didn't even know if she wanted to go to the reading; the fact that Thea had wanted her to have the ring was enough for her.

She gave Henri's another wistful glance as she pressed the brass call button to the left of the black lacquered door. Surely, she was needed for only a signature or something simple, although Colette was the executor of Thea's estate, and it occurred to her suddenly that if that were the case, it was odd she hadn't mentioned anything the night before on the porch.

The door buzzed, and Sabine heard the lock click back. She pushed it open and followed a narrow hall to the last door on the left, also painted in a mirror-finish black enamel and with a gold metal plate engraved with *Ms. Katherine Boudreaux, Esq.* The taller door to her right was the same but marked *Private.*

She smoothed a wisp of hair away from her face, then sighed and tucked it behind her ear when it slipped back.

"Oh, for heaven's sake." The deep, feminine voice from behind the door was as unexpected as a surly ghost popping around the corner. "Just come on in, Sabine."

Sabine looked up and spotted the tiny black camera in the nearest corner. She knocked lightly to be polite and stepped into the office, closing the door after her. The woman behind an expansive mahogany desk looked her up and down and, surprisingly, flashed a genuinely warm smile as she invited Sabine to sit. She was in her late sixties perhaps, with wavy silver hair bobbed to her chin. Perfect lipstick that could only be described as a Parisian scarlet was her only pop of color, although it was all she needed. Her ivory skin was luminous, with beautiful lines around her eyes that made Sabine think she laughed loud and often.

"Well," Katherine said after she'd introduced herself and offered Sabine a coffee. Sabine had politely declined and chosen the glossy tufted-leather chair across from the desk. "You're probably wondering what all this is about."

"A bit," Sabine answered honestly. "Although you mentioned it was something Thea needed from me specifically, so I'm sure she had a reason."

"You could say that." Katherine rolled up the sleeves of her French-cuffed, white, button-up shirt and lifted the collar into a delicate frame for her face as she spoke. "You'll forgive me for the early hour. Thea was quite specific about every detail of this process, so I'm fitting you in before I start seeing my regular clients this morning to ensure absolute privacy."

Sabine squinted as a sudden beam of golden sunlight fell from the window and across her face. She shifted in her seat and leaned out of its path. "What process?"

"First of all, Thea assured me that you are in possession of a valid passport. Is that correct?"

Sabine watched as she opened a leather portfolio and shuffled the papers inside until she found the one she was looking for. She slid on a pair of slim, black-framed, reading glasses and peered over the stack of papers in her hand at Sabine.

"Oh, sorry." Sabine pulled herself back into the present. "She's right, of course. I do have a valid passport, although it's a waste of paper. I've yet to step foot outside the country."

The office door opened suddenly, and a tall, olive-skinned man with chiseled abs and wet, tousled dark hair stepped in, his gaze fixed on Katherine. He was shirtless, wearing just a faded pair of Levi's low on his hips, and carrying a mimosa so cold it had already frosted the slim crystal flute.

"Your mimosa, my love." He held the flute out to Katherine and kissed her hand before he let her take it.

No way that guy is a day past twenty-five, Sabine thought as she directed her attention out the window to hide her smile.

"Horatio, darling." Katherine sat back in her chair and smiled as she gestured to Sabine, whose chair had been mostly obscured behind the door as he opened it. "Please say hello to Sabine Rowan. She's my first client this morning."

Horatio turned around in clear surprise and flashed a bright smile. "And a beautiful one, as well." He paused. "Would you also like a mimosa?"

Sabine smiled in return and shook her head, barely able to contain a subtle snort of laughter until Horatio was safely out the door.

"My apologies," Katherine said, taking a delicate sip of her drink and setting it at the corner of her desk. "I'm not usually meeting with clients until nine o'clock, so he thought I was alone, I'm sure."

"No apologies necessary." Sabine smiled, warming to Katherine in the span of a second. "That's the most entertainment I've had this week."

"Well." Katherine set the sheath of papers between them on her desk and placed a blue-enamel fountain pen on top. "Let's get to it then, shall we?"

Sabine nodded, suddenly very aware of a shift in the energy around them, almost as if Thea had walked into the room and perched on the edge of the desk, her gaze fixed on Sabine.

Katherine took her glasses off for a second and looked across the desk, her gaze warm and comfortable, as if they'd known each other for much longer than they had.

"Before I line everything out, I need to tell you that I'm only here to ensure Thea's wishes are carried out, insomuch as possible. So please know that Thea has approved everything we discuss today, but I can't provide insight into the reasoning behind it beyond the legalities of the situation."

"Are you talking about her will?" Sabine asked, suddenly aware that her sister hadn't mentioned the meeting because she wasn't made aware of it. "Shouldn't everyone else be here for this?"

"No. This is just for you. The actual reading of the will isn't until next week."

Sabine shifted in her chair, unable to think of anything to say, despite the swirl of questions clouding her mind like a silent dust storm.

Katherine slid her glasses back on face, then peered over them at Sabine.

"You look pale, dear. Would you like a glass of water?"

Sabine shook her head.

"Well, let's get on with it, then, shall we?" Katherine looked at the brass diver's clock on her desk and turned it around to face Sabine. "It's 8:10 a.m. now, and you have a lot to do in the next three hours."

"What are you talking about? I have to be at the theater in—" Sabine glanced at her bare wrist out of habit. "Well, at some point this evening anyway, and I'm already behind because of the funeral."

"You may wish you'd said yes to that mimosa after you hear what I'm about to say." Katherine passed an identical leather folder across the desk to her and waited until she picked it up. "Your aunt is leaving a portion of her estate to your sister, of course, as well as paying off her mortgage and setting up trusts for her children. But for you, she wanted to do something different."

"She knows I hate surprises." Sabine felt the blood drain from her face. "Why would she do this to me?"

Katherine walked around to the front of the desk and sat in the other leather chair next to Sabine. "She told me as much. It may make you feel better here that she's giving you a choice with this bequest." She paused, clearly choosing her words carefully.

"But if you'll take some advice from someone who knew Thea very well?"

Sabine nodded and glanced at the ceiling, fighting a ridiculous urge to cry.

"Instead of asking why Thea would do this *to* you—" Katherine reached over her desk for a tissue and handed it to Sabine. "Perhaps consider why Thea would do this *for* you."

"Of course." Sabine nodded, trying to calm her breathing. "I must sound like an ungrateful child."

Katherine shook her head, her voice softening. "What it sounds like is that you've had a lot on your plate for way too long. You're overwhelmed, and it makes sense that you would be."

"Oh, God." Sabine looked up slowly, shame draping itself like a weighted blanket across her shoulders. "You were at the funeral yesterday, weren't you?"

Katherine nodded, then returned to her chair on the other side of the desk. "I'll get straight to the point. Your aunt has a proposition for you." She took one stack of stapled papers out of her leather folder and put it on one side of the desk in front of Sabine. "When you leave this office today, you can choose to stay in New Orleans and return to life as you know it. If you do that, your inheritance from your aunt will be set at the sum of $5,000, which you will receive immediately."

Sabine nodded. The idea of living returning to normal sounded fine. Whatever that was.

"If you decide to be brave, and I highly recommend you do, the situation will be very different." She paused as if weighing every word. "In typical Thea style, your aunt has thrown down a challenge for you."

"A challenge?"

"Yes." Katherine picked up an engraved chrome pen from her desk and spun it slowly through her fingers. "Starting now, you'll have three hours to go home, pack a bag, and gather your travel documents. I'll send a car and driver to collect you at precisely 11:15 a.m. at the door of your house to take you to the airport, where a ticket will be waiting for you. Your driver will have the details of which airline when you get there. You must tell no one that you're leaving, including Celestine or your sister."

"No one?" Sabine realized her mouth was open and closed it, shaking her head slowly as if that might clear the fog. "You *must* be joking."

"I assure you, Ms. Rowan, that I am not." Katherine took a sip of her mimosa and then another, pausing to admire it before she set it back down. "Your aunt chose your destination. You'll stay for the duration of one year, and you're free to return on November 1st, 2024."

Sabine sighed and dropped her gaze to the leather folder in her lap. She used to dream of traveling, and Thea had always encouraged her to, but no way in hell was she leaving now.

"In addition, for the next year, you must communicate only with your mother through handwritten letters. You may call or email anyone else at your discretion once at your destination." She paused, slowly closing the leather folder. "And I will, of course, pay a visit to your family this evening and let them know what's going on, as well as your employer. I assume you have an assistant set dresser that can take over?"

Sabine nodded. "Work isn't the issue. I have a capable assistant who is ready to step up. But I can't just walk out." She realized too late she was talking more to herself than Katherine. "My mother would literally fall apart."

Katherine held Sabine's gaze until it dawned on her, layer by layer, that her mother was the reason Thea wanted her to get the hell out of the country. Her mother was the reason for *all* of this.

"Rest assured, Thea left directives for proper medical care for your mother, as well as provisions for rehab and counseling should she choose to take advantage of it. But ultimately, it's her choice."

"Yeah," Sabine said, her voice heavy with worry. "That's what I'm afraid of."

"If you follow your aunt's directions, $500,000 will be deposited into your bank account at the end of the year, whether you choose to stay or leave. In addition, you'll have a generous monthly stipend while you're there."

Katherine pulled a separate sheath of papers from the folder and looked them over before she went on.

"Thea signed a contract for the sale of her house a few weeks ago. I understand you and Colette were informed of that fact?"

Sabine nodded, gripping the arms of the chair to stop her mind from spinning.

"That money will be split between you and your sister and will be available to you should you choose to purchase your own real estate either during your year abroad or when you return to New Orleans." She paused. "I'll handle those details should that situation arise."

Thea had always been good with money and investments and had taught Sabine to follow in her footsteps. Money like that could set her up for life if she invested it wisely, and all it would take was a year of her life. The first ripple of excitement moved through her chest like breath, then stilled instantly when she remembered Celestine at the funeral.

Katherine nodded toward the brown leather folder still in Sabine's hands. "I know this must feel overwhelming, but everything you need to take the first steps is in that folder." She looked intently at Sabine. "Your aunt set up an account for you with her bank here in New Orleans. You'll find the debit card inside. I'll use that account for the stipend deposits, so you'll have instant access via the card wherever you are."

Sabine sat back in the chair and closed her eyes. The words felt stuck in her throat.

"So, she expects me just to pack a bag and leave for an entire year?" She paused, staring out the window until she could string together the words. "Why would she offer me an opportunity like this when she knows I can't take it? She knows how bad my mother's gotten. She'll drink herself to death if I leave."

"Sabine." Katherine stood and came around to lean against the front of her desk. It was a while before she answered. "May I be frank?"

Sabine nodded, half wishing she'd ditched this trainwreck of a meeting and gone to Café du Monde when she had the chance.

Katherine met her gaze with kind eyes, and her voice was the type of soft that you offer when you know the words have sharp edges.

"It's not your job to fix your mother's alcoholism."

"But—"

Katherine held up her hand, and Sabine had the good sense to close her open mouth.

"I know it feels like that right now, but if you continue to enable her and let her live with no consequences, she *will* drink herself to death. Celestine must choose to come out on the other side of this and fix what's really wrong. She either will or she won't. You can't do it for her."

Katherine walked back around her desk and sat, pushing a discreet black, leather-covered box of tissues across the desk to her.

Sabine took two, knowing there was nothing else to say. Katherine and Thea were adamant that she flit off to God knows where; Sabine was certain that wasn't an option. She saw no middle ground.

"I think I understand everything as well as I can at this point." She kept her eyes on the folder in her hand. "I'll think on it."

"You don't have long. The driver will be in front of your house at 11:15 a.m. and will wait for exactly five minutes. After that, the opportunity will no longer be available to you."

"I understand."

Sabine stood, slipping the leather folder into her bag. Just as she touched the door, she heard Katherine clear her throat, and she turned to look back at her.

Katherine slid the brass cap back on her fountain pen and met her eyes. "It's not often someone works their entire life to make sure you don't miss out on yours." She hesitated. "Don't let her down."

Sabine started to reply but had nothing left to say. She stepped through the door and closed it behind her, the click echoing in the empty hallway.

CHAPTER THREE

A fter she'd let herself into the house, Sabine stopped on the way to her room to check on her mother. Celestine still wore the dress from the day before, but she'd managed to twist the blankets around herself and pull her pillow over her head to block the sunlight. Sabine walked in, just close enough to be sure she was still breathing, and looked at her watch. She had just over two hours now.

Why am I even checking the time? She backed out of the room as her mother stirred in her bed. *It's not like I can go.*

When she got to her room, she had to tell herself not to slam the door behind her. Everything looked smaller, somehow, a little worn at the edges. She opened the chipped wooden shutter doors to the narrow, ivy-covered balcony overlooking the street and squinted in the sudden sunlight. Dust drifted silently in the wide beam of light that poured like liquid over her bed, coming to rest in a warm pool on the hardwood floor.

Sabine pulled open her desk drawer and rifled around until she finally found her passport in the back corner. The fantasy travel itineraries she'd been planning for months before the accident had been shoved to the back of the desk drawer with her passport. Sabine picked it up carefully and turned it over in her hand, leafing through the pages. They were all blank, the pages crisp and perfect, not stained with off-center ink stamps and creased edges from being tossed back in a travel bag. She'd always thought that seemed wrong; passports were meant to be a creased, inky jumble, not perfect, lonely squares kept in a dark drawer for the someday that would never arrive.

She tossed it onto her bed and dug the rucksack she'd bought for her trips out of the back of the closet. It still had the tags on it. The sunlight dappled the surface, and Sabine brushed the cobwebs from the shoulder straps, the sound of her fingertips moving across the rough nylon jarring and out of place in the silence.

I can't possibly be thinking about this.

Sabine picked up the bag but stopped just before she tossed it back inside, her fingers tense and white around the cool edge of the closet door. Something was rising in the back of her mind, moving swiftly toward the surface, like air bubbles billowing to the surface of the ocean. The accident had been the start of Celestine's downward spiral, but the sudden realization that there might not be an end filled her with a bright flash of anger, the ripples spreading like fire, destroying the glassy surface of denial she'd worked so hard to protect.

Sabine stepped back, closed her fingers around the rucksack tags, and ripped them off. The stiff paper sliced her hand as it jerked through it, and blood dripped down her palm. She stood there, staring, until the first drop landed on the splintered hardwood floor. Then she looked at her watch.

❖

Two hours later, Sabine threw the overfilled rucksack over her shoulder and raced down the stairs as quietly as possible. She peered through the front window to see that the driver was already parked outside of her door in a black Escalade, talking on his phone as he glanced at his watch. The minutes pounded in Sabine's chest like a second heartbeat; she didn't need to look at her watch again to know it was 11:17 a.m. She had exactly three minutes to open the door and walk down the front steps of her house. The bag felt foreign and heavy on her shoulder as she reached for the doorknob.

"Sabine!"

Sabine curled her fingers around the cold metal and pressed her eyes shut against the sound.

"Don't try to act like you're not there." Her mother's voice hardened midair. "I heard you come down the stairs."

The rucksack dug into Sabine's shoulder, and she switched it to the other side as she glanced back at her mother's open bedroom door. She traced the outline of the passport in her pocket with her fingers and felt the pages bend under her touch.

"I've had an accident, darling. Can you come help me?"

Sabine let the rucksack fall off her shoulder and walked to the open door. A surge of anger welled inside her, but she shoved it down just as quickly, forcing herself to shake it off. *She can't know what's going on. It's not like she's doing it on purpose.*

And maybe it was a sign, anyway. Sabine looked back at the overstuffed rucksack on the floor. What was she thinking? As much as she loved Thea, she couldn't just abandon her entire life in New Orleans and run off to God knows where. Maybe her mother was saving her from a moment of insanity before it was too late.

She took a long breath and stepped into Celestine's bedroom. The bed was bare, stripped down to the mattress with a dark yellow stain in the middle, the sheets in a lifeless tangle on the floor. Her mother was sitting in the darkest corner of the room with the curtains drawn, smacking a box of Camel Lights against the palm of her hand.

"Sab, love, I've had a little accident." She crossed her legs, her unzipped funeral dress from the day before falling off the sharp edge of her shoulder. "I'll just sit over here until you get it changed."

Celestine didn't look at her as she spoke. She clicked the chrome lighter over and over until it finally it flamed to life, then leaned back in the chair as she inhaled the acrid first drag, exhaling silken gray smoke through her nostrils toward the ceiling like some medieval dragon.

Sabine looked at the latest stain, overlapping the previous ones by a wide margin.

"Sabine?" Her mother flicked her cigarette into an imaginary ashtray, rubbing her forehead hard with her fingertips. "I'd like to get back into bed. I feel like I've been run over by a truck."

Sabine waited until her mother looked up before she answered.

"No."

Celestine's head whipped around. "What do you mean, 'no'?"

The smell of urine rose with the late morning heat, and Sabine met her mother's gaze before she replied. "Just…no. I'm done."

Sabine felt the world turn under her foot as she whirled around and walked out the front door, only to sink slowly down to the steps as she closed it behind her.

The driver was gone.

CHAPTER FOUR

*F*uck. Sabine leaned back against the door and shut her eyes. *I can't believe I finally stood up to her, and it doesn't even matter. It's too late.*

She let the rucksack fall off her shoulder and pulled her passport out of her pocket, swiping at the sudden burn of tears falling past her lashes with the heel of her hand. She opened the stiff cover and turned the blank pages slowly. Suddenly, the only thing she wanted in the world was to see them smudged with stamps, like she'd seen when she leafed through Thea's passport as a child. She wanted to know what it felt like to walk off a plane into a country she'd never been to, to create her own life somewhere like she conjured theater sets from blank backdrops, from the sheer expanse of nothing. But most of all she wanted not to have let Thea down.

"If you want to catch that plane, you're going to have to get in the car."

Sabine's head snapped up to see Katherine leaning against the door of a gunmetal gray BMW in glossy black stilettos, leather folder in hand.

"But it's past time." Sabine's words fell out in a rush as she scrambled to her feet. "I missed the driver."

Katherine pointed to her watch and waved her toward the car as she opened her door. "You didn't miss him. He left early.

He called me before you got out here and told me he forgot to pick up your damn travel folder, so I came for you myself."

Sabine heard the front door of the house open as she reached the car. She turned back around and locked eyes with her mother for just a moment. A bottle of vodka already dangled from her fingers. Sabine slid onto the cool leather of the backseat and shut the door.

Katherine turned around, her voice gentle. "Stay or go, Sabine?"

Sabine didn't look at her, and she didn't look at her mother. She kept her eyes locked on the road ahead until she heard herself say the only two words that mattered. "Just go."

"Here you are, ma'am." The airline receptionist, or whatever the hell they were called, handed Sabine two boarding passes. "One of the boarding passes is for your flight to Atlanta, that's the one on the top, and the second is for your flight to Edinburgh. Looks like there are no delays for either at the moment, so it should be a smooth trip."

"As in Scotland?" Sabine turned the boarding passes over in her hand. "Edinburgh, Scotland?"

"Yes, ma'am."

The woman looked pointedly over Sabine's shoulder to the next person in line. Sabine stepped away as she folded the boarding passes into her passport and dropped them into the interior pocket of her jacket. Given what Katherine had told her, she knew she'd be heading out of the country, but now it was loudly real. It was on the paper in her hand. She was all in, and there was no going back.

It's not like she'd never traveled. She'd been to New York twice to visit Thea while she was working Broadway shows. But she'd never traveled alone, and she'd never set foot outside the

US. As she dropped her backpack, jacket and shoes into the pale-gray plastic bin at security, she tried not to focus on the fact that she still had time to walk back out of the airport like a sensible person.

Thea had spent her junior year of college abroad at Aberdeen University, and when Sabine was little, she'd tell her wild stories about her time there, weaving in tales of dragons, her favorite castle in Edinburgh, and fantastic mythical creatures. They'd always planned to go back together, but after the accident that killed her father, everything changed, and then Thea was diagnosed with lung cancer. It just never happened.

By the time Sabine found her gate they were already boarding the last rows. She didn't have time to think, not that she could have if she wanted to. The second she clicked the seat belt across her lap she felt like she couldn't keep her eyes open. She leaned her head against the cool glass of the window and closed her eyes to stave off the headache brewing like a dark windstorm, not opening them again until the plane touched down in Atlanta.

Sabine had only a short window to catch her connecting flight at the Atlanta airport, which turned out to be the size of a small country. By the time she reached the right terminal, she was out of breath from sprinting through the halls, and the rucksack filled with lead on her back was digging permanent ruts in her shoulders. She slowed when she spotted her gate, dug her boarding pass out of her jacket pocket, and checked the number. E13. She joined the line of shuffling travelers already boarding and tried to ignore how her heart was pounding and tightening at the same time. The scanner beeped, the flight attendant waved her on, and Sabine slipped out of her pack to carry it by hand.

The crush of people through the walkway was intense, and the air seemed to thin the closer she got to the arched entrance of the plane. She moved to the side to catch her breath, which seemed to make it worse. The more she tried, the more breathless she grew, and she slid down the makeshift wall of the walkway to the ground. A few of the last passengers to board stopped to ask if she needed help, but Sabine just shook her head and did her best to look normal. She waited until everyone had gone and the walkway was empty before she stood.

How do you make yourself do something that will change every single thing about your life?

A male flight attendant who looked like he belonged on the cover of a Harlequin paperback leaned out of the entrance and caught her eye before he walked over to where she stood and held out a bottle of cold water with one hand and a mini bottle of Jack Daniels with the other.

"Scared to fly?"

Something about his soft Southern accent made her take a deep breath before she answered. "I know this sounds crazy, but I'm more scared of the destination." She took the water bottle and twisted off the cap. "I'm scared this is all just too hard. Once I step onto that plane there's kind of no going back."

Sabine was suddenly very aware that she was talking to a stranger and must sound insane. Well, not quite a stranger. His name tag said Britney B., and he was clearly as gay as the locker room of the Ice Capades. That was something.

"I get it." He nodded, polishing the face of his watch with his shirtsleeve as if the plane had suddenly been delayed by an hour. "My dad's a preacher here in Atlanta, and he had big dreams about me becoming the next Jerry Falwell or some shit." He looked over at her and dropped the tiny bottle of bourbon into her jacket pocket. "Change is hard. But so is staying where you don't belong." He paused, then smiled as he picked up her rucksack and held it out to her. "You've just gotta choose your hard."

❖

The second Sabine landed in Edinburgh, her phone vibrated with a stream of texts from her sister.

She ignored the alerts, scanning the terminal for a place to sit and get her bearings. She dodged an onslaught of laughing tourists streaming out of duty-free and ducked into Costa Coffee. There was no line, which seemed like a miracle, so she ordered and sank into the last empty seat, a small corner booth with an empty paper cup in the center. A server dropped off her coffee, and Sabine had just wound her hair into a soft bun when the phone in the pocket started ringing again.

"Hey, Colette," she said as she picked up the phone, then had the good sense to immediately hold it away from her ear.

"Oh my God. Where the hell are you?" Colette paused for a sudden gulp of air. "I've been losing my mind since that woman showed up and said you'd made a break for it." Colette's trademark half-shout half-whisper kicked into gear, almost certainly a vain attempt at not waking her toddler. "What the hell *happened*? Tell me everything!"

Sabine sank down into the seat, braced her knees on the back of the seat in front of her, and rubbed her forehead. "First, tell me what you know so far."

"Nothing." Colette paused for dramatic effect. "I know jack shit. Thanks for that."

"Colette. Surely you know I had no choice."

"Well, that's what that fancy lawyer who showed up to my house last night said. That, and that you're out of the country for the next year, courtesy of Thea."

"Well, congratulations." Sabine unrolled the top of her rucksack and peered inside, hoping she'd had the sense to pack some aspirin close to the top. "You now know everything I know."

"Bullshit. You're not getting off that easy. She wasn't telling us something. I saw it in her face, so spill it." Her staccato stream of words skidded to a sudden stop. "Wait. First tell me where the hell you are right now."

"I just flew into Scotland." Sabine glanced at the only signs she saw from inside the coffee shop, one directing travelers to

Customs, and another to Ground Transportation, both with arrows pointing in the same direction. "And I guess I'm going to find a place to stay until my head stops spinning, and maybe see that castle Thea always talked about. Edinburgh Castle, I suppose." She paused, pulling her rucksack closer as a cluster of people pressed by her on the way to the counter. "And after that, I don't know. I guess I'll just figure it out."

Sabine heard her sister tapping her nails, as she always had when nervous, and pictured her sitting in the dark at her kitchen table, absentmindedly flicking her children's toys onto the floor.

"So, the lawyer said Thea chose the destination, and all this has something to do with Mom." Colette took a long breath, and her voice softened. "You're going to have to connect the dots for me here because I'm lost."

"I honestly don't know much more than what you just said, but I'll fill you in on the details I do have." Sabine blew the surface of her coffee, then put Colette on speaker as she took the first sip and scalded the hell out of her tongue. She fanned at her mouth with her hand for a few seconds, which did absolutely nothing, then went on. "Thea set it up so I'd inherit a small sum from her estate if I stayed in New Orleans, or I could pack a bag and leave the country for a year. If I chose to do that, I'd inherit a shit ton of money at the end of that time." She paused. "Oh, and I can't call or email Mom for the entire year. We can communicate through letters, but apparently, that's it."

The phone was suddenly quiet. Sabine pushed her cup to the center of the table and rubbed her tired eyes with the heel of her hand. She decided to just let the silence settle. She didn't have the energy for anything else.

"Thea is a goddamn genius." Colette's voice sounded like her smile. "I think I get it now."

"Really? Well, that makes one of us." All the breath in Sabine's body drained out in a slow sigh as she leaned back in the booth, staring at the buzzing fluorescent strip light above her.

"Keep me posted on everything, okay?" She took a deep breath, unsure if she wanted an answer to her next question. "And you are going to check in on Mom, right?"

"I will. I promise." The softness in Colette's voice hardened, as if it might shatter and fall to the floor. "Not that she deserves it. After you left yesterday, she walked right into my house and raided my liquor cabinet. I found her passed out under the kitchen table when I came back from the park with the kids." Colette started to go on, then paused. "So just for the record, you made the right choice."

"I don't know, Coco." Sabine stared at the blur of people rushing past the coffee shop. "I don't have a clue what the hell I'm doing here."

"You'll figure it out." Sabine closed her eyes and smiled at the warmth in her sister's words. "If there's one person in the world who can make something beautiful from nothing, it's you."

CHAPTER FIVE

After the disaster that was Customs and Immigration, where Sabine nearly had a heart attack digging for her missing passport at the very bottom of her bag, she finally found the signs for Ground Transport and followed them out of the airport. Frozen diesel fumes clung to her as she walked past taxis waiting in a queue along the curb and buses that rushed by at lightning speed with a permanent lean on their horns. An attendant pointed her to the next taxi in line, and she slid into the backseat, slamming her door shut against the chaos outside. The driver looked back and reached for his seatbelt.

"Where to, love?"

Sabine's mind was blank. She had no idea, which was clearly not the answer the driver was waiting for as he continued to peer back at her from the rearview mirror. He spotted a break in the traffic and merged into the undulating flux of vehicles headed for the exit, then looked back at her again, his gaze flicking between the front window and the rearview mirror.

"Shit, I don't know." Sabine braced herself for him to roll his eyes, but he just nodded as he unwrapped a caramel he'd plucked from the pile in his cup holder and popped it into his mouth. He was older, with a gray beard and a bright, quick smile.

"Aye," he said, whipping them into the center lane as they approached the airport exit. "Let's go at this a different way, then." He looked up as she nodded. "I assume yer headed toward Edinburgh proper?"

"I think so." She paused. "Yes."

"Alreet. Da ye 'ave a place ta stay lined up?"

Sabine shook her head, suddenly overwhelmed with all the change. She felt frozen, like she was watching a rising wave gather power and loom over her in the dark, shifting sea. She tried to focus, tried to just seem normal, but tears burned her eyes as she braced for the impact of yet another wave.

"Na worries, lass. That's an easy one." He smiled into the mirror and shot her a wink. "Let's start there, yeah?"

He explained the difference between hotels and hostels as he wove in and out of traffic, and she chose the hostel option. Sleeping in a dorm with people she'd never met was the least weird thing to happen in the last twenty-four hours, so why not? Being alone in a hotel room in a foreign country was only going to make her feel lonelier. She stared out of the window, watching the cars pass, letting herself sink into the feeling she'd been fighting. She was tired. The kind of tired that makes your mind race and your stomach churn, and the only thing you can do to block it out is close your eyes.

By the time she felt the taxi rolling to a stop and the driver shift into Park, there was a pile of cellophane wrappers in the cup holder, and the sun had set, the buildings around them slicked with rain that reflected the amber glow of the streetlights. She shook the sleep from her head and handed him her debit card, looking up at the soaring stone cathedral to her right.

"That's it, are you sure? It looks like a church."

"Aye." He reached into his glove box and pulled out a new bag of caramels, pausing to rip into the bag with his teeth. "A private citizen bought the cathedral thirty years ago from the city and turned it into a hostel. I worked night shifts here at the front desk when me bairns were just wee things." He handed her back the card and receipt and nodded up at the glossy black Gothic doors with hammered-silver hardware. "They'll take good care of ye in there, and trust me, 'tis the safest place in Edinburgh."

Sabine thanked him and stepped out gingerly, lifting her rucksack onto her shoulder, a move she immediately regretted. Her back and shoulder felt bruised, as if she'd walked to Scotland the day before, carrying a pack filled with stones.

She watched the taxi pull away as she climbed the limestone steps to the enormous doors, which were surprisingly easy to open. The lobby was bustling in every direction as she entered, and the couches in the waiting area to her left were draped with people, the air littered with accents Sabine couldn't quite catch. A reception area sat to the right, and a long, curved railing, like the bow of the *Titanic*, loomed directly ahead. Sabine let her bag drop from her shoulder as she walked forward and peered over the railing into a bright lower level. It was scattered with worn, mismatched couches and warmed by the glow of bohemian lamps, the air charged with laughter and the clink of ceramic teacups settling onto saucers. At the far end of the space was a small café tucked into what looked like choir lofts, with a few bistro tables in front and the scent of freshly ground espresso drifting to the second level.

She looked back to the reception area where someone finally stood behind the desk, although whoever it was on the phone. Sabine walked up and leaned lightly on the edge of the desk, which didn't seem to faze the person behind it. She was tall and slender, with dark hair cut close over her ears and longer top layers swept back from her face with a glossy pomade. She held up her one finger with a glance in Sabine's direction, then turned away. The language she was speaking sounded like Italian, but the flow was so swift she couldn't be sure; whomever she was speaking to, though, it sounded an awful lot like an argument.

Sabine noticed her name tag, *André,* as she reluctantly clicked off her phone and tucked it into her back pocket. She took a deep breath and her eyes fluttered closed for a second before she opened them. "How can I help?"

Sabine hesitated, trying to remember exactly what the cab driver had told her. "I guess I need a room?"

"I'm afraid all of our private rooms are booked, but we do still have several bunks available on the upper level, although it may not be what you're used to." André clicked through several screens on her computer and looked up. "American, right?" Her deep brown eyes were framed with long, dark lashes, but the angles of her face were sharply masculine, softened by the full, sensual curves of her lips.

Sabine said that she'd take whatever was available and tried to pay attention as André told her something about a code to get into the front door, but her accent was so thick it was hard to catch the words before they slipped away. André wrote the number on Sabine's card receipt and handed it to her, then directed her up the left bank of stairs.

By the time she'd found her bed on the top level, which turned out to be a long, narrow room that looked down on the two floors below, Sabine was beyond ready for a shower. The showers turned out to be in a large, communal room lined with showerheads along every wall, but she felt surprisingly comfortable. No one even glanced in her direction, at least until she realized that she hadn't brought a towel and stood there naked and dripping as she read the sign posted by the door. *Towels are available to rent at the front desk.*

She yanked the clean clothes she'd brought onto her still-wet body, located a blow dryer she'd seen attached to a wall, and hoped the shampoo had been enough to wash the airport smell out of her hair. Her body and hair dried in about the same amount of time, and as she stashed everything back into her pack and pushed it into the far corner of her bunk, she glanced at her phone to check the time. She hadn't thought about food since she left New Orleans, but now hunger was suddenly clawing at her stomach with sharp, urgent swipes. She leaned over the railing lining the narrow upper level to see if any actual food was coming out of that café, but all she saw were bistro tables scattered with espresso cups and half-empty pints of beer.

She finally left the hostel and turned toward the center of town. After about twenty minutes of searching, she passed a busy pub with both doors thrown open to the sidewalk. A circular mahogany bar took up most of the open space, but live Celtic music was coming from the corner stage, and quilted-leather booths were tucked into every available space. The rich, comforting scent of roasting meat drifting from the open doors was like a siren's call, and she stood on the steps and drew in a long breath, relaxing into the warmth.

"Will it be one fer dinner, then?"

Sabine snapped open her eyes to see a blond young woman smiling and motioning her inside, and for no reason at all, following her seemed to be the exact right thing to do. Sabine slid off her jacket as the woman led her back to the last cherry-leather booth in the corner. She handed Sabine a menu and nodded to the chalkboard over the bar.

"Ye can order off the menu, unless ye'd rather 'ave the roast. It's a pork roast tonight, I think, which is always lovely."

"It smells like heaven." Sabine pulled the length of her hair over her shoulder and glanced at the stage in the corner. A semicircle of players undulated with the movement of the music, like the wings of some mythical beast, mostly fiddles with the firm undercurrent of a handheld drum. The high resonance of a single flute floated above, making the music seem almost haunted. Sabine leaned back in her seat, realizing suddenly she hadn't ordered. "Sorry," she said, nodding to the chalkboard over the bar. "I'll take the roast."

The woman smiled and took the menu as Sabine shrugged off her jacket and leaned back in the booth, letting the music wash over her as she rubbed the tired burn from her eyes. Despite being in a country she'd never visited before, with no one she knew, this was as relaxed as she could remember being for a long time. Her muscles slowly unfolded onto her bones as she melted into the rhythm of the pub, soaking in the laughter and clink of glasses. The music seemed achingly familiar, as if she'd known it all her life.

For the first time in forever, she had nothing to manage. No Celestine drama, no drunken accidents to prevent, no sharp words slicing through the air like thrown knives. She couldn't remember the last time she hadn't felt tensed against something and now suddenly, nothing. It was almost unsettling.

"So, you made it out for dinner?" Sabine opened her eyes. It was the Italian from the hostel, this time with a bottle of beer in her hand. She looked at her watch before she continued. "I'm impressed. You looked down for the count when you got here."

Sabine hesitated, then gestured for her to sit. Somehow André's accent was smoother now, her voice sanded and smoky at the edges. The scent of cold November air clung to her clothes, as if she'd just ducked in the door, followed by the scent of sandalwood she'd worn long enough to meld with the warmth of her skin. "I'm pretty sure that's not a compliment, but since you're correct, I'll let it slide."

André laughed and slid into the other side of the circular booth. A charcoal turtleneck sweater clung to her impressively defined arms and the black jeans she'd paired it with made her look, well, Italian. Her hands were square, with long, bronzed fingers and a single sterling signet ring on her left hand. A second too late, Sabine realized she was staring.

The server came back and placed a pint on the table. "Oh no. I actually didn't order that," Sabine said, pushing it to the edge.

"I know," she said with a glance at André. "Someone ordered it for you."

"Thanks, I think." Sabine smiled warily and pulled it back. "What is this?"

"She said you hadn't ordered a drink, so I ordered you what I'm having. It's Peroni, an Italian lager."

Sabine smiled. "Well, that tracks with the accent." The pub lights glittered across André's dark eyes, and Sabine looked away to take a long swig of the beer. It hit her almost instantly, a wave of warmth rolling over her. She felt André's gaze and looked up. "What are you doing in Edinburgh?"

Sabine decided to answer honestly. She didn't have the energy to make the truth sound normal. "I have absolutely no idea."

André laughed, sinking the rest of her beer and catching the server's eye for another. "Spontaneous trip, huh?"

"Sure." Sabine slid a hand around the back of her neck and squeezed gently to loosen the tight knots under her fingers. "Let's call it that. Sounds better than the dumpster fire the last twenty-four hours have actually been."

"Whatever it is," André smiled and reached out to take her beer from the server as she passed. "I bet my last twenty-four hours can beat it."

"That's cute." Sabine smiled and leaned back into the worn-leather softness of the booth. "But unlikely. Let's hear what you got."

"Kidding." André's smile was flat and so quick Sabine wasn't sure she'd seen it. "I won't bore you with my romantic tragedies."

"Why not? You'll probably never see me again." Sabine traced a cold drop of condensation with her finger as it rolled down the side of the glass. "Hit me."

The server reappeared and slid two plates of sliced pork roast, drizzled with silky mushroom gravy, onto their table before she hurried back to the bar. The rosemary-scented steam rose like temple incense, heady with the decadent scent of perfectly roasted pork loin, creamy red potatoes, and tender-crisp rainbow carrots, the leafy green tops still attached.

"This is the first real meal I've had in ages." Sabine cut a bite of the delicate roast, which turned out to have a perfectly buttery texture and crispy, herb-crusted skin. She looked up at André. "Go on. You were just about to tell me about your romantic tragedies. If I had to guess I'd say it had something to do with the person you were on the phone with today when I arrived."

André looked up, her fork poised in the air. "You speak Italian?"

"God, no." Sabine let the honey-glazed carrots melt in her mouth before she went on. "But I know what lesbian drama sounds like."

"Fair enough." André sipped her beer slowly, as if using the time to choose her words. "I was in a five-year relationship with someone who cheated on me. We've been thinking about getting back together lately, but the person on the phone was a friend who told me she'd hit on her at a party a few days ago."

"Damn."

"Yeah." André picked at the edge of the label on the beer bottle, slowly folding over the corner. "I thought I knew who she was now, that she'd changed."

Sabine took a sip of her beer and set it down, catching André's eye before she spoke. "It sounds like she's shown you who she is." Sabine softened her voice. "Twice."

"Jesus." André flinched dramatically, with the barest hint of a smile. "Don't hold back. Tell me how you really feel."

"So," Sabine looked into her eyes, then went back to her roast. "Why do you not believe her?"

"I don't know." She laid her fork and knife across her plate. "I think I was just waiting for her to love me…" André paused. "Like I loved her."

Sabine nodded. She knew how it felt to do everything for someone hoping they'd love you back. She touched André's hand, as light as air. "She's doing you a favor. She's shown you who she is and what she's capable of for the future." She pulled her hand back and picked up André's beer. She held her gaze as she took a swig, putting it back down between them. "It's time to believe her."

André laughed, swiping back her bottle with a wink. "I don't usually let people talk to me this way." She shook her head, holding Sabine's gaze. "But maybe I should." She lifted two fingers when the waitress looked their way. "Are you always in control like this?" She looked her up and down, pausing before she went on. "And don't say that it's just your personality, because I'm not buying it."

"Pretty much." Sabine flashed back to her job in the theatre, which now seemed like a lifetime ago, where she always called the shots, and her romantic relationships hadn't been much different. "I've had to be."

It was velvet-black night when they finally walked out of the pub, and the air had a frosty edge to it that Sabine's thin denim jacket didn't begin to ward off. "I have a feeling I'm going to need to do some coat shopping." Sabine looked up at the silvery mist beginning to creep across the moon, and as her gaze lowered to the streetlights, the light glittered gold on the rain-slicked cobblestones under their feet.

André dodged a teenager racing toward them on a bike and slowed her steps. "How long are you in Scotland?"

"A year, though I'll probably move around the country a bit." Sabine paused as she realized that was literally her only plan, if it could even be called a plan. "I have no idea actually."

"Well, I'd get an overcoat as soon as possible." André looked her up and down. "It's November. That little situation you've got going on there wouldn't keep you warm in the dead of Scottish summer."

Sabine stopped abruptly and peered up at an immensely tall octagon-shaped building looming over the street about a block away. The moon glowed behind the domed glass top, made of randomly shaped panes of blue glass that amplified the light and made it look more like a ghostly apparition than a building.

"What's that?"

"The National Library of Scotland." André pressed her hand gently into the small of Sabine's back and guided her across the street. "It's one of the most unique buildings in Edinburgh."

"How long have you lived here?" Sabine smiled as André pulled her gently to the inside of the sidewalk and stepped across to walk on the outside. "Not that I'm an expert or anything, but I don't detect even a hint of a Scottish accent in all that sexy Italian you've got going there."

"And you never will." André looked over and smiled, leading her to the front of the building she'd been looking at and up the dark granite steps. "But you are correct about the sexy Italian."

Sabine peered up to the top of the building they were now standing in front of. The moon was hovering above it now, and the glass panes refracted its light like a shattered mercury mirror. The air was still and cold, and a group of young people in dark overcoats passed on the sidewalk below the steps, laughter tinkling with the click of their heels as they turned the corner and disappeared. André pulled a set of keys from her jacket pocket and opened the ancient, carved walnut doors, holding them open for Sabine.

"Would you like to see inside?"

Sabine instantly sensed the vastness of the space as the lights clicked on one by one around the enormous room. Beautifully dark wooden desks and tables were arranged in a double line down the center of the circular room, with brass desk lamps glowing gently against the green glass shades, illuminating the scars and character in each piece as if they were brushstrokes. But it was the shelves—all the glorious bookshelves lining the room, rising from the first story into the next and nearly touching the blue glass ceiling of the library–that took Sabine's breath away. Ladders on rails lined the shelves and a walkway on every level led completely around then up to the next. The air hovered still and silent around them, heavy with the scent of old paper, dust-shrouded leather and long-buried secrets.

Sabine walked to the center of the first floor and gazed up at the moonlight, sensing the weight of the centuries of history lining the walls around her. "How do you have a key to this place?"

André smiled, still leaning against the entry doorframe, and pointed to a polished brass sign on a marble column in the entryway. Sabine walked closer. *Master Librarian and Curator, André Tosca.*

"I've never even heard of that title." She paused, turning back toward André. "So why in the world were you working behind the desk of the hostel?"

"Library science seems to exist on a much smaller scale in the States, but Scotland is serious about its literary history. I got my PhD at Edinburgh University, and they hired me the next week." André smiled. "My brother owns the hostel. Both of his front-desk attendants called in sick for tonight, so I did him a favor."

Sabine turned where she was and looked up the walls to scan the thousands of books around them as André dimmed the lights and led her up a wrought-iron spiral staircase to the second level, then on to the third. The blue mosaic-glass tiles now just above their heads glowed with a pale, otherworldly light, as if filtered through sheets of ice. Now that they were closer, Sabine could just make out a few lines in black script within each one.

"What's written inside the glass tiles?"

"They're quotes from famous Scottish novelists. Over the last hundred years the glass has clouded just enough to obscure the actual words, which to me makes it even more romantic."

André stopped at a tall, narrow door with her name on it and unlocked it, gesturing for Sabine to step through. She hesitated, but she was too curious to stop now, and as the lights clicked on, she realized it must be André's office. A smooth, cognac leather sofa lined one wall, with two matching chairs across from it and a lush sheepskin warming the space between. Amber glass sconces dripped light down the walls, and a large Scotch-pine desk took up most of the back wall, painted a deep navy blue with delicate gold trim. André set her keys on a small table near the chairs and poured whiskey from a decanter into two cut-crystal tumblers she took out of the bookshelves. She handed one to Sabine, gently clinking the edge of her glass with her own.

"You should taste that," she said, her gaze locked on Sabine, her voice deep and smooth. "And then taste it again."

Sabine took a sip of the whiskey that exploded like a flash fire in her mouth, then settled into an intense, ashy vapor. She finally found her breath as the last of it faded, and she raised her eyes to André. "And why would I want to do that?"

André set her glass down on the end table beside her. When she looked back at Sabine the light found the gold specks in her eyes and lingered there. "Because I'm about to take it out of your hand."

Energy crackled in the space between them. Sabine took another sip, then closed her eyes as André's fingers brushed hers as she grasped the glass. The light in the room was bronze and silent as André raked a hand through her hair, her eyes locked onto Sabine's.

"In the next few seconds, you're going to feel that wall against your back, and every inch of my body holding you to it." The words settled between them, intense and palpable. "If at any time, you want me to stop, say the word 'whiskey,' and I'll step back immediately." André paused, her voice dropping to a whisper. "Do you understand?"

Sabine nodded, biting her lip, her breath caught in her chest, silent and waiting.

"Now," André said, closing the gap between them, her hand warm on Sabine's cheek, thumb stroking her lower lip as she spoke. "What's your word?"

Sabine's stomach dropped, her breath disappearing with it. She closed her eyes against the shocking push of arousal that gripped her, shook her, and made her heart pound within her clit.

"Tell me your word, Sabine."

André placed her hand warm in the center of her chest until she drew a breath. Sabine's eyes fluttered closed. "It's 'whiskey.' My word is 'whiskey.'"

Suddenly her back was against the wall. André held both of Sabine's wrists above her head in one hand, the other warm and soft at the base of her neck. Her thumb was under Sabine's chin, gently tipping it to the side as she followed the heated slope of Sabine's neck with her tongue.

Sabine's nipples tensed as André unbuttoned the front of her shirt and dropped one of her bra straps down her shoulder. She slipped her finger under the sheer edge of the fabric until it fell off her nipple, which was flushed and tensing harder with every breath. André lowered her mouth and touched her first with the heat of her breath, then pulled it into her mouth, swirling her tongue and stroking until Sabine's breath caught in her throat.

André lifted her head and flicked the gold clasp between Sabine's breasts with her fingers. The bra fell to her sides, and André moved to the other side and pulled her nipple into her mouth, hard, scraping it lightly with her teeth as she let it go. Sabine felt her knees weaken and she fought the orgasm she was suddenly on the edge of. She managed only a single word when she tried to speak.

"This—"

André's voice was a whisper, equally gentle and powerful. Her gaze locked onto Sabine.

"Did I tell you to speak?"

Sabine's clit throbbed with another rush of deep, heavy arousal. "No."

"I'm going to let you answer that question again." André held her eyes, her hand tightening around Sabine's wrists. "Properly, this time."

Sabine slowed her breath. "No, sir."

"That's better." The button on her jeans slipped through André's fingers. "Good girl."

Sabine closed her eyes as André edged down the zipper. Slow, deliberate fingertips slid behind the soaked lace of her panties to graze her clit as Sabine groaned and leaned into André's shoulder, wrists straining above her head. She needed André closer. She needed her inside.

André whispered against her neck in Italian as she slicked her fingertips over Sabine's straining clit, the intensity catching fire as she slipped deep inside. She started fucking her with two fingers, then three, still holding Sabine's wrists above her head. The intensity was far beyond what Sabine had ever given in to, and the deep ache of pleasure was heightened by the fact that she could do nothing, absolutely nothing, but feel.

"I'm going to kiss you, Sabine, and the second I do, I want you to come for me." The heel of André's hand moved rhythmically across Sabine's clit with every thrust. "Do you understand?"

Sabine's knees went weak as André kissed her. Her hand stilled, then moved inside with an intensity that exploded into the achingly deep, endless pleasure of an orgasm Sabine couldn't control. Her knees failed her this time, and André held her up until the last wave shook her, then gently let her hands down and wrapped Sabine in her arms.

"Good girl," she whispered, her voice a low scrape against Sabine's ear. "That was an excellent start."

CHAPTER SIX

The next day, after she'd woken up in the late morning, Sabine found a nearby café for breakfast, and as she rounded the corner of a street on the other side, she saw Edinburgh Castle for the first time. It sat on the rocky bluff at the edge of the sea, as if carved from the stone, the waves crashing below, swirling and retreating only to return with more white force. *This is it. This is the castle that Thea loved.*

She walked toward it and finally found the road to the gates, then spent the day wandering around the interior, trailing her fingertips over the rough stone walls. She leaned over the railings to stare at the sea below and closed her eyes to listen, awash in the ancient energy. She read all the posted metal plates that told of its history, but the thought that it looked exactly as it had when her aunt was here was never far from her mind. Thea had sent her to Scotland because she'd loved it so much; suddenly, the importance of soaking in the experience the way she'd intended became much more real.

That night, as she was re-packing her bag, she leafed through the contents of the leather folder Katherine had given her. All the details she'd outlined in her office were there, of course, but as she stacked the papers and started to slide them back into the folder, she saw it. A yellow Post-it note at the very bottom. She pulled it out and looked at what was written on it, in faded pencil script. *Muir Rothesay.* She looked out the window beside her bunk and tried to remember if she'd ever heard of it before. *Had*

Katherine mentioned it and she'd just forgotten? What the hell was Muir Rothesay?

The next morning she finally decided to try the café downstairs, and on her way back upstairs with her latte, she asked the guy at the front desk what Muir Rothesay meant. He looked to the map of Scotland mounted on the desktop and pointed near the top, then went back to his computer.

"That's a wee village in the North, in the Highlands. There's only one train there a day, so if yer wantin' to go, I'd get a move on, lass. It's Friday and if ye miss it t'day, there won't be another till Monday." He looked around the computer at her and raised an eyebrow. "It's Waverly Station you'll be wantin'."

Sabine hurriedly packed her things and made her way to Waverly Train Station, but by the time she found the train she needed, to go to some town she'd never heard of, she felt like she'd circled the globe at least twice. She'd managed to jump on the northbound train to the Highlands just in time, and as the train rolled out of the station and picked up speed, she rested her head against the window, hoping to grab a quick nap in the empty car. It was a crisp blue-sky morning in Scotland but still the wee hours of the day in New Orleans and she'd felt shattered since she landed in Scotland. It was strange, the second she no longer had the manage the world on her own, she felt like she couldn't keep her eyes open.

She'd just nodded off when a transit employee pushed open the sliding door separating the cars and asked to see her ticket. He punched it with a chrome clicker before disappearing smoothly into the next car.

For most of the nearly six-hour journey, the train car remained empty, with just the rhythmic clackety-clack of the rails beneath the train car, so Sabine finally slipped into a deep sleep. When they abruptly jerked to a stop at Rothsay Station, she gathered her bag and jacket, checked twice to make sure she had her bank card and passport, then stepped off the train steps into what felt like Antarctica. Cold wind whipped her hair around her face as she stepped onto the open-air platform. She checked to be sure it was the right stop and hurried toward the enclosed area of the station ahead, dodging sea gulls and narrowly escaping a wet chunk of snow that slid from the roof and landed beside her as she pulled the glass door open.

Rothsay Station turned out to be roughly the size of her living room at home, but much, much colder. The kind of cold that circles your neck with an icy, sandpaper grip.

"Excuse me." An older gentleman wrapped up in what appeared to be a dozen layers of mismatched wool took his time looking up from the computer screen behind the ticket desk.

"What cannae help ya wit, love?"

"I was just wondering where I'd catch a taxi into town?"

The man smiled, pulled a leather tobacco pouch out of his coat pocket, and nodded toward the exit. "Ya'd be hard pressed to find a lad that'd get his taxi out in this muck. Only ganna get worse in the next few hours so I'd just get somewhere ya can put yer head down, if I was ye."

The wind whipped in from the open front of the station and wrapped Sabine's hair around her face. She managed to pull it to one side and tuck it inside her jacket collar before she spoke. "So, there's no transport to town at all?"

The man held up one finger and picked up the station landline, pressing the grubby first key on the speed dial with a gloved finger.

"Aye, Dalton! Is yer man Barton down the pub at the moment?" He paused, covering his other ear and leaning into the headset. "Alreet, ya, that's what I thought, but there's an American lass here lookin' fer the taxi. D'ya tink he's in any shape ta drive 'er anyway?"

Sabine caught only about five of the words that rose to the surface from the sea of Scottish brogue, and only because she'd once painted sets for a theater doing *Brigadoon*. It didn't matter anyway; the handful she did understand was enough to let her know she was shit out of luck. As if she didn't know that already.

"Aye now." The gentleman put down the phone with a chuckle and gave Sabine a wink. A wavy shock of hair fell out of his cap, which he tossed onto the counter behind the window. Ironically, his hair was the same color as the snow that had attacked Sabine on the way into the station. "I've bad news and worse news for ye."

Sabine drew in a long breath and looked longingly back at the heated train car. "Let me have it."

"Are ye in town fer a bit?"

Sabine nodded. "You could say that."

"Might wanna get a jump on accommodation, then. The hotel is under renovation, and I 'appen to be privy to the fact the lodging house is shut. Busted pipes."

"You're kidding." Sabine narrowly resisted the urge to roll her eyes. "That's the only two places to stay in the whole town?"

"Aye. Ya might wanna ask at the lodgers though. They may let ye stay if ya don't need water." He paused to pull a pipe from his other pocket. "Bad luck, I'm afraid. It hasn't snowed this early for the last fifty years or so. The wee ones are thrilled, but none of us were ready for it. In fact, yours was the last train. They've shut us down until at least tomorrow."

Sabine thanked him and picked up her pack, pulling her thin jean jacket tighter around her.

"Pardon." He looked her up and down through the smudged glass of the ticket window. "But is that what yer callin' an overcoat, miss?"

Sabine looked down, then outside at the thick snow blowing sideways across the road.

"I'm from New Orleans, and I guess I didn't expect…" She shook her head. "…all of this."

"From the States, eh?"

Sabine nodded, watching him unwind a thick, charcoal-gray scarf from around his neck. He pushed it under the glass partition as she shook her head.

"Take it, lassie." He smiled, his bright blue eyes twinkling under his gray brows. "Ye'll freeze before ya even get inta town. The missus will only make me another."

Exhausted tears burned the back of Sabine's eyelids, and she smiled, willing them away. "You're so nice, thank you, but I can't take your scarf." She paused. "You don't even know me."

"Well." He gave her a kind glance. "Ye look enough like one o' us anyway, with that wild red hair. Can't have ya freezin' before ye even make it to the pub." He winked at her. "Just in case."

Sabine thanked him and wrapped it around her neck, throwing her pack over her shoulder. It was two in the afternoon according to the clock in the station, but it looked more like evening as she walked out to the road from the strangely castle-like stone archway of the station. As the road unfolded in front of her, she had to smile; she hadn't thought to ask the way into the village from the station, but there was literally no way to miss it. The tire tracks crisscrossing the single road faded rapidly under new snowfall as she added her footfalls to the mix, pulling the scarf closer around her neck and tucking the ends into the buttoned front of her jacket.

The scarf smelled faintly of woodsmoke and cherry pipe tobacco, and as she pulled it over her nose, Sabine felt suddenly off balance with the sense that she'd been where she stood before. For a few seconds, everything was familiar: the road, the icy wind, even the crumbling rock wall lining the road to town. She stopped, the snow crunching under her feet, and drew in the scent of the scarf; the icy air only sharpened it, like wet flint across metal. She closed her eyes as she inhaled. It was familiar, but fading fast and hazier by the second, like a familiar memory that turns out to be just a dream you had once.

She tucked her scarf back into the jacket and stared at the low, slate-gray clouds that hung low over the churning sea, hiding the distant, pale-yellow suggestion of the sun. The air was dropping lower and colder as she neared the village, footprints were few and far between, and the evergreens hung low with the weight of the glittering snow.

The train-station attendant wasn't kidding. The entire village was deserted. Off-center *Closed* signs dangled in the butcher's window and a tiny cafe, and even the grocery store was dark as night behind the front windows. Despite the growing panic twisting in her stomach, she found something beautiful about the tall, quiet, gray, stone buildings lining the road. Most of them were either two or three stories tall, with expansive front windows of wavy, settled glass, some crisscrossed with lead, forming the panes into small diamond shapes that held the light. They were almost warm under Sabine's fingers as she walked past.

What if I'm stuck here and have nowhere to stay? She tried not to think about the news that hers had been the last train of the day, or that the attendant had not been sure they'd even start back up tomorrow. She could possibly pass the night in the open station building if she had to, but that sounded colder than where she was standing now. It served her right. She'd traveled across the world to Rothesay because she'd seen the name of the village scrawled on a Post-it note. *Obviously excellent planning on my part.*

The sea sounded angry as Sabine walked through town. She leaned over the rock wall lining the sidewalk and watched the waves crash over the wide stone pier below the road, tossing a wall of water so high that every breath of air tasted faintly of salt, and the ground under her feet rumbled like it might split in two and fall into the water. She was almost to the end of the dark buildings on either side when she noticed a sheer curtain of woodsmoke swirling toward the sky. She ducked down a side street and wandered down the crumbling brick alley until she came to an alcove. The Woolpack Inn.

This must be the place with the burst pipes he was talking about.

A *Closed* sign hung on the door to the Inn, but someone had to be inside; it was the only place in town with smoke rising from a chimney. Sabine took a moment to count her options, which went quickly since they totaled a big fat zero, then knocked on the door, shifting her pack to the other shoulder.

Hearing no answer, she stepped to the side to peer into the window. The place was clearly ancient and had probably been ensconced in that corner of the alley for at least a few hundred years. The low, narrow doorway featured a thick plank of glossy petrified wood above it. The stones around the doorframe were worn smooth by a thousand hands, creating a bare, luminous sheen, and the inside, or as much as Sabine could see from the main window, was far smaller than she'd expected. A single fire crackled in a hearth along the back wall, and to the right of that stretched a bar, simply built, with an impressive array of whiskies on raw oak shelves behind it. Just a few tables were scattered about, and the light came only from the electric sconces on the walls and the firelight.

She jumped as the black wooden door opened in suddenly, the hinges screeching from the cold.

"Whit can I do fer ya, love?"

She stepped back a step and pointed to the sign above the door. "I was just wondering if you had any rooms for rent still? I heard there's a pipe issue, but I don't mind not having water." She took a deep breath, trying to reel back the panic that resonated in her words. "I thought I'd ask, just in case."

The man stepped out to glance at the sign above the door and shook his head. "That's just the name of the pub, lass. The original owners might have rented rooms as well, but it hasn't been a proper inn in quite some time."

"That's okay. I'll ask down the—" Sabine was turning to leave when a piercing alarm cut through the pub. The man looked as perplexed as she felt until...he wasn't.

"Oh, bollocks. I forgot the feckin' oven!" He turned back toward the bar and not so much motioned as pulled her through the door. "Come on in while I sort this out. You'll freeze out there, love."

Sabine stepped inside as he disappeared through the double doors behind the bar. She had to cover her mouth not to laugh at the stream of colorful Scottish profanities that floated over the top of them, and after a few seconds she peeked in to see him swatting a flaming baking pan. She hesitated, then grabbed a towel from the counter and fanned the ancient fire alarm in the corner until it stopped screaming. The silence seemed to echo around the walls as the last of the flames coming from the stainless-steel baking pan subsided into a thin puff of smoke.

"How have I managed to catch the bleedin' t'ing on fire without cooking the veg?" The man looked genuinely dismayed as he poked a huge chunk of raw potato with a fork. "They're still raw. Everything's raw."

Sabine fanned her towel at the remaining smoke and inspected the pan. "It looks like you lined the pan with paper?"

"Aye." He nodded at a box of parchment on the counter. "Didn't want to spend all night here cleanin', ya see."

"It's actually the paper, not the food, that caught fire." She poked a black edge of parchment paper, and it crumbled into an ash pile on the counter. "I think the vegetables are actually fine if you want to try again."

The man ran his hand over his hair and laughed. He was older, sixties maybe, with wrinkles across his face in the shape of laughter. His ash-silver hair was gathered in a ponytail at the base of his neck and wrapped with a strip of worn black leather. "Well, that's the first good news I've had all day, so if that doesn't entitle us to a whiskey, I don't know what does."

He reached up to the wooden shelves above the oven and plunked a bottle between them, then snagged a couple of clean glasses from the drying rack.

"I'm Morgan Wallace, by the way." He uncorked the bottle and flashed her a grin. "And I don't know what possessed me to even start this. I'm a bleedin' disaster in the kitchen. I've a cook for the pub, of course, but she fucked off up to the Hebridian Islands ta see her sister Thursday last, so she's as much use ta me as a flamingo's left leg."

He splashed a generous amount of whiskey in each glass and pushed hers toward her with a nod.

"My name is Sabine." She inhaled a rush of dark smoke from the whiskey as she took the first sip, which scorched her throat like a forgotten campfire. "Christ. What the hell is this?" She tried to catch the words before they scattered across the counter, but she was too busy trying to choke down the liquid smoke in her glass.

Fortunately, judging from his rumbling laugh, Morgan somehow found her remark hilarious and plunked his glass down on the table. "God. I love an American doesn't pretend to know their way around a dram."

"You know what though?" She swirled the amber whiskey up the side of her glass. "I can't believe I'm saying this, but I like it. I think. I couldn't tell you why though."

"That's how ye know yer onta somethin' great." He gave his glass a final swirl and finished it before he topped up both glasses. "Whether it's whiskey or people."

The liquor started to warm her chest from the inside out, and she unwound the scarf from her neck as she tried another sip and looked around at the countertops scattered with wrinkled brown bags of groceries. "So, what's with all the food? You can't be open tonight. It looks like the entire town has rolled up the sidewalks."

"Ah, right you are." Morgan drained the last of his whiskey and plunked his glass down with a lingering glance of affection. "But some of the older folks in the village haven't been able to get out, an' I want to be sure they get a hot meal tonight, at least.

I called my daughter to help, but she didn't answer, stuck at work most likely, so chances are I'm on me own."

Sabine folded her scarf and jacket onto a stool by the door. "How much food do you have?"

Morgan looked around the countertops and was silent for a second. "Hoping for about forty dinners, maybe more if I can stretch it, but I'm startin' to realize I shouldn't have bothered. I'm used to cooking for family, but I don't always do well at that, if I'm honest."

Sabine peeked into the stainless-steel oven and drew in the deeply warming scent of roasting meat. "Well, the beef roast looks beautiful. You'll need to turn up the heat in about twenty minutes to finish it, but it smells like it should be done in an hour." She rolled up her sleeves and turned on the tap to wash her hands.

"A roast is the one thing I can pull off on the odd Sunday, but in fairness, any Scotsman worth his salt should be able ta say that." Morgan paused as she turned off the tap and peeked into the oven again. "Are ya sayin' yer willin' ta help, lass? You dan' even know me."

"You don't know me either, but here I am." She arched an eyebrow as she dried her hands and reached for one of the two black canvas aprons hanging from a hook on the wall. "A random American drinking your whiskey."

"Excellent point." A smile like wildfire flashed across Morgan's face, and he pulled on the other apron, raising his glass and handing Sabine hers, both shimmering with a fresh splash of whiskey. "What the hell? Let's get stuck in."

CHAPTER SEVEN

Alden slammed the door of her Land Rover and leaned her head back onto the worn leather headrest. She turned the key with her eyes still closed and pulled off her gloves, dropping the left one into the passenger's seat while she tried to ease the other down over the gash on her hand.

"For fuck's sake. I should have thought about the blood freezing solid out there."

The words fell flat in the empty cab as she held her hand up to the heat blast from the vent and waited for her glove to thaw enough to peel it from her skin.

She'd had better days. Alden was the only certified historic preservationist in the Highlands, where the ancient homes and historic buildings outnumbered people, so she was used to working in driving rain or snow. But she was not used to being stuck on the gabled roof of a medieval abbey with her ladder flat on the ground three stories below. A rogue gust of wind had pushed the aluminum ladder slowly across the icy roofline, and she'd held her breath as the wind stilled, then tipped the ladder over into a silent drift of snow forty feet below. Alden had no choice but to watch it go and wonder how long it would take her to get frostbite. She'd been replacing broken slate tiles for two hours when it happened, so by the time she heard the muffled sound of the ladder disappearing into the snowbank, she was already damp and chilled through.

Her phone was in her truck, so she'd halfheartedly called out for help, but the nearest home was at the far end of the road, and everyone in Rothesay with even a crumb of common sense was huddled inside by the fire. Eventually, she'd broken a hundred-year-old loft window with her boot and lowered herself through it, but not without slicing the hell out of her palm and leaving a ruby slick of blood on the glass like a scene in a damn horror movie.

"Fucking hell. I've really got to start wearing leather gloves." She peeled the last of the frozen glove from the cut and held it up to the truck's interior light. It wasn't dangerously long, but just deep enough to require some Highland stitches before she went anywhere else. She dug her icy phone out of the glove box and dialed her da.

"Alden! Where the hell ya been?" Alden switched her da's rumbling bass voice to speakerphone and set it on the dash. "I called ye over an hour ago."

"Da, are you down the pub?" Alden rubbed her forehead with her good hand and laid her head back on the seat. "I've got a little situation here."

Her da knew better than to press her for details when stress was grating her voice into shards, so she was off the phone in less than thirty seconds. The snow was blowing sideways as she drove the buried one-lane road from the outskirts of the village into the center, but at least the heat was beginning to melt the frost from the dash of the Land Rover. Alden glanced down briefly to make sure the bleeding had stopped and managed to wrap her hand loosely with her scarf before she looked back up and jerked the steering wheel to the right.

"Oh, *come on!*"

Alden pumped her brakes and skidded to a sideways stop directly in front of a massive red Highland cow and her calf, serenely standing in the center of the road, both covered in a lofty blanket of snow. Long red hair usually hung straight down over their faces, hiding their eyes, but the wind was blowing it to the side, and Alden noticed with dissipating annoyance that they looked delighted to see her. The mother had an impressive set of horns that narrowed at the tip and turned toward the sky in a deep bend, with a meter spread between them. She nudged her baby to follow and ambled over to the driver's side of the Land Rover.

"Aye, you brought yer baby to be beggin' now." Alden rolled down her window and rubbed the wide bridge of the cow's nose, feeling her face melt into a smile against her will. "Startin' 'em early, I see."

Alden reached into the backseat for the lunch she'd forgotten to eat. When she turned back around, the cow had wedged her entire snowy head past the window and into the cab.

"Ya know I don't have time for this madness, don't ye?" Alden handed over her sandwich, loaded with thick slices of sharp cheddar and Branston's sweet-pickle relish, then rubbed her snout as she chewed. "Is ya wee one ready for the good stuff yet?"

She leaned past the cow and looked down at the baby straining to see into the window, her soft brown eyes wide with curiosity and a calm, slow blink that fluttered her long, red-blond eyelashes. Alden dug into the small drawstring muslin bag in her lunch satchel and grabbed a handful of whole rainbow carrots. She was getting to the last of the sweet summer carrot and parsnip stash from her garden, which was an undeniable seasonal tragedy, but she couldn't possibly resist the little chubby bandit on the other side of the door.

"Now don't come cryin' ta me if ye get a stomachache, ya little thief."

The cow finished the last of the sandwich, leaving an impressive pile of crumbs on Alden's lap. She stepped back to let Alden hand the carrots out the window to her baby, grunting until she got the last one for herself. She scraped her fuzzy cheek against the windowsill and nudged her calf back slowly from the car after Alden held up both hands to show that they were empty. She laughed despite herself at the look of serene bliss on their faces. "You know that's called highway robbery, ye little villains? I should call the law on ya."

Alden waited until they had ambled back to the side of the snowy road to carefully turn her vehicle around and start toward the village again. Gray-velvet smoke rose from a single chimney down the alleyways, but not a single light shone in the shops lining the sidewalks, the windows all black with wavy slicks of ice across the glass. She climbed the nearest sidewalk with the left side of her truck, dropping the right side back onto the road, then shifted into Park and cut the engine.

Not a single footprint marred the smooth expanse of airy white as Alden got out and buttoned her coat, which wasn't a surprise given the blowing snow. The sea crashed against the concrete pier, and Alden walked the few steps to the corner, just in time to see it rush through the black iron railing and over the opposite side. The sound of the crash thundered up the hill and reverberated under her feet, as if the silence of the snow had emboldened it.

The power of the ocean had always resonated with Alden, and the pier below Muir Rothesay was an unforgettable example of it. The centuries-old concrete structure was lined with rough, hand-forged iron railings on all sides, extending about twenty yards into the water even at low tide. When the sea was angry, the water pounded the sides relentlessly, eventually retreating in iridescent layers of silver green that swirled over the somber blue depths with a foamy hiss.

Alden turned up the collar on her canvas overcoat and buttoned the top button over her scarf. The sea mist had already dampened her hair, and the warm interior of the truck seemed like a distant memory as she hurried across the main street and into Oliver's Alley. It was a definite stretch to call the cobblestone path that led to her family's pub an alley; tourists always seemed to learn the hard way that it was just wide enough for one person or a bicycle, not both.

The peat fire in the pub was blazing as Alden let herself in, and after she closed the door against the still-falling snow, she stopped to hang her overcoat by the fire to dry. Iron hooks had been built into the sides of the brick hearth, as well as arched cubbies for stacks of firewood on either side. Alden tossed another log on the fire and tried to pull her hair back into a ponytail with one hand.

"Alden, love." Alden spun around as her da came through the kitchen doors. "Will ye look at the state of ya. Have ye been out in the weather all day again?"

"I have, although not by choice." Alden held up her hand. "Do ya have that first-aid kit behind the bar still? I had a little scuffle with the abbey down the road and lost the final round."

"Ya need to watch yourself." Morgan rifled through the drawers behind the bar and held up a steel box as he slipped into his coat. "How many times have I told ye that place is haunted?"

"Da, if you're talking about your tall tales for the tourists about topless female ghosts, they aren't exactly having the effect you're hoping for." Alden flipped the latch on the box and pulled out a roll of gauze. "Besides the fact that you've been telling me that story for the last thirty-seven years and I have yet to see a single one."

"Well, I may be exaggerating a wee bit for the odd American in the pub, but you know the monks are a mischievous lot, to be sure." Morgan leaned in for a closer look at her hand as he wound his chunky green scarf around his neck and picked up the keys hanging behind the bar. "If you can wait a few minutes to patch that up, I can do it for ye. I just have to pick up Declan from the train station and drop 'im home."

"What's he doing there?" Alden ripped open a disinfectant wipe packet with her teeth. "I heard on the radio that the trains have been canceled for the next two days at least."

"I don't know exactly, but Patrick just called me from the ticket station. He said Declan's been sitting on the bench for about twenty minutes."

Alden nodded, wincing as the alcohol hit the open wound. "Are ya bringin' him back to the pub?" She handed her dad the gauze roll. "I can look after him if you're busy here. I'm done for the day." She paused and looked toward the kitchen doors as the sound of dropped silverware came out of nowhere. "What are you doin' here, by the way? Ye can't possibly be thinking about opening just for Patrick and your buddies?"

Morgan opened the roll of gauze and set it on the bar as he headed for the door. "Who said anything about opening? Sabine will tell ya all about it. I've got to go collect your nephew before he decides to walk into Aberdeen."

"Sabine?" Alden looked up and tossed a bloody pad of gauze into the trash behind the bar. "Who the hell is that?"

Morgan opened the door, the wind instantly whipping his hair out of its leather binding as he pulled a wool cap down over it. "Alden, I want ya to be nice to that lass and do what she tells ye. We're nearly done back there. She's helping me for no good reason whatsoever, and yer mother is out of town until tonight, so don't go ruinin' it."

Alden looked around at the deserted pub. "Helping you with what—?"

Morgan pulled the pub door shut against the wind, and Alden watched him walk past the windows and down the alley. Alden muttered to herself as she wound half the roll of gauze around her hand, tucking the end under and pulling it through to the other side. "Hail Mary bandage it is then." The cut was still bleeding, and wrestling butterfly stitches with one hand was not something she wanted to attempt after the day she'd had.

She heard the oven door squeak open and shut. *So, he's just leaving me here with some random woman?* She slipped behind the bar and headed for the doors, but they opened suddenly from the other side and swung toward her, colliding with her face hard enough to send her to her knees.

"Oh my God. I'm so sorry!"

It was a moment before Alden looked up, but when she did, a woman stood over her holding a cardboard box. She finally reached over her to set it on the bar and offered Alden her hand, but from the look on her face, Alden made a mental note to avoid mirrors for a few days. Mirrors and clueless Americans. Both.

"The radio is on in the kitchen." The words of the woman named Sabine fell over each other in a rush. "I had no idea anyone else was here." She pulled her hand back and stopped suddenly, her head tilted to one side. "Oh, God. I think I gave you a black eye. It's swelling up already."

Alden closed her eyes, her fingertips tracing the spot where the edge of the door had squared up with her cheek. "See that clear area in the door there?" Alden opened her eyes long enough to see Sabine's hesitant nod. "That's called a window." She let out a slow breath and considered the mandatory sentence for murder. "You don't have those in America?"

"We do. It's just that box is so tall, and I guess I was trying not to drop it." Sabine reached for Alden's bandaged hand to help her up just as Alden managed to pull it out of her reach.

"Your name is Sabine, right?" The girl nodded silently this time. "Great." Alden paused to gather the last of her patience. "Can you do me a favor? Fuck off over to the other side of the bar, so I have a chance of getting up from the floor without another black eye."

"Sorry, I just…" She rounded the corner of the bar and watched from a safe distance. Alden stood and pushed open the kitchen door, remembering after she stepped in that she'd been headed to the kitchen in the first place to find out who Sabine was. *And now I know. Another clueless American collecting Instagram pictures.*

Alden rubbed her temples and took a deep breath, holding it for a second too long before she let it out. Her da had specifically asked her to be nice, and to be fair, he rarely asked for anything. She caught her reflection in the kitchen chrome and rolled her eyes as she pushed open the doors.

"So, it's Sabine, right?" Alden pulled a bottle of Coke out of the cooler behind the bar. "What's with all the boxes in the kitchen?"

The words echoed in the empty room. Alden looked down the hall, but there wasn't anywhere else to hide in a tiny sixteenth-century pub. It looked like Sabine had taken her request to fuck off seriously. Alden opened the door and looked down the alley in both directions. She considered calling for her, but only because she had no idea how to explain to her da how she'd managed to make a girl disappear in less than thirty seconds.

"Well, that has to be a record," Alden muttered as she stepped back into the pub, glancing down at the blood that had soaked through the gauze on her hand. "It usually takes me at least sixty seconds to scare off a beautiful woman."

CHAPTER EIGHT

Alden latched the door behind her and rested her head against it for a moment before she turned around.

"So, you think I'm beautiful, huh?"

Alden froze, then turned slowly to find Sabine leaning against the hearth, smiling.

"Where did you go? I thought you left."

"Well," Sabine glanced down at the blood-soaked bandage on Alden's hand, "I considered it. But it looks like that black eye I gave you isn't your only problem."

Alden's phone rang, and she patted down her pockets until she found it. "Hang on. This is Morgan." She clicked it on and watched as Sabine slipped behind the bar. "Da, did ya find him?"

"That I did, but it's a bit of a tricky situation. Are ye all right to stay on there for a bit?"

"Aye, I'm fine, but what in the world is going on in the kitchen? I was just in there, and it looks like ye emptied the walk-in refrigerator into boxes."

"Let me talk to Sabine."

"What?" Alden hesitated. "You mean the—"

"Aye, and dan't even tell me you've scared her off already." Morgan paused. "'Ave ya really?"

Alden shook her head to stave off the mother of all headaches and clicked on the speakerphone. "I just put you on speaker. She's standing right here."

"Hi, Morgan." Sabine's voice was cheerful, as if she were speaking to an old friend, and he answered just as warmly.

"Would ya ever think about helping my Alden deliver those meals for me, lass? I've got a little family situation I've got to handle down the train station, and I don't know that I can be back for a while."

"Of course. No worries. They're packed and ready to go. Does…" The American paused and calmly arched an eyebrow in her direction.

"Alden. My name is Alden."

"Does Alden know what families they go to?"

This is just surreal. Alden started to unwind the gauze from her hand. *I go to work for a couple of hours, and Da plucks a random American out of a blizzard to be his assistant.*

"Aye. She'd better know. She's lived here all her life," Morgan said. "Listen. I'll be back as soon as I can, and I'll join you two to finish the deliveries. In the meantime, don't be lendin' yer ear ta—"

Alden hurriedly clicked off the speakerphone and held it back up to her ear. "Jaysus, Mary, Joseph, and the wee donkey, Da. I'm not *that* bad."

"Ye certainly are." Alden heard the smile in his voice and turned toward the door to hide her own as he continued. "Just be nice. That's all I'm sayin'."

Alden said a quick good-bye and dropped the phone back into her pocket, which loosened the end of the gauze wrap enough to make it sink like a bloody party streamer to the floor.

"I assume that crime scene on your hand—" Sabine glanced over her shoulder as she washed her own hands in the small ceramic sink behind the bar. "—is why you have the first-aid kit out?"

"Aye." Alden reclaimed her seat at the bar and unwound the rest of the gauze, dropping it into the trash on the other side of the bar. "It looks worse than it is. It's only still bleeding because I haven't stopped to bandage it properly. It'll be fine once I get it done."

Sabine spread a bar towel on the bar and motioned for Alden to give her the hand. "How did you do it?"

"I cut myself at work. That's all you're getting." Alden extended her hand and looked up at Sabine warily. "You could be some ax murderer for all I know."

"Ah, so now I'm a beautiful ax murderer." Sabine looked up and smiled as she opened a yellowing packet of butterfly stitches from the bottom of the first-aid kit. "Lucky you. What else you got?"

Alden almost laughed, then winced as Sabine carefully pulled the edges of the cut together and placed the first butterfly stitch. She stared at the kitchen door to distract herself. "So I guess we're delivering boxes after this. What the hell is in them, anyway?"

"Your dad made a roast to pack up and deliver to people that might be running low on food with the snow." Sabine tucked a stray lock of hair behind her ear and leaned closer to Alden's hand. "And I happened to come by just as he was attempting to burn down the kitchen."

"Aye. That sounds about right. My mam is a lovely cook, but Dad gets in over his head like it's his job. Something's usually on fire within about five minutes or so."

"Your mam." Sabine placed the last stitch and looked up. "Is that your grandma?"

"No. My mam." She paused. "You pronounce it 'mom' in the States, or so it seems on the telly." Alden looked longingly at the scotch decanter behind Sabine and tried to keep her face neutral as Sabine wrapped her hand in fresh gauze. "I'll try to dial down the Highlands accent for ye so you have an outside chance of understanding me. How do you know my da?"

"I was trying to find a hotel with vacancies, and the 'Inn' part of the pub sign threw me off. He was nice enough to invite me in, and I stayed to help when I saw what he was trying to put together."

Sabine finished and secured the gauze with tape, then gathered the supplies and repacked the kit. The hair she had wound around a pencil fell down her back as she leaned over to stash the box under the counter, falling to her waist like weighted satin. It was deep red with flashes of gold that caught the light, and a perfect match to the amber freckles dusted across her face.

"I promised Morgan I'd help deliver, but if you'd rather do it yourself, I understand." Sabine pushed through the kitchen doors and came back with an enormous scarf, winding it around her neck like a noose. She stopped, looked confused as to what to do with it all, and finally just jammed the ends down into the front of her denim jacket and tried to button it up to her neck.

"What the hell are you doin', ya dafty?" Alden laughed despite herself and leaned back to get a better look. "Have you never worn a scarf before today?"

"Of course, I have." Sabine sniffed, pressing down the enormous lump of scarf under her jacket. "I mean, like when I was a kid or something. It never really gets cold in New Orleans."

"Come here." Alden stood and undid the top bronze button of Sabine's jean jacket, suddenly very aware of how close she was standing. "There's a right way and a wrong way to wear a handknit scarf, especially a wool one. If you do it wrong, it's like trying to wrap a mattress around your neck and then button your coat over it." She unwound the chunky wool from the delicate slope of Sabine's neck, then held it up. "Fold it in half so the ends meet, then put that double layer around your neck." She laid the doubled scarf across her shoulders. "Then just take the ends and pull them down through that loop, and you're done." Alden pulled them through and adjusted the scarf until the loop was just under her neck, trying not to notice the clean scent of roses that clung to the warmth of Sabine's skin.

Alden finished with the scarf and stepped back, looking around the room. "Okay. Where's your overcoat?"

Sabine shoved her hands into the pockets of her jacket and shook her head. "Why does everyone keep asking me that?"

Alden realized then that Sabine was already wearing what she thought was a coat. "Damn, girl. You're going to need more than that if we're going to be traipsing around the village delivering your dinners. There's almost a meter of fresh fall out there." She grabbed her jacket from the hearth and shook it out, knocking off the slate dust and any remaining glass shards. "Wear this. I've got another one in the truck. It's not fancy, but yer legit going to freeze out there in five minutes if you try to make do with whatever the hell that is."

Sabine took it and put it on, rolling up the sleeves that hung three inches past her fingertips. "Are you sure?" Sabine looked up at her, clearly doubtful. "Or are you just saying you have another one in the truck so I won't feel bad for taking yours?"

"Good Lord. You really haven't lived in a cold climate, have ye? We literally stash coats and scarves everywhere in case we get caught out." Alden slipped behind the bar and looked through the kitchen doors. "That's an impressive stack of boxes, although I'm not sure we have that many people in the village. You and Da weren't messing, were ya?" She looked back over her shoulder. "I'd let you go get the Land Rover while I get all that stacked at the door to load, but something tells me you can't drive a stick."

Sabine sniffed, suddenly very interested in the sleeve of the jacket. "I can load the boxes. I'm stronger than I look." She looked up and met Alden's eyes. "You just go get the truck. If we get going, most of what we packed up will still be hot when it gets to them."

"All right, then." Alden dug for the keys in the pocket of her jeans. The sooner she delivered those dinners, the quicker she could go home and forget about the day from hell. "Yes, ma'am."

Twenty minutes later all the meals were loaded in the back of the Land Rover, wedged between random window frames and a few ancient bricks Alden was taking home to repair for the chapel's belfry at the edge of town. Sabine settled into the passenger's seat like it might bite her, and Alden glanced in her direction as she shifted into first gear. It was an effort not to roll her eyes.

"Looking for something?"

Sabine twisted in her seat and peered down into the gap between the edge of the seat and the scarred leather console. "Just the seat belt. Are you hiding it?"

"Nope." Alden revved the engine and pulled away from the curb, carving a fresh path through the snow. "I took them out a few years ago to make a climbing harness for work."

"Seriously?" Sabine sat back slowly and closed her eyes for a tense few seconds before she gripped the dash. "Isn't that illegal?"

"Maybe in California, lass, but you're in the Highlands now."

Alden just shook her head and smiled as she watched Sabine's fingertips on the dash slowly turn white.

❖

Alden tapped her thumb on the steering wheel and watched through the window of the snow-covered cottage with the thatched roof that had seen better days. Worn whitewashed boards framed the windows in front, forming a perfect square of golden light under the clusters of sparkling icicles hanging from the eaves. She made a mental note to circle back tomorrow and shovel the snow from Mrs. Macgowan's walkway. She'd lost her husband the previous summer to dementia, and almost every day, someone in the village would call in on her, just to see if she needed anything done. And, just as Alden anticipated, she'd taken to Sabine like a long-lost relative.

Alden rubbed her temples, willing away the headache forming behind her eyes. She'd gone out to warm up the truck again while Sabine said her good-byes, and Alden watched through the windshield as Mrs. Macgowan wrapped a handful of oat cookies in a tea towel for Sabine as she walked her to the door. Sabine left her with a hug, and the widow was beaming by the time she reached the end of the walk.

"Thank baby Jesus. It's about time," Alden muttered as she leaned over and opened the passenger door, waving to Mrs. Macgowan as Sabine made her way to the truck. She slid in quickly, pausing to knock the snow off her shoes before she shut the door.

"Saints be praised, I think that was the last box." Alden lowered her lights as the snow fell in a dense, glittering curtain. "Although, I have to say, Da was right about some of them needing someone to drop by. I got the feeling a few were on their last loaf of bread." Alden's phone pinged, and she picked it up, glancing at the text that flashed onto her screen. "It looks like Da got my nephew sorted, so they're home now. He said to say thank you again for your help." Another ping and Alden rolled her eyes as she turned her phone toward Sabine. "And apparently he's got a bottle of whiskey with your name on it for putting up with me."

"It was actually a lot of fun." Sabine held her hands up to the heat blowing out of the dash vents. "I was worried, but everyone honestly couldn't have been nicer about a stranger showing up at their door."

"Aye, because you're not a stranger if you're with me," Alden said, tapping the brakes when she hit a slick patch of wet ice. The blurred streetlights of the main street glowed in the distance like a glittering tabletop Christmas village. "In a village of four hundred, especially in Scotland, there are no strangers. More like an enormous family you wish would stay out of your business."

"So, you grew up here?"

Alden nodded, cautiously shifting into second as the road cleared. "Aye, for the most part. I went to boarding school for secondary studies and then Edinburgh for university. I guess I always knew I wanted to come back though. I just needed the skills for what I wanted to do."

Sabine pulled off the knit cap Alden had insisted she wear and placed it on the dash, smoothing her hands over her hair and tucking it behind her ears as she stared out the windshield. The ocean was surprisingly still, the moon low and heavy over the dark rippled surface, and the church bells rang out and echoed through the silence as they drove slowly into town.

"Where are you staying?" Alden glanced into the rearview mirror at the rucksack Sabine had thrown in the backseat as they were loading up. "I'm surprised anything is open. The boardinghouse and hotel are closed, aren't they?"

"I'm staying with a friend." Sabine reached into the back of the truck and dragged her rucksack though the seats to her lap. "You can just drop me at the front door of the pub. I know my way from there."

Alden turned down the alley, headlights bouncing off the wet brick buildings on either side. The flurry of footprints they'd left in front of the door had disappeared under fresh snowfall as Alden pulled up to the door and cut the engine. Sudden quiet fell around them, and the town seemed even more deserted with the pub empty and dark. "Are ye sure about this? Unless she lives above a shop, all the houses are back where we just came from. I can drive you. You just have to tell me the address." Sabine shook her head and the silence thickened. Alden glanced up into the rearview at the deserted alley behind them. "I can't just leave ye at the pub until I know you've got a ride."

Sabine opened the door and tossed out her rucksack, shrugging off Alden's coat and folding it carefully onto the passenger seat. The wind whipped around the corner of the pub and blew snow between them. Sabine shut the door, then shoved her hands down in her pockets as Alden rolled down the window. "I'll call her to pick me up. Take care of that hand." Sabine's hair blew across her face as she picked up her rucksack and threw it over one shoulder. "Ax murderers who know their way around a medical kit are few and far between. Or so I hear."

Alden watched her walk back down the alley in the direction of their tire tracks. She pulled the collar of her denim jacket around her neck and lowered her head into the wind, hair billowing behind like a scarlet castle flag as she rounded the corner and disappeared.

CHAPTER NINE

S abine leaned against the wind and walked up the alley, but the cold funneled around her like she was walking through an ice tunnel. The snow was deeper now and crept into the tops of her running shoes, caking around her thin cotton socks, so cold it clung like fire on her skin. She pulled her collar up and wound her scarf around it so that it covered at least some of her ears.

She'd clearly packed all wrong for Scotland, and now no shops were open to buy warm clothes and there were no trains to get back to a bigger city where they didn't roll the sidewalks up when it snowed. She should have shopped in Edinburgh before she took the train north, but after the encounter with André, her thoughts had been elsewhere, and then she'd been even more distracted when she found the note from Thea. A quick mental inventory of her rucksack offered a jumble of T-shirts and jeans, a couple of hoodies, and no shoes but the low-top, white leather Pumas on her feet. She'd been in such a rush that last morning at home that it hadn't occurred to her to pack any jackets, or even a second pair of shoes.

She'd just rounded the corner of the alley when she heard Alden's truck start up again, so she slipped behind a bookshop and pressed her back against the wet stone wall. Her stomach was rumbling with hunger or worry, she wasn't sure which, but she couldn't remember what country she was in the last time she'd eaten. The red glow of Alden's taillights was just visible at the edge of the darkness as she took a cautious step out, and the only sounds were the shifting of the snow on the trees and the muffled slip of the seawater against the pier. More snow dusted her hair as she started up the hill toward the train station, which suddenly looked like an abandoned castle, the Gothic arches disappearing into the sheer gray clouds that obscured the moon. It wasn't an ideal plan, sleeping in an open station, but it was the only one she had. She couldn't have told Alden she didn't have a plan for the night; Alden had already assumed she was another entitled tourist who had no business being in town. Other than telling her to fuck off three seconds after they'd met, Alden hadn't been rude, but she hadn't been friendly either, and Sabine wasn't about to hand her more ammunition.

She made it to the top of the hill and across the lot to the station, but she was so busy scanning the waiting area beyond the front arches that she didn't even realize she'd slipped on the ice until she was flat on her back, staring at the sky. She lay dead center in a puddle of motor-oil slush, which instantly soaked through the length of her hair and every inch of her jacket. She let out a long, slow breath, watching it rise like smoke from her mouth and disappear into the endless navy-blue expanse of sky. There was no point to getting up before she was ready; it was impossible to be wetter than she already was.

Well, fuck. She reached gingerly up to touch the back of her head where it had collided with the frozen concrete. *At least it won't take me as long to die of hypothermia.* She finally stood and threw her rucksack onto her shoulder. It landed on her back with a thud as the wind whistled up the hill to wind her wet hair around her face and turn her jacket into a sheet of stiffening ice.

The station was deserted, which Sabine took as a sign of a benevolent god, and she chose a seat in the corner to block the wind still pushing its way through the open building. A sign written in Sharpie was taped to the ticket-counter window.

Station is closed until further notice. Service will resume when it is safe to do so.

It was an odd feeling, being alone in an open public space. A single light fixture hung in the center of the lobby, the fluorescent bulb buzzing intermittently like a warning. Transit posters in frames, curled at the edges, cautioned about pickpockets and the dangers of trying to board a train without a ticket. Various warnings and notices dotted the three walls of the waiting area, and seagulls sailed through the arches of the entrance wall, gliding close enough to Sabine to determine she didn't have any food before disappearing into the darkness again. The scent of iron and grease hovered in the air from the tracks, and she looked around for vending machines, but one glance told her they were as dark as the shop windows.

She tried to unzip her rucksack to retrieve one of her hoodies, but the tiny metal pull on the zipper kept falling from the numb stumps of her fingers. She sat back in her chair and closed her eyes, trying to imagine being on the porch swing at home with the soft brush of a Southern September evening on her skin, the delicate scent of night-blooming jasmine rising from the nightshade garden below. She had a strange feeling of being adrift, but she'd been drifting since the moment she boarded the plane. She couldn't remember when it started, when she'd decided that her own life wasn't as important as Celestine's, but she'd been placating her long before her father's death. Her mother's drama and narcissism had always been jarring and painful, and she'd learned early on that keeping Celestine happy was basic self-preservation.

As she lay down on the row of uneven plastic chairs, she let herself melt slowly into sleep, pushing thoughts of her mother from her mind and telling herself it would be warmer when she woke up.

"Well, now, whadda we 'ave ere?"

Sabine's eyes snapped open. She knew right away she'd been asleep for hours; she was so cold her body felt weighted and weak at the same time, and she wasn't alone. Two men were walking into the station, younger, maybe late teens or early twenties. The one wearing track-suit bottoms and a puffer jacket was hanging back by the entrance, glancing around from side to side, and the other was walking toward her.

"Oi, I asked ya a question." Dirty jeans hung too low on his hips, and there was a cigarette burn on the sleeve of his jacket. "Anyone ever tell you it's rude to ignore people?" He waited, as if his question was real, as if Sabine should respond. His eyes narrowed and he looked back to the other man, who stepped into the station and started inching toward them. "Aye. I know what it is, Callum." The words were aimed at the man behind him, but his gaze never left Sabine's face. "She's fuckin' deaf." He leaned into her, so close she smelled the stench of cigarette smoke and soured laundry rising around him. "Or at least she better fuckin' be, ta be disrespectin' her betters like that."

Sabine lowered her eyes to her hands that were wound around each other in her lap, the fingers white and tense enough to snap the tendons off the bone.

"She wouldn't be here all alone if she dinnae want a wee bit a company. Right, lassie?" He stepped between her knees and leaned down to grab the front of her jacket. Sabine scrambled to her feet and backed over to the nearest wall, hands braced behind her. She jerked her head to the side when he laughed and stepped up to her, his breath hot and acrid on her neck. "I'll take that as a yes." His hand was searching for the button to her jeans as Sabine squeezed her eyes shut and pressed herself harder into the wall.

"Please don't. Just leave me alone."

Her voice was dampened somehow, as powerless as she felt. She wanted to scream, to curse, to say a thousand things, but as soon as the words were out of her mouth, they froze in the air and clattered to the floor. Her limbs were limp and useless as he tore open the zipper on her jeans and shoved his icy hands under her shirt. She gathered all the strength she had left and wrapped it around one word, screaming it so loud that it reverberated around the concrete walls.

The man ripped open her jacket and tore her shirt from the neckline to the hem, leaving it gaping open. He stepped back leisurely, tilting his head to the side as he took out a knife and sliced through the center of her bra. "Let's see if you got anything I want, sweetheart."

Sabine pressed her eyes shut as hard as she could, the stale cigarette stench of his clothes coating the air between them. She felt frozen, and her limbs didn't work when she tried to push him off her. The only thing she could do was repeat the same word over and over, like a chant, barely loud enough to hear. *No.*

"Ah. I think yer gonna regret sayin' no ta me, lass." He jerked his head from side to side to force Sabine to look at him, but she refused. He started to say something else, but a sudden voice sounded behind him, and he whipped his head around. "Wait yer fuckin turn, mate." His words were a gravely hiss. "She's good for more than the first round. She's a fuckin' American."

CHAPTER TEN

Fuck me. Alden watched Sabine walk until she turned the corner, then smacked the steering wheel with the heel of her hand. *I can't just follow her around a deserted village like some kind of creeper, but damn. That girl is a really bad liar.*

She pulled out slowly and looked for Sabine as she turned onto the main road, but she'd already disappeared. Alden accelerated slowly back onto the road along the rocky shore that led to the north village, where the sky was inky black and starless, and the truck lights illuminated the thickly falling snow that blurred the image of the main street in her rearview mirror.

She's a grown woman, and it's clearly feckin' freezin' out. She wouldn't have left if she didn't have somewhere to stay, right?

Alden tried to shake the uneasy memory of watching Sabine walk down the alley and turn the corner as the road ahead curved itself around the restless sea. As she climbed the hill toward home, pinpricks of light in the darkness drew closer to become windows in houses, framing the families gathered around tables and busy kitchens, gold light spilling out onto the drifts of snow beneath.

Almost all Muir Rothesay locals lived outside of the commercial portion of the village, and apart from a few expensive summer rentals along the beach, their homes were all stacked in rows up the face of a steep hill. Most of them were modest row houses and whitewashed cottages set back from the shore, with cobblestone streets and faded green-and-white metal street signs from the last century. An arc of dark forest at the top of the hill created a perfect backdrop, and from the path at the edge of the trees, all the colorful houses and thatched roofs below seemed to fall directly into the whitecapped sea, which had become a famous Instagram opportunity for tourists.

Alden turned up the hill, shifting into a lower gear as her tires threatened to spin, then took a right onto All Saints Street. The house she grew up in was the last home on the block, a tall, slender, three-story row house with a bright yellow door. She made a mental note to fix one of the third-floor shutters hanging askew as she pulled into the brick driveway and cut the engine, listening to the clicks and hiss of the engine as it cooled in the night air. Just to the left, her mother's greenhouse, constructed of recycled windows and doors and held together by a crazy array of hinges, was fogged up from a collection of heaters and humidifiers. The warmth was fading fast in the cab of the truck; frozen wind crept into the cracks and wrapped around her legs as Alden leaned back, mentally sorting through Sabine's story.

Didn't she say she found the pub only because she was looking for a place to stay? Alden tried to ignore the twist in her stomach as she looked at her watch and then to the rising moon just visible through the smudge of clouds. *It doesn't matter anyway. Even if I went back, I'd never find her now. She could be anywhere.*

Alden looked up to see her mother leaning out the door and frantically gesturing her inside. She shouted something about Alden "catching her death" as she stared dramatically to the heavens and waved her in again. Alden nodded and gathered her things from the backseat of the truck. She'd moved home over a year ago to help her parents care for her nephew when her sister Eileen had died suddenly. It hadn't been easy, and to be honest, things were getting harder by the day. It was difficult to reach a grieving twelve-year-old when you hadn't had a chance to grieve yourself.

Alden slung her bag and metal lunch box over her shoulder and headed toward the house, dropping everything on the hall bench as she came in. The air was warm with the scent of Guinness stew, and bubbling laughter bounced down the hall from the kitchen. Like most row houses, theirs had been built back in the day with traditional closed-off communal spaces, punctuated with hallways and doors, meant to give big Catholic families some peace and privacy.

When Alden was about her nephew's age, she'd helped her dad gut the lower level and remodel it into a bright, open living area with the kitchen to the left, a massive stone fireplace in the center surrounded by cozy couches, and tall windows that flooded the space with natural light, even during the short days of winter.

Morgan glanced over his shoulder from his post at the sink when Alden walked in, wet potato peeler in hand. "There's a pint waitin' on the counter for ya. I'd pour it, but yer mother tells me I can't leave the sink until I've peeled every spud in the country." He winked at her and continued. "Thank the blessed Lord we're not in Ireland."

"Well, since he can't talk and peel at the same time..." Her mother poured Alden the pint of lager and kissed her cheek. "We'll be waiting for dinner till next week. I'll tell ye that fer free."

Alden smiled and shrugged off her coat as she sank down into a mismatched chair at the kitchen table and watched her parents tease and banter in their familiar rhythm. The warmth and love between them had always been palpable, and Alden had just assumed that was the way love was—that once you found it, it grew, forging roots strong enough to hold the family together no matter what the wind blew their way. She'd been wrong.

"Stop in to yer nephew's room, will ye?" Worry colored Morgan's voice as he glanced back over his shoulder at Alden. "He's had a rough one today."

Alden swallowed half her beer in a long gulp and set it on the table. "He was at the train station, right? What the hell was he doing there? The trains aren't even running."

"Jesus, Mary, and Joseph. I don't feckin' know." Morgan turned around and ran his hands through his hair before he leaned back onto the sink. "You know I have such a hard time communicating with him—"

"We all do, to be fair." Gwen crumpled some dried red chilis in her hand and sprinkled them into her favorite orange enamel pot. "And if ye ask me, we're the root of the problem, not him."

"Anyway, I tried for the better part of an hour, and he never did tell me what's going on in that head." Morgan reached across the counter for his own pint. "When I got there, he was just sitting on the landing bench, staring down at the rails."

Alden shook her head, pushing a pile of notepaper to the center of the table. "Well, I don't know what that means, but it can't be good." She finished the last of her pint, and it was a moment before she continued. "I know it doesn't help that he does school at home, either. I know when I was twelve, everything revolved around your mates. Or it should, anyway."

"Aye, an' there's the thing." Gwen took the peeler out of Morgan's hand and got started on the three remaining potatoes. "He doesn't have any mates way up here in Rothesay, and for the life o' me, I don't know how he'd even go about making any."

Morgan opened another can of Guinness and picked up Alden's pint, carefully pouring down the side of the glass. "That reminds me. Where did the American end up staying tonight?"

Alden shrugged. "With her friend in town, I guess."

"What friend?" Morgan dropped the bottle in the trash. "She said she didn't know anyone in town."

"She said that?" Alden shook her head and reached for her keys. "Are ya sure?"

"Aye. That was the whole problem. She said she assumed there'd be accommodation available in town, as you would, of course, and then the poor thing got here only to find everything closed because of the weather. When you walked in without her, I thought she must have gotten lucky and found a place that was still open."

"Ye left the poor girl in town? What was her name, Sabine?" Alden's mother whipped her head around, peeler lofted in the air. "Your da told me she was just lovely and saved the food delivery he had goin' today. She'd be more than welcome here anytime." Gwen paused to drop the peeler back into the sink and planted her hand on her hip. "What were ye thinking?"

"Damn it. I knew she was lying." Alden stood and slid back into her jacket. "I had a bad feeling when I left her, but she insisted she didn't need help, that she had a friend in town she could call."

"And you believed her? D'ye know nothing about women?" Gwen shook her head as she dried her hands on her apron. "I love ye like you're my own daughter, but you can be a right eejit sometimes."

"Mam, I am your own daughter." Alden smiled and stopped to kiss her cheek as she headed for the door. "I'll be back."

"Don't ye come back here without the American!" Gwen's voice echoed in hallway as Alden ran out and slammed the door behind her.

The truck was still warm so it started right up, and Alden drove faster than she should have down the hill and back out to North Road. She mentally sifted through all the places Sabine could be on the way back into town, but beyond churches or the picnic gazebo in the village park, nowhere was remotely warm or sheltered. She knew for a fact that every pub and restaurant was closed, and when she dialed the two places she thought might be open for accommodation, the call went straight to answer phone.

"Goddamn it."

Alden's stomach sank as she clicked off the phone and tossed it back onto her passenger seat. She slowed as she rolled into town, looking for new footfalls, but the drifts were fresh, as if no one had been there for days. She turned down the alley leading to the pub, but even her own tire tracks from earlier had disappeared. As a last resort she checked the Catholic cathedral and Anglican church, but other than porchlights and a few notices tacked to the doors, even they were dark and locked up. Alden pulled her truck over by the pier and killed her lights. She rubbed her temples too hard, staring out the window at nothing. *There's nowhere for her to go. How could she have disappeared without so much as leaving a footprint?*

The moon broke free from a pewter cluster of clouds, and the sudden light illuminated the crystalline snow the wind swirled into the air. Alden cut her fog lights and stared up the hill. The snow in the air settled to the ground as the wind changed direction and the moonlight fell onto the street, reflecting shadows into footprints that had been invisible under the headlights. Alden fired up the engine and followed them carefully up the hill, getting out twice to get a closer look at the path. She flicked her lights back on the second she realized where they led.

"Train station," she muttered. "Smart lass."

She locked the truck and dropped the keys into her pocket as she walked toward the entrance.

❖

Sabine's eyes were still shut as the man shouted over at someone over his shoulder. She tensed to stone when she heard the metallic clank of his belt buckle, followed by the low hiss of his zipper. She tried to push him off but had no strength in her arms, and her knees began to buckle as he sank his teeth into her shoulder. Then, time strangely seemed to slow, intensifying the strange sensation of the man being literally ripped off her. Sabine felt the weight of his body as it left hers, and then icy air rushed in to claim the space.

She opened her eyes as he fell violently back onto the concrete, the knife skittering across the floor and coming to rest under a row of plastic seats. His gaze was still locked on her. Her lungs strained to fill as she pulled her shirt together and realized it was Alden who had thrown the man onto the ground.

"Who are you, her boyfriend or sumthin'?" The man's eyes narrowed, and he spat the words in Alden's direction as he scrambled to his feet. "Ya need to learn to share your toys. I told ye I'll give 'er back when I'm finished—"

Alden's fist knocked the last word out of his mouth, and the impact reverberated like a loose echo, bouncing around the station walls before it faded. He fell backward again, blood streaming from his nose down the front of his shirt. He scanned the room for backup, but his friend was long gone. Alden took another step toward him, and he held up his hand, half scrambling, half running as he backed out of the station and into the darkness, still holding his nose and cursing. Sabine finally drew a breath, listening to his footsteps grow fainter, muffled by the snow.

Alden shook off her jacket and draped it around Sabine's shoulders. She was shaking so violently that Alden pulled her into her chest and wrapped her arms around her, holding her tight until Sabine softened in her arms. Her words were a whisper when she finally spoke. "Are you all right? Did he hurt you?"

Sabine pulled her torn shirt together, but all the buttons had been ripped off. She eased the collar of her jacket down her shoulder. An angry red bite mark at the base of her neck was swelling, but the skin didn't look broken.

"Sabine, I'm so sorry." Frustration crept into Alden's words, and she gently pulled the coat back over Sabine's bare shoulder. "I can't believe I let this happen."

Sabine didn't say anything, just leaned in slowly until her forehead touched Alden's chest. Alden wrapped her arms around her and stood there as Sabine's taut muscles started to unfold onto her bones, until her breath didn't sound like knives, until she remembered no one but Alden was there.

Sabine drew in a deep breath, then finally took a step back. "But you didn't."

Alden hesitated, frustration still lingering at the edges of her words. "What do you mean?"

"You didn't—" Sabine let her words fade as she pulled Alden's jacket together and tried to zip it up over her bare skin, but her fingers felt wooden and frozen into place. "Let anything happen to me."

Alden met her gaze for a long second, then zipped the jacket to the top. She took both of Sabine's hands in hers and turned them over. "Can you feel this?"

Sabine shook her head as Alden gently pressed each of her fingertips, then her palm, watching her intently. When Alden reached the back of her hand near her wrist, she told Alden she felt the touch, but it didn't feel normal. Her skin looked waxy, almost gray, and her fingers didn't move when she told them to.

"Sabine." Alden's voice was low and even. "I think you might have frostbite. We've got to get you warmed up, and hopefully we'll have caught it in time. We need to go now, though."

"Maybe." Sabine narrowed her eyes, and she hesitated. "Where are you taking me?"

"Home. Where I should have taken your stubborn ass in the first place." Alden picked her up by the waist and stood her on one of the plastic chairs. "Hop on my back. If your feet are frostbitten too, you don't want to be walking on 'em. You can give yourself nerve damage going from here to the truck."

Sabine wrapped her legs around Alden's waist and leaned into the warmth of her body. Alden picked up her rucksack in her free hand, and they walked out of the station, Sabine's head heavy and silent on Alden's shoulder.

CHAPTER ELEVEN

Sabine reached for her rucksack in the backseat of the truck as Alden turned into a brick driveway and switched off the engine.

"This is your house?"

She took her time studying the tall, slender home with off-center windows and light spilling out in every direction. It looked to be leaning slightly to the right, but that could have been a trick of the enormous moon hanging as if by a silver thread behind it.

"It looks like something out of a Dr. Seuss fairy tale."

"Aye. You're not the first person to say that." Alden smiled, slipping the keys into her pocket. "It's my parents' home. They adopted my nephew last year, and I moved back to help until they find their feet with him." Alden took Sabine's rucksack out of her hands and put it on her own shoulder. "And it's almost cute that you'd think I'd let you carry that." She got out and walked around to open Sabine's door. "Are you always this stubborn?"

"Do all Americans annoy you, or is it just the beautiful ax murderers? We get a bad rap, you know."

Alden laughed and shook her head. "My da let ya in on that one, did he?" She held out her hand to steady Sabine as she stepped out of the truck. "It's all Americans, by the way. Every one of 'em."

Sabine smiled and stepped onto the stone path to the door. "Are you coming?"

"Are you sure you're all right to walk? How do you feel?" Alden slid the rucksack onto her shoulder and shut the truck door. "I mean, besides ridiculous for wearing wee cotton trainers to the north side o' Scotland. That would be understandable."

"Honestly, they're fine. Cold, but fine. It's my hands that still feel weird." She looked to the front door and hesitated, her hands shoved deep into the jacket pockets. A dog barked near the bottom of the hill, the sound echoing up and around them in the cold, still air. "Alden, could we maybe not tell your parents what just happened?" She paused, looking back at the truck as steam escaped the hood and disappeared into the night. "It's just...a lot."

"Of course, I'm not going to tell anyone." Alden put a hand on the small of her back and guided her onto the path. "That way, when I hunt him down and bury him under the pier tomorrow, it'll go off without a hitch."

The front door swung open suddenly, and a short, plump woman with silver waves cut to her chin rushed out wearing an apron and snow boots, pulling Sabine into her arms for a tight hug.

"Thank the baby Jesus!" She let her go, leaned back to get a good look at her, and pulled her in again. "I was about to go down to the church and light a candle for ye, and I hadn't even met ya!"

"Sabine, the strange woman hugging you is my mother, Gwendolyn Wallace." Obvious warmth colored Alden's words as she swung the rucksack in and dropped it by the door. Morgan rounded the corner into view and clapped his hand over his heart, cell phone in hand. He held it up to Alden and cocked one eyebrow. "I've been calling ye since half-seven, ya wee bastard." He motioned everyone in and shut the door against the cold. "But no matter, yer both here now, and that's all that matters."

Sabine followed everyone down the hall until it opened into a beautifully warm and rumpled family room centered around a massive, crackling fireplace with a bright, homey kitchen to the left. Something on the stove smelled like heaven, and her stomach twisted with the memory of how hungry she'd been in the station.

"Get yerself sat down, dear. Let's warm ye up." Sabine had changed her ripped shirt for a hoodie in the truck, which was lucky since the first thing Alden's mother did was take her coat and drape a wonderfully cozy tartan blanket around her shoulders. "We'll have ye fixed up and fed in no time. We were just about to dish up the stew, so you've perfect timing."

"Mam, will ya take a look at her fingers? I think she's got some frostbite set in." Alden took the kettle to the sink and filled it, setting it onto the stove and flicking the switch before she turned back around.

Both of Alden's parents leaned over her to check out her fingers, then stood up without a word and looked at each other. Morgan shook his head and put a steadying hand on Sabine's shoulder.

"That's going to hurt like hellfire when it comes back to life, love, but I think you might have just avoided any permanent damage. Let's get ya warmed up and see what yer dealin' with."

The tea kettle started a slow whistle, and within three minutes, Sabine had a steaming cup of sweet, milky tea in front of her and a hot-water bottle clad in a hilarious handknit cardigan meant to warm her hands. Gwendolyn even covered her hands and the hot-water bottle with a wool scarf to help hold the heat in.

"Thank you, Mrs. Wallace." Sabine had a sudden maddening urge to cry and looked down to hide the tears burning her eyes. "This is really kind. I'm sorry to cause such a fuss."

"Just call me Gwen, dear, and I'm delighted to have someone to fuss over." She looked at Alden pulling soup bowls and plates out of the cupboard and smiled. "That one hasn't let me lift a finger since she moved back home, and my grandson Declan, well, he doesn't come out of his room unless dragged, so I'm at perpetual loose ends."

Alden came back to the table and cleared away the tilted pile of notepaper and pens, tucking them away on the counter. "Declan is my nephew, my late sister Eileen's son. He's twelve." Gwen put down five mismatched pottery plates and topped each with a wide, shallow bowl. Alden followed behind, tucking a linen napkin and silverware beside each place setting. After she distributed the last of them, she looked around like she'd lost something. "Where did your father disappear to?"

The front door creaked open right on cue, and Morgan appeared with a dusty bottle in his hand and a beaming smile. "I've been waiting for an excuse to break out the good whiskey." He winked over his shoulder as he dusted the snowflakes from the tops of his shoulders. "And hopefully, you're going to understand why we need it inna few minutes, love."

"Aye." Gwen unwrapped the scarf around the hot-water bottle and had Sabine turn her hands over. She pulled a pair of round, gold-rimmed glasses out of her apron pocket and slipped them on, leaning in to look more closely. "I hope so, anyway."

"Any color coming back?" Morgan shook his head as he took four crystal whiskey tumblers out of the cabinet and placed them on the table.

"Saints preserve us, not even a smidge yet." Gwen wrapped her hands up a bit tighter and put her arm around Sabine's shoulder. "You let me know when ye start to feel 'em again, yeah?"

Alden lifted the lid of a pot on the stove and looked at her mother. "I might see how Declan is for a minute, if you're settled here, then. Do you want me to do anything to the stew before I go, Mam?"

"Just pop that loaf of bread in the oven for me, love." Gwen pointed at the dough in a dented tin bread pan on the counter and turned back to Sabine. "Now you tell me a little about yerself, poppet. How long ye in town for?"

"I'm not sure." Sabine hadn't even had time to wrap her own head around the shitstorm her life had become, much less thought about a way to explain it to other people. "I do know I'll be in Scotland for a year, though." She paused, noticing the sensation of pinpricks beginning to start on her fingers. "I'm from New Orleans. My aunt died recently, and I..." The tears started to build again behind her eyelids.

"And ye thought it might be time for a change?" Morgan pulled out a chair and plunked three of the crystal tumblers on the table, filled almost to the halfway point with whiskey.

Sabine wiped her eyes with her sleeve and nodded. "I'm sorry. I don't know why I'm getting emotional. It's just been a long day, I guess."

Morgan squeezed her shoulder and waited until she met his gaze. "There's never a reason to apologize for tears, love. You can press things down only so long before yer heart decides to clear the deck. We celebrate feelings in this house." He nudged her glass toward her. "It takes courage to go through something rather than around it."

The warmth in Morgan's smile washed over her like a wide swath of sunlight, immersing her in the same feeling of déjà vu she'd had walking into Rothesay for the first time.

"Now, let's see how those hands are doing," Gwen said as she unwrapped them and held out her own hands for Sabine to lay hers on top.

"They certainly aren't numb anymore. In fact, they're starting to feel like they're on fire."

"Yes!" Morgan slapped the table and handed out the glasses. "That's what we've been waiting for. That just means the tissue is still alive, which is a very good thing." He took a closer look at the slightly mottled pattern on Sabine's hands and glanced up at Gwen. "There's still a few dodgy spots though, do ye think? Best keep them on the heat, but start shifting them around a mite if ya can, to get the blood moving a wee bit."

"Wow." Sabine took a long breath and let it out slowly. "They feel like they work again finally, but seriously, it's like I'm holding them over flames. I can see why you went for the whiskey."

"Never fear. We are a country that has an answer for everything." Morgan rifled through a drawer in the kitchen before he came back to the table. Sabine laughed as he plunked a red-and-white paper straw into her glass. "And that answer is whiskey. Welcome to Scotland, lass."

Once her fingers felt almost normal again, Sabine tucked into two bowls of rich Guinness stew. It was heaven, with tender chunks of beef and colorful veggies simmered in an impossibly rich brown broth, and the homemade bread Gwen had pulled from the oven at the last second was nothing short of gorgeous. A generous slab of handmade butter slicked the golden crust, and steam rose like magic around the knife as Morgan cut into it. He kept passing Sabine another slice until she had to hold up a hand in surrender.

"I can't. I don't think I've ever been this full, but this is the best meal I've eaten in ages."

"I married her for cooking," Morgan dished up another bowl of stew for himself and gazed down the table at Gwen. "The fact that she's the best-looking lass in the Highlands is just a bonus."

"Oh, God." Alden rolled her eyes good-naturedly and glanced down the table at Sabine. "Living with these two is like being stuck in a never-ending romance novel. Poor Declan. No wonder he never comes out of his room. He's afraid he'll get sugar shock."

"Where is Declan?" Sabine glanced at his empty place setting. "Is he scared of Americans like Alden is?"

Morgan nearly choked himself laughing, but Alden just shook her head and appeared offended. "I can't believe you said that after I left ya in a deserted town and gifted you authentic Scottish frostbite." She popped the last bite of bread into her mouth. "Some people have no gratitude whatsoever."

"Hey. There's Decs." Morgan pushed back from the table and motioned over a thin boy in faded jeans and a rugby shirt who shuffled down the stairs toward the kitchen. He looked a little like a young Harry Styles, but with better hair. "I was wondering if he was ever going to get hungry."

Gwen made an eating motion with her spoon and pulled out the chair next to her. He hesitated, then shrugged and sat, looking at Alden for a moment before he glanced over to Sabine.

"Oh, that's…" Alden went to the counter and returned with a pen and notepaper, then paused and pointed to Sabine. "Um…" She held up her hand and made the hand shapes of S-A-B-I-N-E in sign language so slowly that Sabine had forgotten how to spell her own name by the time Alden reached the last glacially slow letter.

Sabine smiled and waved in Declan's direction to get his attention before she put down her spoon. *That was legit the slowest hand-lettering I've ever seen. I'm like a year older now.* Declan's face lit up when he saw her signing, and he laughed, signing back with lightning speed. *Is your name really Samimee? I'm guessing my aunt tanked that?*

"Bloody hell." Alden was staring at them in shock. "You know sign language?"

"Well, it's American Sign Language, or ASL, so technically it's superior to whatever you just did there, but yes."

"Sweet Mother o' God." Morgan laughed, shaking his head as he watched Sabine sign what she'd said to Declan. "Wow. I did not see that one coming."

Gwen dished up Declan's stew and squeezed Sabine's shoulder as she sat back down. Her voice seemed far away when she finally spoke, and she was still looking across the table at Declan, who was making handshapes in exaggerated slow motion to tease Alden. "You're an angel. I haven't seen a smile like that from him in ages."

So, what's your name sign? Sabine asked, saying the words out loud to the rest of the table as she spoke to Declan, then doing the same as he signed back to her.

What do you mean, my name sign? Declan looked confused.

"That was my question." Morgan leaned forward on his elbows, his whiskey forgotten. "What's a name sign?"

"Well." Sabine signed and spoke at the same time. "Every deaf and hearing-impaired person who uses sign language has the option to choose a sign for themselves, something that represents who they are. It's a lot faster than hand-lettering everyone's name and always handy if two people have the same name."

Alden got up, cleared everyone's dishes but Declan's, and returned to the table, picking up the whiskey tumbler Morgan slid down to her. "Aye. Seems a damn sight better than pointing at people, which is what I've been doing."

Declan looked thoughtful as he spooned the last of his stew into his mouth and set down his spoon to sign. *Will you ask them if—*

Sign it to them, and I'll say it out loud so they see both together. Sabine signed and spoke as she kept eye contact with Declan. *It looks like you've been too easy on them. They've got to learn sometime.*

That made everyone laugh, and Declan smiled as he paused, pushing a shiny wave of dark brown hair behind his ear. *I want to choose everyone's name signs for them. Is that okay?* He looked at Morgan and Gwen, excitement flickering in his eyes, and they agreed.

"Wait," Alden interjected, rolling her eyes. "Don't I get a say in this?"

Sabine looked at Declan and smiled, then both turned back and signed *no*.

"Aye. I see how it is." Alden sniffed and leaned back in her chair, whiskey in hand and sarcasm dripping. "I can already tell this is going to go well for me."

Declan attentively watched Sabine sign Alden's words and laughed before he headed back to his room with his stew, looking excited to start working on the name signs. He was halfway down the hall when he turned around and got Sabine's attention.

Wait. What's yours?

Sabine made the handshape for the letter S, then tapped it twice on her heart.

That fits you. Declan signed, then flashed them all a smile before he turned and took the stairs two at a time.

❖

By the time the dishes had been done and Alden showed Sabine to her room, it was nearly midnight. Gwen had insisted on rubbing Sabine's hands with a tincture of olive oil and black pepper and sent her up to bed with a hot-water bottle, but the burning had cooled by the end of dinner, and other than being a bit stiff, they felt almost normal again.

Alden led the way up the staircase, made of glossy oak beams and square peg nails, looking back over her shoulder at Sabine. "Mam has been obsessed with growing microgreens and God knows what else in every available space for the last year, so the safest thing to do was put you in my room in the attic." Alden led her up the last short staircase to the attic door. "Don't worry. I'm sleeping on the couch downstairs."

The door at the end of the staircase had a rounded top and was barely tall enough for Sabine to walk through, and she was only a couple of inches over five feet on a good day. Alden grabbed the top trim and ducked to follow her into an arched attic bedroom with wide wood-plank floors painted black and warm maple boards lining the high-pitched ceiling. A double bed with a horizonal door for a headboard was piled with cozy, rumpled wool blankets and aged linen sheets. The tall window on the far center wall framed the starry sky like a painting, and a chandelier made of iron pipe and Edison bulbs flared to life with the click of a switch. The light dimmed as Alden turned a dial on the wall, and just enough remained to illuminate a worn, cognac-leather couch tucked under the eaves opposite the bed.

"You'll be safe from the jungle up here." Alden dropped her rucksack under the eave by the bed and pulled a stack of extra blankets out of a steamer trunk that served as a footboard. She stood, glancing at the door like she was making sure it was still there, before she continued. "And Mam told me to tell you you're welcome to stay as long as ye like."

"Your parents have been so kind, but I'll be out of your hair soon. Well, as soon as town comes back to life." Sabine sat on the bed and ran her hand over a striped wool blanket with a handstitched navy hem. "It's a strange feeling to have the money to buy what I need here, but literally nowhere to get it."

Alden opened a narrow door near the one leading to the stairs and leaned inside, flicking a light switch on the wall. "This is your water closet, by the way. That cast-iron tub is way too heavy to be in any attic, much less a three-hundred-year-old one, but at least the microgreens on the second floor will break your fall."

Sabine went to check it out, instantly charmed by the antique tub that looked like it belonged in a doll house. "This is adorable. I've never seen such a tiny tub."

"Aye. I guess it is. People were smaller back then. The tub is older than the house." Alden motioned her out into the main room and pointed to some exposed copper piping with an odd gauge on the wall. "And I happen to know you've had a rough day, so I want to show you something top secret that will help."

"Watch yourself." Sabine stopped and ran her finger over the slightly dented but gleaming pipes. "If I didn't know better, I'd think you were warming up to me." She paused, looking around the attic. "And why do I smell lemongrass?"

"Don't count on it. I'm just being hospitable." Alden resisted the urge to roll her eyes. Barely. "Or it's possible I may feel a bit guilty for leaving you in the village when I knew you were lying." She polished the crystal case of an old-fashioned pressure gauge hung above the pipes, using her shirtsleeve. "Also, when did you learn what lemongrass smells like? Don't most Americans think herbs come from the supermarket?"

"Oh my God. You're relentless." Sabine playfully punched Alden in the arm and instantly regretted it, shaking out her tender fingers as she shook her head. "What did we ever do to you?"

Alden just pointed to the pipes. "Tap the top bolt twice."

Sabine gingerly reached out and tapped it lightly. Nothing happened.

"Okay." Alden obviously tried but failed to keep a straight face. "Now tap it like it's not a poisonous snake."

Sabine tapped it harder, and the maze of copper piping swung open via hidden hinges on a wooden panel door. Inside was a roomy mahogany box and silver tray, with two cut-crystal glasses and a dark bottle of something too small to be wine. It had a wax seal over the cork and a faded parchment label in a foreign language that was peeling at the edges. The only word she could make out was Port. A small bunch of dried lemongrass flower, accented with lavender, hung on the back of the door, tied with green hemp twine.

"Wow. If you're trying to impress me," Sabine said, picking up the bottle to take a close look, "it's working. How did you even find out this was here?"

"It wasn't. I designed it for Da when I was still at university." Alden split the seal on the bottle, poured into one of the glasses, and handed it to Sabine. "At the time he was still teaching at a university in Aberdeen, and the attic served as his office. I cleared the space behind the wall and built it in for him for Christmas one year. He loved it."

"Wait." Sabine looked at the second glass still empty on the tray. "You're not drinking?"

"No. I'm headed back downstairs so you can get some sleep." She glanced at the small copper alarm clock on the nightstand. "I just wanted you to know it was there if you fancied a nightcap."

"I slept for a while at the train station." Sabine tried to rub the dull ache from her forehead, but the pressure only pushed it deeper. "I don't even know what day it is anymore, so I'm not really on a schedule."

She looked out the window to the moon, trying to quell a sudden feeling of panic at being alone. What had happened in the train station still clung to her like acrid smoke from burning trash. She hadn't planned to tell Alden, but if she didn't, she wouldn't be able to close her eyes. It made it too easy to remember the station: the grease-soaked scent of the iron rails, the hollow thud of her back hitting the wall when he ripped her shirt open, even the indescribable feeling of not being able to fight back, to suddenly feel like a lifeless rag doll.

"Hey. Are you okay?" Alden caught her gaze and put a hand on her back to steady her. "You went pale all of a sudden."

She pulled a cozy throw off the coach and draped it around Sabine's shoulders, then poured her own glass of port and led Sabine over to the sofa. Alden settled into the opposite corner of the couch from Sabine, who wrapped the throw around her legs and gingerly tasted the port. It was surprisingly rich, with a spiced sweetness and a long, slow burn as it sank down the entire length of her chest.

"So, Da tells me you're in Scotland for a year?" Alden set her glass on the small wooden coffee table beside them. She hesitated. "But it seems to me you're not the kind of girl to just pick up and move to a different country."

Sabine nodded, slipping off her shoes and tucking her legs up underneath her on the couch. "Yeah. Good guess."

"So, you're not going to tell me?"

"You say that like you were expecting me to just spill it." Sabine swirled the port up around the sides of the glass. It thinned to a sheer, hypnotic, cherry hue that would be perfect to paint into a sunset backdrop at the theater. If it weren't a million miles away now. "Do you always get everything you want?"

"Fine." Alden ran both hands through her hair. "You've got a bit about ye, I'll give ya that. If you tell me, then you can ask me something you want to know." She seemed to catch herself as soon as she spoke and added, "Something innocuous like what size my boots are or something."

"Oh yeah. I've been dying to know that all day." Sabine set her drink down, piled her hair on top of her head, and secured it with the elastic she'd had around her wrist since she left New Orleans. "Always my first question when I meet a mysterious butch."

"I can't believe ye just called me a butch." Alden seemed shocked for a moment, then rolled her eyes and stretched her legs out, plunking her boots on the wood-plank table. "I'm clearly high femme. My stilettos are just in the shop." She shot Sabine an actual smile and paused. "How do you know those terms, anyway? You don't exactly give off gay vibes."

"Why? Because we've known each other for almost a day now, and I'm not sitting in your lap, unbuttoning your shirt?"

"Damn." Alden let out a low whistle and laced her fingers behind her neck, leaning back in the crook of the sofa and locking her gaze on Sabine. "Ya don't mince words, do you?"

"Not usually." Sabine closed her eyes and drew in the scent of the port, the heat of her hand around the glass raising smooth notes of dark cherry and cacao to her nose. "People tend to underestimate me, so I make sure it's clear they shouldn't."

Sabine held Alden's gaze until Alden smiled, rolling up her shirtsleeves to her elbow. A tattoo of a nautical compass, in intricate black and smoke tones, covered the inside of her left forearm.

"You don't date much, do you, Sabine?"

"Why would you say that?"

"Listen. Apparently, I've already let the cat out of the bag, so I'll just say it. You're the kind of beautiful that people write poetry about, but I think to most, you might come off as intimidating." Alden rolled the glass between her palms, the port climbing the sides of the crystal and scattering the golden light from the chandelier. "But then again, I hear that's common for ax murderers."

"Enough about me." Sabine arched an eyebrow and sank the rest of her port. "Let's talk about you, Lothario."

"Lothario, huh? Jesus. I see my reputation precedes me. I'll have to thank Da personally tomorrow." Alden leaned back and laughed, then downed the rest of her port and reached out for Sabine's empty glass. "I have a feeling I may need a top-up for this line of questioning." She walked over to her stash cabinet and poured, then kept her gaze on Sabine as she walked back. "Aye. I guess I promised you a question." She leaned back into the sofa, returning her feet to the table. "Hit me."

"How old are you?"

Sabine waited for her to answer, although she had a pretty good idea already by the traces of silver at Alden's temples and the magnetic crinkles around her eyes, too distinct to be anything but decades of laughter.

"Thirty-seven." Alden smiled. "And you?"

"Thirty-three, but we're talking about you here." She leaned back and studied Alden's face for a long moment. "And what do you do for a living that you came into the pub dripping blood today?" Sabine leaned back and swept Alden with her eyes. "Organized crime?"

Alden smiled, then looked into the rafters and rested her glass on her knee before she answered. "I'm an architect, but I specialize in the preservation of historic buildings, specifically in the Highlands." Her voice softened and slowed, as if she were narrating a silent film in an empty theater. "I've loved them since I was a kid. There's just something so...energetically dense about them. They absorb centuries of energy, all the history of the people that lived there, prayed or died there. It seeps into the stones and timbers, the very bones of the place." Silence fell around them, and the brush of the wind against the window was the only sound. "That's too sacred not to preserve."

"Ah." Sabine smiled, pulling the tie out of her hair and letting it fall to her waist before she draped it over one shoulder. "An undercover romantic."

"Aye," Alden said, with no trace of a smile. "Although if you tell anyone, I'll have to kill you."

"And bury me under the pier?"

"Exactly."

The port started to warm Sabine's cheeks, and she stretched her legs out beside Alden's. Alden took the glass out of her hand and turned one palm over, brushing her fingertip slowly over each of Sabine's. "Can you feel this?" Sabine nodded, watching Alden's face as she traced the tips of each finger, then down to the center of her palm. "I'm not going to pretend it wasn't a close call with that frostbite, but I think you're safe." Alden brushed the inside of Sabine's wrist with her thumb as she gave her hand back and tucked a stray lock of hair behind her ear. "No sign of permanent damage."

"I get the feeling you never wear your hair down." Sabine sat back and smiled, leaning slightly to look at the back of Alden's neck. "Will you show me?"

"Correct." Alden touched the leather wrap she'd bound it in that morning at the base of her neck. "And...no."

Sabine thought for a moment, then said, "If you show me, you can ask me one more question before I go to bed."

Alden hesitated, then reached back and unraveled the leather strip. Her dark chestnut hair fell around her shoulders with its own movement, wild, as if Alden's bare hands were the only thing to ever tame it. Sabine leaned forward and ran her fingers through the waves, watching the light glint across the dark, textured layers as it fell around Alden's face.

"I've never seen longer hair that makes someone look even more masculine." She tucked a piece of it behind Alden's ear, her fingertips grazing the strong slope of her neck. "When it's loose, you look...savage." She paused, choosing each word. "Dangerous, maybe."

"You're in Scotland." Alden held her gaze, her voice low and rough at the edges like charred wood. "All the beauty here is savage."

Alden's eyes were a silky honey brown, streaked with gold, a stark contrast to her bare, dark lashes and wild hair. Sabine caught herself staring and looked down, intensity crackling in the air between them.

"You need to get some sleep." Alden took her empty glass gently and put it on the nightstand, then finished the last of her own port, picking up both glasses as she left. She'd almost reached the door before Sabine said the word she'd braced herself not to say. "Wait."

Alden paused and looked back, clutching the open door.

"I know this is a lot to ask." Sabine took a deep breath and let it settle in her chest. "But I was asleep when—" She tried to wrap words around how she felt. "—at the train station."

Alden's voice was soft. "When you were attacked?"

Sabine nodded. She knew Alden was waiting for her to continue, but she couldn't. The memory of how it felt to wake up in fear, to have all her choices ripped away before she even opened her eyes, settled onto her chest, pressing all the air from her lungs.

"Are you saying you'd feel safer if I slept up here on the couch?"

Sabine nodded again, hating the sudden tears burning the backs of her eyes. She wiped the first to fall to her cheek with the heel of her hand, harder than she'd meant to. "How did you know?"

"Because I was there." Alden's gaze softened, and Sabine felt the weight of the images playing in both their minds. "I get it. I'll be back up in a few minutes."

Sabine nodded and watched the door close behind her. She found her toiletry bag in her rucksack, then brushed her teeth and finger-combed the tangles out of her hair with weak arms. She had a brush somewhere, but suddenly she was too tired to look, too tired to do anything but pull back the covers and slip into bed. The attic was so silent she heard snowflakes brushing past the dark window behind her. Her eyes fluttered closed as she drew in the sheer rosewater scent that lingered on the linen pillow like a faded garden memory.

When she opened them again, Alden was turning off the chandelier. Sabine turned onto her side to watch as she placed a small brass candlestick on the nightstand. She struck a match and lit the candle, then made up her bed on the couch.

Sabine watched the amber flame rise and fall, the tension in her body softening with the sweet scent of warming beeswax. "Why did you bring me this candle?"

Alden pulled her sweater over her head, tugging down the T-shirt she wore underneath, then climbed under the duvet on the couch. She turned onto her side to face Sabine. "Because I thought you might not want it to be completely dark. There's another in the water closet, just in case." Alden smiled. "Are you ready for your question?"

Sabine nodded, already awash in the seductive darkness.

"Beyond Scotland, where is the one place you've always wanted to go?"

"Paris," Sabine said softly. "Always Paris. I want to sketch it."

Alden turned over onto her back, and Sabine had almost drifted to sleep when she heard her own voice again. This time, it was just a whisper.

"Alden?"

When Sabine opened her eyes, Alden was staring into the rafters.

"I have one more question."

"Aye." Alden paused, running a hand through her hair. "Go on."

Sabine's eyes fluttered closed. "Are you still in love with the American who broke your heart?"

It was a moment before Alden answered, each word suspended in the air between them as if they were unfolding onto an empty stage.

"No." Alden's voice was softer than her words. "I'm not sure I ever was."

CHAPTER TWELVE

The next morning, Alden was gone by the time Sabine opened her eyes. Her duvet was folded neatly at the foot of the couch, and the sun shone liquid gold through the window, dust motes floating across the wide, translucent beam like dappled leaves on a river.

Sabine drew a bath and had just sunk into the rose-scented bubbles up to her chin when her phone rang. She clicked on speakerphone, setting it back down carefully where it had been lying on the bath stool.

"Oh my God, I'm so glad you answered!" Colette's voice cracked, and Sabine heard her plunk down into one of her kitchen chairs. "I was just checking out the weather, and there's supposed to be an absolute blizzard happening in the north of Scotland right now. Are you okay?"

Sabine smiled, stretching out her fingers in the warm water. "I'm totally fine. At least one of us checked the weather."

"Did you find a place to stay at least?"

"For the time being. I need to decide what the hell I'm doing next, but I'll get to that today, I guess."

Sabine listened to Colette tapping her nails on the table. She had something to say, and Sabine knew from experience that quizzing her about it wouldn't move things along.

"It's midnight here now, but the reading of the will was this morning." Colette cleared her throat. "It was a shitshow, predictably."

"I was wondering about that on the plane. Thea's lawyer told me Thea had paid off your mortgage and put together trusts for the boys, and obviously she sent me halfway across the world for a year. I knew Celestine was expecting way more of Thea's money than she actually got." Sabine shook her head as a vivid memory of her mother trying to pry her aunt's ring off her finger at the funeral washed over her and dug in. "How did she take it?"

Colette was silent for a moment and drew in a shaky breath before she put the words together. "She lost her shit. I was so mortified." Her voice was tense and thin, which was always how it sounded when she was talking about their mother. "She was drunk, of course, and refused to ride with us, so she showed up twenty minutes late. She started off demanding to know where you were—"

"What did Katherine tell her?"

"That you're an adult and it was none of her concern." Colette sighed. "Then she started to get really agitated when she realized Thea had already sold the house and the theater—"

"How could she not know that?" Frustration turned in her chest, scraping her with its sharp edges. "I mean, maybe she didn't realize about the theater. Thea didn't tell anyone until after. But she saw us over at her house for weeks packing up her things and cleaning."

"That's exactly what I thought, but Thea sold the house privately, so I guess there was never a for-sale sign. I think she just assumed the house would be left to her." Sabine heard the refrigerator close, then the familiar pop of Colette uncorking a bottle of sauvignon blanc. "Then Katherine told us that the boys' trusts had been set up with the proceeds from the theater."

"Oh, God."

"She literally jumped over her desk and grabbed Katherine by the collar."

Sabine sat straight up in the tub and picked up the phone, clicking off the speaker. "Please tell me you're kidding."

"I'm not kidding, but Katherine handled the situation like a boss, of course. I apologized afterward, and she couldn't have been more gracious, but I'm still mortified, of course."

"So." Sabine hesitated, not sure if she should ask a question she didn't want the answer to. "What did Thea leave her?"

"Thea left her a trust, which Katherine will control. She didn't say exactly what the amount was, but she did say that the funds were to be used only for rehab, should she choose to go, or medical expenses associated with her recovery. She won't be able to draw on it for any other reason."

"Holy shit." Sabine stood and reached for her towel, the phone balanced between her ear and shoulder. "No wonder she lost it."

"Hey." Colette's voice faded as she turned away from the phone. "I can hear one of the boys in the hall. I probably need to make sure he's okay."

"Of course." Sabine paused, turning the sapphire band on her finger. "Don't let her get to you, okay?"

"Honestly, I had no idea how bad she really was until you left." Colette's voice cracked, and Sabine heard the frustration creep in. "I feel so guilty I just left you over there with her for so long."

"Colette, that was my decision, and you've got your hands full with a husband and two kids." Sabine took a breath, wrapping the towel around herself. "And I wasn't ready to admit this before, but honestly, neither one of us should have to babysit her."

"That's the goddamn truth." Sabine heard one of her nephews chattering to her sister and smiled. "Listen, I have to go, but call me soon, okay?"

Sabine clicked off her phone and pulled a clean pair of jeans from her rucksack. Guilt rushed in that she hadn't been at the reading of the will to manage her mother, then more guilt at the strange sense of relief she felt about being halfway across the globe so that wasn't possible.

When had her world gotten so small?

❖

Alden screwed a misting nozzle onto the hose and adjusted the water temperature to tepid. The sun glowed amber against the greenhouse windowpanes held together by a rusty assortment of antique hardware, most of which she'd brought home from work after upgrading public spaces to code. The body of regulations governing the preservation of historic Scottish buildings had always been its own cutthroat government. On one hand it was vital to keep the buildings as visually authentic as possible. On the other, only slightly less important, was the fact that tourists getting clocked by falling chandeliers and collapsing castle gates was a bad look for the country.

Usually, preservationists reinforced the existing historic materials with more modern hardware and hidden supports, ideally keeping the original look of the structure identical. Alden had spent more than one afternoon in her shop, beating the shine out of new regulation hardware with chains, blowtorches, and hammers, then artificially aging them with acid baths and salt tarnish. The old hinges and window hardware that were no longer up for code on a job were usually gifted to Alden by the owners to take home and repurpose, and over the years, she'd acquired a reputation for her ability to find a new life for anything from hand-forged iron nails to shattered stained glass.

She'd woken before sunrise and gone downstairs to make a cuppa, setting out her mother's morning teapot and favorite cup as she waited for the kettle to boil. Sabine had still been asleep, curled up in the tangle of wool blankets, her hair spilling over the edge of the bed. She was safer to look at when she was asleep. The reflection of the candlelight flickering in her eyes the night before had been dangerous, to say the least. Sabine's eyes had velvet-brown edges, like a damp handful of overturned earth that melted into pale blues and greens, like wet sea glass warming in the sun.

"It's so toasty in here!"

Alden spun around with the water sprayer in her hand, just missing Sabine, who ducked behind the door right before the spray pelted the wall.

"Christ! Ye scared the life out o' me!"

Sabine stepped out from behind the door, one eyebrow raised. "Oh, really? That's all it takes? Good to know."

"Come over here." Alden motioned her over, handing her the patinaed copper sprayer. "Just for that I'm putting you to work."

Sabine laughed and took it, lofting it into a fine mist over Gwen's herbs, each housed in a broken bowl, rusted tin bucket, or chipped mug. "This whole place looks like magic."

"Aye. You're not wrong." Alden picked up a rag and started wiping down the wooden potting benches. "Mom can't bear to have anything go to waste, so she chucks every plant she sees in here and hopes for the best. Even in the winter it's pretty rare that something doesn't thrive in here."

Sabine watered the waiting plants until even the air was damp and humid, the mist warmed by square patches of sunlight the windows cast onto the plants. "Why do I smell patchouli?"

"Probably because you just watered it." Alden crouched down to the lowest table and pinched off a couple of dark leaves from a plant rehomed into a rusted coffee can, then stood, crushing them in her palm. "Patchouli is a love-it-or-hate-it scent, though. Which is it for you?"

"Love it. I love most herbs, but something about patchouli is just deeply earthy, spicy and warm at the same time. One of lighting techs at work wears it, and I always know when she's around."

Alden handed it to her, then rinsed her rag under the tap and wrung it out, hanging it to dry on a peg behind the yellow ceramic sink on the far wall. "What do you do for a living when you're not stranded in Scotland?"

Sabine leaned over the lemon balm, closing her eyes and inhaling the bright, grassy scent that drifted toward the ceiling with the mist. "I'm the lead set dresser at one of the historic theaters in New Orleans. My family's owned it since the early twentieth century."

Alden nodded, pinching dead leaves from a climbing tea rose that took up most of the southern wall, the velvety vines spread out and winding around window frames, searching for sunlight. "What do you love about it?"

"What do you mean?"

"I can tell you love it just from the way you talk about it." She dropped a handful of the trimmed leaves into an empty pot in the corner. "Tell me one thing. The first thing that comes to mind."

Sabine grazed the glossy leaves of a chili plant with the flat of her hand. "I love it when people don't remember the sets."

Alden nodded. "You'd think it'd be the opposite. I went to quite a few plays in university. That has to be a shit ton of work."

"It is." Sabine looked up, watching a sheer white cloud through the glass as it drifted lazily over the sun, stretching like a spiderweb across the light. "But if they notice my sets for themselves, then I'm just making art. And not very good art, if it has to stand alone. When the sets bring the play to life—when they're silent support for the actors and illuminate the story as it unfolds—I know I've done my job."

Sabine brushed a spray of droplets off her sleeve and turned back to Alden. "From what your dad told me about what you do, I'd imagine you'd feel the same way."

"You're right, but instead of a story with characters and a plot, I'm trying to drag history into the present. I want people to feel they're in another time and place, seeing exactly what the building looked like then." Alden coiled up the hose and hung it back on its iron hook. "What else did my da tell you? Or do I even want to know?"

Sabine followed Alden as she walked back through the mud room and into the house. "You definitely don't want to know."

"Fantastic." Alden picked up her coat from the back of a kitchen chair and handed it to Sabine. "Are you ready to go?"

"What? I'm just supposed to follow you into the wilds of Scotland and hope that jalopy outside doesn't break down in a cow field?"

"Oh, sweet Jesus." Alden held the shoulders of the coat up for Sabine to slide into and hit the lights on the way out the door. "I'm going to pretend I didn't hear that crack about Jolene."

"*Jolene?*" Sabine covered her mouth in shock. "Like the Dolly Parton song?"

"I have no idea what you're talking about." Alden opened Sabine's door and walked around to her side, sliding in and starting up the Land Rover.

"Where are we going, anyway?"

"I made a call last night to someone who may be able to help you with your little problem."

"My little problem?" Sabine grabbed the dash as Alden made a sharp left to avoid a pothole and missed. "Obviously you're going to have to narrow that down."

"You'll see." Alden leaned over and popped the glove box, grabbing a pair of charcoal, fingerless gloves.

Sabine smiled and looked out the window to the sea as they pulled onto the road that wound down into the village. Alden was charming. Too charming, which was precisely why Sabine usually dated girls that were Alden's complete opposite. Feminine, unassuming girls that were pleasant but easy not to fall in love with. It just kept things simple. Safe. No surprises.

"It looks like town might be waking up a bit now that the snow's fucked off back where it came from." Alden stopped half on the sidewalk and pulled the gearshift into Park. "Even Da said he might open the pub so the locals can get a wee dram if they're goin' mad in the house."

"Oh my God." Sabine beamed as she got out of the Land Rover, and she pointed at the glass front of one of the shops.

"That store right there, the one with the stack of sweaters in the window. It looks open." She ran up to the door and peeked in. "It *is* open!"

Alden locked the truck and opened the shop door for Sabine, who was still peering through the window like an excited kid. "That's because I called Maeve last night and asked if she'd mind openin' up for ya today for an hour or so. She said it was either that or murder her husband, and she needed longer to plan that particular mission."

Sabine stopped abruptly as they stepped in, her voice dropping to a whisper. "Is she serious?"

"Knowing Maeve, that's a distinct possibility. She's all talk, mind, she loves the bones of him, but she loves to talk some smack even more." Alden stepped up to the counter and rang the bell, looking down the hall that led to a staircase. "You'll see. She has a heart as big as the ocean, though. Her and my mam have been friends since they went to nursery together."

"She can say anything she wants." Sabine ran her hand over a stack of dreamy-looking Shetland sweaters with suede elbow patches. "I need warm clothes slightly more than I need oxygen."

Alden leaned against the counter and nodded to a stack of boot boxes covering the back wall of the tiny shop. "I don't know how much you want to spend." Alden glanced down at her shoes. "But I'd suggest starting with trading in your trainers. What are they made out of, anyway? Paper?"

"They're perfectly appropriate for tropical climates, thank you very much. It's still a hundred degrees where I live."

"Anyway, start with some boots and a proper overcoat. Then you can add to that as you'd like."

Something crashed down the staircase behind the counter, and the door flew open, smacking a dent into the wall behind it. Alden smiled, motioning for Sabine to join her at the counter. A stocky, scowling older woman rubbed her hip as she stared at the door, which now looked like it might be hanging from one hinge.

Her wiry gray hair was as wide as her face, but her smile was brilliant and genuine when she turned to see them standing there.

"Alden, you get more handsome every time I see ya, lad."

"Thank you, Maeve." Alden leaned forward to kiss both of her cheeks with genuine affection. "This is Sabine, the clueless American I was telling you about."

Sabine smacked Alden's arm with the back of her hand and pretended to be offended as she stuck out her hand. "It's very nice to meet you, Maeve. Thank you so much for opening up for me. I was a bit clueless about the weather. Alden's not wrong about that."

"Sweet Mother of God. She looks like a local with an American accent." Maeve took Sabine's hand and squeezed it, nodding in Alden's direction. "Mind yerself around this one. She nearly married up the last one who took a shine to her."

Alden took a sudden interest in the wallet display to the right of the counter and shook her head. "For the love of all that's holy, Maeve. If ya tell that story again—"

"Oh, it was the talk of the town for the next year! Left ye at the altar, didn't she, love?"

"We never made it that far, thank the good Lord." Alden stared at the watch she wasn't wearing and arched an eyebrow. "Would ye look at that? I'm late to check out the boots."

She rounded the corner swiftly, and Maeve leaned into Sabine and dropped her voice. "Ya can't find a truer heart than 'er. That woman was an absolute eejit. Left her for a man too." She patted Sabine's hand again and excused herself to put the kettle on.

Sabine wandered back to the boot section, trailing her palm over a few more stacks of sweaters on the way. Alden saw her and opened her mouth to speak, but Sabine cut in. "Maeve seems lovely, but her accent is so thick, I didn't catch a word she said."

Alden smiled, pulling a box down off the display. "Liar."

"You can't prove that." Sabine bumped her shoulder lightly into Alden's. "If you ever bring this up again, I'll deny it, but my first girlfriend was so pissed off when we broke up that she photocopied a picture of me sitting on the toilet topless after a night out, looking like an absolute drunken wreck, then papered the entire campus with it." Sabine paused, closing her eyes to blot out the memory. "Like every inch of it. I was mortified."

Alden smiled and pulled a box down off the top shelf. "I couldn't hear a word of that through that crazy American accent. But if I had..." She leaned in, the energy crackling between them in the silence as she whispered into her ear. "That story would've made me forget all about mine."

Maeve's head popped around the corner. "What do you take in yer tea, love?"

"Um." Sabine paused. "Milk, extra sugar, thank you."

"Lovely." She started to leave then popped back around the corner. "Alden, love, did ya see Mrs. Yardley up the road lately? The one that runs the café?" Maeve shook her head. "She's been eatin' nonstop since last Christmas, no word of a lie." She paused, smiling and obviously savoring the moment before she continued. "Ya can't help but feel fer her fella, can ye? The poor bastard must not know whether to hump her or harpoon her."

Shock colored Sabine's face as she watched Maeve duck back around the corner, then covered her mouth with both hands and laughed.

Alden just shook her head and started lacing up the first pair of boots.

"I'm tellin' ya. No one's safe."

By the time they finished shopping, Sabine had the gossip on almost everyone in town, in addition to a stack of wool flak sweaters, an overcoat similar to Alden's, wool socks, and a beautiful pair of leather hiking boots with red laces.

"Now don't forget to wax this coat before ye wear it out in the weather, love. I'll throw this tin of wax in fer ya, and get

Alden to do it for ye, since she's no doubt at loose ends with the snow."

"Yes, ma'am." Alden winked at Sabine and nodded to Maeve, who was clearly waiting for an answer. "I'll do it tonight."

After Sabine paid the bill, they walked into the shimmer of bright sunlight sparkling on the snowdrifts. The waves crashed rhythmically into the pier below, and smoke swirled skyward from more than a single chimney. The snow still crunched under her feet, but it seemed much less ominous somehow in the sunlight.

"If I didn't know better, I'd say town might be coming back to life soon. It's starting to look less and less like Antarctica out here." Alden stacked Sabine's bags carefully into the truck and shut the door. "Are you hungry?"

"God. I'm starving." Sabine shot a doubtful glance down the closest side street. "Are any places open yet, though?"

Alden picked up her phone from the dash and nodded toward one of the brick side streets. "Let's take a walk." She locked up the truck and scrolled through her phone for a minute, then dropped it back into her pocket. "Right. We're looking for teddy bears today."

"What?" Sabine stopped and glanced behind them. "Where?"

"Don't worry. They won't sneak up on you." Alden pointed to a closed, dark shop, with a home on the upper level. The windows of the house above were aglow with light, and a small gray stuffed bear sat in the corner of one of them.

"I'm so confused." Sabine squinted up at the teddy and then over at Alden. "You're going to have to be more specific here on why we're shopping for stuffed animals."

"I thought you might want to see a bit of secret Scotland." Alden settled her hand in the small of Sabine's back as they walked farther down the street. "This is literally the Scotland that you have to know a local to experience."

Alden pointed to a second-floor home with a pink teddy bear in the window, then another across the street with a brown bear sporting a red bow. "Because the main industry in Rothesay is tourism, restaurant licenses, especially liquor permits, are tightly controlled and almost impossible to get. Because of that, bigger corporate chains, usually based in London, own most of the restaurants open in season."

"That's a shame. Especially in small villages." Sabine stopped abruptly and pointed to the opposite side of the street with a teddy in the window. "So, they just price the locals out of the market in their own town?"

"Aye." Alden led her to a tall, red, lacquered door beside a dark newsagent. She pressed a button on an intercom installed beside it, and a scratchy voice came on the line. "Yes?"

Alden leaned into the speaker. "Two, please."

The lock on the door clicked, and Alden held it open for Sabine. She walked up a narrow, steep staircase framed by peeling plaster walls, then turned the corner to find a glossy wooden landing and a pale lavender door. Alden lifted a small picture hanging above the brass doorknocker, removed the handwritten note taped underneath, and handed it to Sabine.

Sabine looked at it carefully, then folded the note back up. "I'm not sure what this means, but it says, 'chili chips or chicken pot pie?'"

Alden smiled. "Either of those sound good to you?"

"Going from what I've seen already, I'm assuming the chili chips are fries, and only psychopaths don't like a big plate of those."

"Good answer." Alden laughed, put the note back where it was, and knocked. They heard light running footsteps, a pause, and then someone much shorter than the actual doorknob appeared, a small, rumpled boy in brown corduroy trousers and a Manchester United football jersey. He took his time to look Sabine up and down, as if he knew she was fresh off the train, and he didn't quite like it. "Mam says come in."

Alden gestured for Sabine to follow him, and she brought up the rear, locking the door behind them. A young woman with a baby on her shoulder flashed a bright smile as they passed the kitchen. "Alden, how are ye? Let me put Lucy down, and I'll be right out to help ya."

Alden stopped to give her a short hug, then kissed both cheeks. "No worries, Avril. We've plenty of time and Bert to look after us. Take yer time."

Bert led them down the hall and into the dining room, which contained an enormous table plunked in the center with a mismatched cream and sugar set and one stained-glass lamp in the center. The lamp filtered warm, colorful light onto the oiled wood table, and Sabine rescued a red toy car from her chair and placed it by the lamp, where it blended in perfectly.

The walls were painted a rich, matte green, the perfect backdrop for pictures of the family on one wall, as well as the empty picture frames in shades of ivory on the opposite wall, waiting for their pictures. The table itself was handmade, with love scuffs on the legs and a small heart carved by an unsteady hand near the edge.

Sabine sat down and leaned into Alden, her voice low. "We're in someone's home?"

Alden smiled. "Aye, Avril and Tony's, but we're here as customers. This is how the locals get around all the rules that keep them from starting small businesses and supporting their families, and it gives stay-at-home moms a way to make additional income."

Bert ran in suddenly and didn't say a word, just pulled up his sleeve and showed Alden his muscle, waited expectantly for her to be impressed, then ran off into another room.

"Anyway, instead of having to frequent the tourist traps, residents of Rothesay can opt to eat home-cooked food and visit with their neighbors." Alden draped her coat over the back of her chair. "No self-respecting local would be caught dead darkening the door of the Twisted Kilt or whatever the hell they called the commercial pit of hell they put in last summer."

Bert rounded the corner again with a floral teapot, then returned with two cups and saucers, one in each hand. He was staring at them as he walked, biting his lip and concentrating so hard that the cups were clattering against the saucers.

"Thank you, Bert." Sabine reached out for one of the cups just before he bumped into the table. He set the other down on the edge of the table and let out a sigh of relief before he looked up to her and tilted his head.

"Who are ye?"

"My name is Sabine." She flashed him a smile and tucked a stray lock of hair behind her ear. "And your name is Bert?"

"Aye. But you say it funny." He shoved his hands all the way down in his pockets and stood there for a few more seconds, then ran out of the dining room and down the hall.

"I love this idea." Sabine poured the tea from the steaming teapot as Alden reached for the cream and sugar. "How do you know who's cooking that day?"

"One of the older women in town runs a blog for foodies, she's had it for ages, and she posts every day. Most of the posts are short, just a couple of paragraphs, and usually contain a recipe or a few photos of cakes or the like. But somewhere in the actual text, she mentions what her grandsons are playing with that day, like a paper doll, a wooden spoon, or a teacup…"

"…or a teddy bear?"

"Exactly."

Alden smiled and spooned some sugar into her cup as Sabine sat back in her chair, sipping her tea and thrilled to be in on one of the village secrets.

Avril popped around the corner with Lucy still on her shoulder, although now she'd started crying in earnest. Avril blew a strand of hair out of her face, bouncing lightly to soothe Lucy. "I'm sorry about the delay. Lucy started crying this morning at the crack of bloody dawn and apparently has settled on it as a career choice."

"Don't be silly. We've only just gotten our tea. Take yer time." Alden smiled at Lucy as Avril switched the baby to the other shoulder, which prompted another shriek of protest.

"So ye must be Sabine?"

"Sweet Jesus, Avril. How do you do it?" Alden shook her head. "How do you get hold of news before it even happens?"

Avril unraveled her baby's fist from her hair and arched an eyebrow. "Yer mam was in here a few minutes ago to pick up a takeaway and told me how ya left 'er at the train station to freeze to death."

"Oh, this is fantastic." Sabine leaned forward and smiled, chin in hand. "What else did she tell you?"

"That you whipped out perfect sign language at the table for Declan, with frostbite, no less." She rolled her eyes in Alden's direction before she went on. "And Declan was delighted. Honestly, she couldn't stop talking about it. She said she hasn't seen him light up like that since forever."

The doorbell rang, and Lucy responded with a wail. She was already gearing up for another as Avril leaned out into the hall and shouted.

"Bertie, will ya get that for me, love?"

Avril waited until she heard Bert open the door and turned back to the table, her cheeks flushed. "Now where were we?"

"Would you like me to take Lucy for you for a bit?" Sabine asked, shrugging out of her jacket. "It's purely selfish, of course. I love babies. I have two nephews I can't get enough of."

"Are ya sure?" Avril glanced down the hall. "I think that's just someone here for a takeaway, but if ye don't mind that would be brilliant."

"Take as long as you need." Sabine came around the table and reached for Lucy, cuddling her to her chest and resuming the bounce. "We'll be just fine, won't we, gorgeous?"

"Thank baby Jesus." Avril smoothed her apron and handed Sabine the towel from her shoulder. "Now, what can I make you two for lunch?"

"Definitely the pot pie." Alden leaned back in her chair and looked over at Sabine. "Were you thinking about the chili chips?"

Avril nodded and glanced at Alden before she went on. "It may not be what yer used to though, lass. Do ye like Indian food, like curries?"

Sabine placed a gentle hand behind Lucy's head as it dropped onto her shoulder, her cries slowly melting into soft sleep sounds. "Oh, God. I love curry. I'm in."

"How has she been crying for a hundred hours and now she's asleep? You must be magic." Avril smiled at her daughter, rounding the corner to the hall and popping her head back in. "And has Alden told ye yet we used to go out back in the day?"

"What is this today, a conspiracy?" Alden rolled her eyes. "And don't you have a takeaway to get to?"

"Oh, this just gets better and better." Sabine smiled, swaying gently, gently patting Lucy's back. She checked to see that she was almost asleep, then sat carefully back at the table. "But I'd actually rather know more about Declan."

"Good answer." Alden smiled as she glanced back at the door and lowered her voice. "But there's no drama with me and Avril. We went out for the better part of a year, but at the very core of her, she wanted a house bursting with children, so it just wasn't to be."

"So, you split on good terms?"

"Great terms. She's still one of my favorite people, and she and Tony are perfect together. He's a mate of mine and even consults on some of my restoration jobs."

Lucy stirred on Sabine's shoulder, then quickly settled again. Alden reached out and stroked her cheek with the back of her hand, looking thoughtful. "So, you asked about Declan."

Sabine nodded, stirring sugar into her tea as Bert topped it off from the pot. "You said he recently came to live with your parents?"

"It's been about a year and a half now. He's my little sister Eileen's son, and when she passed away, he came to live with my parents. It was a lot for them, so I sold my house and moved home to help." Silence settled heavily between them, and Alden's jaw tensed. "She and I were close growing up, but I was away in grad school when she went off to university and got into drugs."

Sabine nodded, smoothing a hand over Lucy's downy head.

"I think it was the hardest on my mam. She's a therapist, a great one, but nothing she did seemed to get my sister back on track. She literally tried everything." Alden pushed her cup away, and her face brightened. "But then one day Eileen came home pregnant, and everything changed. She got sober, was a brilliant mum, and even moved back to Glasgow and trained as a hairstylist. We kept in close contact with Declan, but he always seemed happy and healthy." Alden followed a crack in the tabletop with her thumb. "Then all hell broke loose."

"I can relate to that." Sabine waited for a moment, until Alden looked up. "Tell me."

Alden cleared her throat, her fingertips white against the edge of the table, her voice tense and thinning with every word. "Declan came down with meningitis, and my parents drove down to Glasgow to be with them in hospital. Mam told Eileen to go home and get some rest, that they'd stay with him overnight."

"Your sister must have been so worried."

Alden nodded. "Aye. Declan was everything to her, and he wasn't responding to the medication as quickly as they'd hoped." Alden raked a hand through her hair. "But the next morning, my parents got a visit from a Glasgow detective." Alden's voice cracked, and she picked up her teacup and set it back in the saucer without drinking. "Eileen had overdosed on heroin at a friend's flat the night before."

"Oh my God." Sabine's voice was just breath in the silence. "What happened?"

"I think she took the drugs her friend offered because she was in such a state over Declan, but she'd been clean for years at that point and misjudged the amount her body could handle.

Declan pulled through, but he was in a coma for a week, and the virus severely damaged his auditory nerves. Took them out, really."

Sabine laid her hand over Alden's just as Bert came around the corner with the pot pie and the chili chips. He placed both carefully on the table and stepped back to admire his work as Avril leaned around the corner holding two sets of silverware wrapped in napkins. Bert plunked them both on the edge of the table before he disappeared again, and Avril whispered "thank you" as she took a sleeping Lucy from Sabine.

"So, we've been learning to deal with everything together." Alden passed one of the silverware wraps to Sabine. "The national health service supplied him with a private sign tutor, who has been amazing, but it's been hard for Declan to grieve the loss of his hearing and his mother at the same time. "

Alden unwrapped her silverware and pierced the crust on her pot pie, releasing a waft of savory steam into the air. "Which reminds me." Delicate cream gravy flowed down the side of the pie and onto the plate as Alden speared her first bite. "Mam said he's all excited because he came up with our name signs and wants to show us."

Sabine nodded, folded a chunky homemade chip covered in rich curry sauce into her mouth, and swooned, closing her eyes to take it all in. "This is incredible. The sauce is to die for." She smiled, reaching over to steal a piece of flaky crust off Alden's plate. "It's official. Secret Scotland is my favorite restaurant."

Sabine, wrapped up in her new coat in the passenger's seat, smiled as Alden clicked on her wipers against a sprinkling of snowflakes. "I'm not sure I've ever seen someone appreciate chili chips like that." Alden glanced in her direction. "Certainly not an American."

"It was incredible. Thai coconut curry, scallions, fresh sliced red chilis…I'm pretty sure that's one of my favorite meals ever."

Alden got out to scrape the ice off the back window, letting in a gust of frosty air as Sabine stared through the glass, watching the trees on either side of the pier bend and shift in the rustle of wind that swept up from the sea. She was still tense all over; she had been since the second she stepped onto the plane, braced so tightly against the next disaster that it was painful to draw a breath.

In New Orleans, her world had been tightly controlled, like a play she'd written for herself and restarted every day, but that had been just self-preservation with Celestine in the house. Sabine had learned early on to control everything she possibly could and not let anyone swan in and make changes. That way she had no surprises, no unknown actors, nothing that might alter the storyline and disrupt her world. No chaos, as much as that was possible. And then Thea died.

Thea was born deaf and always said that navigating the hearing world made her feel invisible, like traveling in a foreign country where everyone had a map but her. To her credit, she'd also flatly refused to let her deafness narrow her options in life. She won a theater internship in Scotland the year between high school and college, apprenticing as a costumer, then went on to be one of the most in-demand costumers in the theater world, traveling frequently from New York to New Orleans.

Since she died, a single memory had played in a loop in Sabine's mind. She'd been at her house for dinner, just after Thea received her cancer diagnosis. Afterward, they'd sat on the back porch drinking Thea's signature sweet tea, which was just regular sweet tea with a healthy splash of bourbon, but Sabine was the only one who knew that secret.

The porch floor was still warm from the July sunset, worn wood planks painted gray with a black, iron, New Orleans-style railing. Two wide rattan chairs sat under a ceiling fan, the fan blades shaped like giant palm leaves, and jazz music from down the street floated in and out, as if it were a hazy ghost from the French Quarter.

That night at dinner, Sabine had asked her why she'd never married. Thea didn't answer right away, just looked away and reached for her tea. It was only later, when the silver moon had risen and the silence fallen, that she'd put her glass on the table to sign.

Sabine. Sometimes love happens only once in a lifetime, and you don't realize it was yours until it's too late. She paused, her fingertips together in a steeple shape, before she went on. *I do know one thing for sure, though.*

Sabine nodded, slowly shaping the sign for *What?*

Tears shimmered in Thea's eyes. *I know that love never dies. It only changes form.* Her hands settled back into her lap, and she slowly turned the sapphire-and-diamond band on her finger.

Alden slid back into the truck and seemed to jolt Sabine out of a daydream as snow flew off the jacket she tossed into the back.

"So where is this place you and Maeve were talking about?"

Alden pointed down a street just off the main road through the village. "It's just a wee walk from here, but with the slush and all these bags, we might want to drive." She stacked Sabine's new acquisitions in the truck and fired it up, pulling a knit beanie out her pocket and handing it over. "I brought that from home for ye. It'll have some sawdust in it, mind, but it might be handy if hell continues to freeze over in Rothesay."

Sabine smiled and took it, smoothing it down over her hair. "How do I look?"

Alden turned onto Kingstown Street and pulled it down a bit on both sides. "Well, as long as ya don't perch it on the very top of your head like that, it almost makes you—"

"—blend?"

Alden laughed, pulling up to a curb outside The Loch & Beadle. "Oh yeah. You blend. That's exactly what I was going to say." She nodded toward the door and cut the engine. "This is the boarding house Maeve was talking about. Her sister runs it, so if she says it's open, there's a good chance it is, and Rose is just as demure and charming as Maeve, so she'll keep ye laughing if nothing else."

The door opened just then, and Rose stepped out onto the slushy walk in her fuzzy, pink house shoes, waving her arms like her wiry gray hair was on fire. Alden pointed to the door and nodded. "Looks like Maeve called ahead."

"Git yerself in here, lass!" Rose wrapped her macrame duster around herself and upped the volume. "Ye sit in Alden's rig one more minute, and you'll be up the duff wit' twins, sure as I live and breathe!"

Alden rolled her eyes as she reached back to get her shopping bags and found Sabine's rucksack behind the seat. She turned around and arched an eyebrow in her direction. "Aye. You snuck your bag in here this mornin'. Trying to get rid of me already. I see how it is."

Sabine gave her an angelic smile. "Well, the scotch was lovely, but rumor has it you don't like American girls in your bed, so I figured I had to make a run for it."

"You know you're welcome at our house anytime, right?"

"I know." Sabine leaned forward and kissed her cheek. "I'm just yanking your chain. Thank you." Her eyes softened, and she laid her hand on Alden's arm. "For what you did. All of it."

"Whatever." Alden smiled. "All Scottish butches have a thing for stranded ax murderers. Everyone knows that."

Alden retrieved her bags and carried them into the waiting area while Sabine checked in with Rose. When everything was settled, she came back over with her keys and held them up for Alden to see.

"Aye, the lass actually has a place to stay this time. God bless variety."

Sabine rolled her eyes and handed Alden a sticky note from the front desk with a phone number on it. "In case you have any trouble with Declan." She paused. "Seriously, I'd love to help, so share it with your mom and dad. Don't hesitate to let me know if he needs a little help."

Alden walked over to the front desk and took the pen that Mary was already holding out, seeing as she was chin in hand, listening intently to every word of their conversation. Alden tore the note in half and wrote her own number on the other side, handing it back to Sabine.

"And here's my number, in case you have trouble with..." Alden smiled. "Scotland."

"Cheeky bastard," Rose said affectionately, shaking her head. "Handsome as a film star but been that cheeky since she was a wee thing, so no chance o' beatin' it outta her now."

Sabine laughed and threw her rucksack over her shoulder. "You'd better leave now, before I tell Rose you tried to give me frostbite."

Sabine picked up her bags with her other hand and turned toward the staircase, but Alden stepped close and put a hand on her shoulder from behind. "That rumor isn't true. Just so ye know."

"What rumor—"

Sabine melted into a smile, and then she was gone.

CHAPTER THIRTEEN

Sabine turned the key and opened the door to her room, which turned out to be sunny and cozy, on the very top floor with a single bed piled with fluffy white duvets and tucked under the eaves of the roof. An antique, freestanding mirror reflected the last of the sunlight from the front windows, and a small mahogany desk rounded out the corner, complete with a pad of paper with charmingly curled edges and a black enamel fountain pen.

She plunked her bags on the bed and sank back into the pillows, staring at the beam of sunlight between her and the ceiling. She hadn't had a moment to think about anything but not freezing to death since she landed in Scotland, but now time had started to slow. And then her phone rang. She'd dropped it into one of the inner pockets of her new jacket, and it was on the last ring before she found it.

"Katherine?"

"I'm so glad I reached you."

Sabine could sense her smile through the phone.

"I'm just checking in on you to see how you're getting along."

"I can't believe I'm saying this, but I landed in a really interesting little town and met some great people. I mean, I'm sure I'll travel more later, but—" She looked around the simple, cozy room that already felt more welcoming than her room in New Orleans ever had. "For now, I like this place."

Katherine cleared her throat. "And what town is that?"

"It's Muir Rothesay." Sabine ran her fingertips lightly over the edge of the wardrobe door, worn smooth by a hundred years of touch. "I found the name written on a Post-it in the folder you gave me. So, I just bought a train ticket here."

The line was strangely silent for a moment until Katherine spoke again. "I thought you might. That's a perfect choice."

"Can I ask you something though? When I looked closer at the note, I noticed it's not your handwriting. Some of yours is on the documents you gave me." Sabine laid her hand over her heart, not sure if she wanted to know the answer to the question and, if she did find out, what it even meant. "It's Thea's, isn't it?"

"You're right. It is." Katherine paused. "Thea gave it to me to include in the packet."

"Why, though? I know she was in Scotland for a year, but that university was in Aberdeen. I've never heard her talk about this village."

"That doesn't surprise me, but I'm afraid I can't tell you anything else."

Sabine looked through the ceiling windows into the dusky sky, wishing she knew what to ask. And why. "Okay. I understand."

"I'll let you go. I know it's late there." Sabine listened to the sound of papers shuffling on Katherine's desk. "And I'm here if you need me."

"Katherine?" She chose her words carefully. "I know you can't tell me much, but if there's one piece of advice you can give me, what would it be?"

The line was silent for so long Sabine started to wonder if Katherine intended to answer. "That note that had Muir Rothesay on it..." She paused, her voice softening. "Turn it over."

Sabine listened, thanked her, and clicked the phone off.

Katherine's advice hadn't really been a surprise. The moment she'd realized Thea had written *Muir Rothesay* on that scrap of paper, she knew she'd had a reason. Thea never did anything without one, and Sabine needed to find it, even if she didn't have a clue what she was looking for. She was too tired to try to find the note in the folder now, but she made a mental note to look for it later.

❖

Hours later, after a fitful nap, Sabine had just managed to unpack her rucksack and hang up her new clothes in the tiny wooden wardrobe with the squeaky door that didn't quite shut. She pulled her boots back on and selected one of sweaters with suede elbow patches. After she pulled it over her head, she tried to calm the static in her hair as she peered out the arched window down to the street three stories below. The sun was starting to set, but people were outside finally, chatting and sweeping the slush from their steps.

She locked up her room and ventured down the steps, where Rose still stood at the front desk, taking one measured bite from each chocolate in a gold box, examining it closely, then putting it back in its place.

"Ya wouldn't know ya from a local now, lass!" Rose looked almost proud as she picked up the next chocolate. "Me sister told me ye came over from America in nothing more than a bikini, mind."

"She's not far wrong. Thank God she let me come in and shop." Sabine smiled, thinking about how her socks had been freezing to her ankles a day ago. "Hey. Would you know any cafés or restaurants that might be open?"

"Well now." Rose found the chocolate she was evidently looking for and bit into it with a look of pure religious joy. She took her time enjoying it, popped the other half of it into her mouth, then offered Sabine the tray of previously bitten confections. Sabine shook her head.

"Me son went down the chippy at the end of the road this afternoon, so that's open." Rose rolled her eyes before she went on. "Bless the saints and spirits too. I was about to feed him to the banshees if we'd one more feckin' day holed up together in this madhouse." She licked a smudge of chocolate off her thumb and pointed to the door. "Just left out the door here and then it's the second alley on your right." She paused. "Mind Mrs. O'Clarney's cat though. She hides under the grate and swipes at yer feet." She shook her head and popped the lid back on the chocolates. "Those talons will slice the blood right out yer veins. Not unlike her owner, come to think of it." She tilted her chin up as she stashed the box on top of the filing cabinet. "She loves a spot o' gossip, but not me. That's the devil's pastime, and I'm a churchgoing woman." She smiled beatifically and smoothed down her hair as if adjusting a halo.

Sabine struggled to keep a straight face as she thanked her and headed out the door. Once she was outside, and after dodging the slush pooling among the cobblestones, she found herself continuing to smile at nothing. Somehow Scotland seemed warmer, and not just because the snow was melting. She felt free, and it wasn't lost on her that the strangers here were kinder than Celestine had ever been.

It had never been a secret that Colette had been Celestine's favorite, and her father was so busy with the theater he never noticed. She and Colette became closer as they got older, but Thea had always taken a special interest in Sabine, and she went across to her house to spend the night more often than not. Celestine seemed to resent it but also couldn't be bothered to sign to Thea to discuss it, so she just let her go.

Sabine counted the alleys and turned down the second one, dodging a puddle of water as she stepped off the cobblestones. Thea had been right to give her the choice to come to Scotland,

and even smarter to put a time limit on the decision. If Sabine had had even one more minute to think, her mother would have pulled her right back into her vortex, and she'd be in her sweltering upstairs bedroom in New Orleans, counting the hours until she could leave for the theater and repeat the same day.

The delicious aromas from what Rose had referred to as "the chippy" wafted up the alley and announced its presence long before she actually saw it. Gareth's Chips N' More was not much bigger than a bus stop, with a tiny stainless-steel kitchen in the back and faded, garish pictures of the menu above the counter. An older man wearing a white paper hat greeted her as she stepped in.

"We don't have the full menu, love. The food trucks won't be here till tomorrow, but I can still do ya a pepperoni pizza or a plate of lasagna and chips to take away."

"Lasagna and chips, please."

He nodded and got to work as Sabine sat in one of the plastic chairs attached to the wall. In only a few minutes he handed her a brown-paper-wrapped package that smelled like heaven.

"That'll be seven-pound fifty, please, lass."

Sabine paid him and walked back out to the alley, where darkness was falling swiftly, the puddles on the cobblestones starting to shimmer in the streetlights. The air smelled like diesel and woodsmoke, and the sidewalks were dotted all over with a random assortment of cars. She had stopped to tear a hole in the paper, wedging out a few hot, chunky wedges, when she looked up and saw it—a white wood sign with ornate golden lettering. *Rothesay Estate Agents.*

The inside was dark, but dozens of printed real-estate listings were taped up across the front windows. Sabine dug for another chip and scanned the homes, most of them on North Hill where Alden lived. The last one was different. It was the oldest listing on the window, judging by the posting dates and the tagline across the top in dark-red letters: *Reduced for Quick Sale.*

She leaned closer to make out the description in the streetlight, read every word and memorized the picture, her heart threatening to beat out of her chest, but she didn't need to know anything beyond what she saw in the photo.

A painting of that lighthouse, in an antique driftwood frame, had hung in her Aunt Thea's living room for as long as she could remember.

CHAPTER FOURTEEN

The next morning, Sabine ran down the staircase and headed out into the village, which was busy making up for lost time in earnest. Shops and cafés were open, the sidewalks dry and swept, and sunlight was filtering through the snow still blanketing the tree branches.

Sabine had called Katherine the night before, after she saw the listing, and told her about the lighthouse. After a long pause, she'd said it was well within the price range Thea had allotted for a real-estate purchase and even offered to handle the sale as her attorney. Still, Sabine had tossed and turned, trying to make sense of the photo. The listing had to be for a different lighthouse. Thea's painting was an original, done in oil, so it probably wasn't a reproduction of a famous photo. When she and Colette had taken the art down in Thea's house after she died, they both kept a few of the pieces and put them in the attic of Colette's house to use later in their own homes. Sabine had kept that painting specifically because it was Thea's favorite. She'd asked about it once as a child, and Thea had only signed back that it reminded her of *"the day she wished she could live again."*

Now she was standing outside the Estate Agents, takeaway coffee in hand, staring at the black-and-white photo in the daylight and waiting for someone to open the doors. The more she looked at it, though, the more she convinced herself she'd made a mistake. Little things were different, like the lanterns hanging around the exterior, and the trim and shutters surrounding the three windows on the third level that hadn't been there before.

But the sea, and the outline of the cliff to the right of the lighthouse, was identical. Even the cedar tree in the foreground, although much taller now, seemed eerily familiar. Sabine dug for her phone and snapped a picture, then texted it to Collette.

Remember that picture from Thea's living room I kept and stored in your attic?

She started to tell Colette more, but the door suddenly swung open, and she only had time to press *send* and drop her phone into her pocket.

"Merry morning ta ya, lass." The older gentleman that opened the door for her had a red beard that nearly touched the center of his chest, sparkling blue eyes, and a quick smile. "Are ye havin' a wee look at the properties or here to enquire about one in particular?" He waved her inside to a bright office with an orange kettle screaming in the corner and a comforting waft of vanilla pipe smoke coming from one of the two desks. "Either way you'll have a tea then, won't cha? I can tell ye a lot more about the properties in the window than a picture can. They don't talk much, the rude bastards."

Sabine laughed and lifted her cup. "I've got coffee, but thank you very much for the offer."

"Ah, an American." He switched off the kettle and motioned her over to his desk by the window, offering her a seat in the leather chair opposite. "Lovely to meet you. I'm Martin Abernathy."

"Sabine Rowan."

She smiled as he turned his attention to his smoldering pipe, puffing enough to fire the ember and watching it with genuine admiration before he set it back on his desk.

"Now, what can I help you with, today, lass? Was there a particular listing ye had yer eye on?"

"It's the lighthouse." Sabine turned in her chair and pointed at the listing. "The one on the end there? Is it still available?"

"Are ye kiddin'?" A tall, slender young woman with a ruffled auburn pixie cut walked through the room and flipped the *Open* sign on the door. "He rips 'em off the wall the second the sale goes through and does a little jig in the street. If it's up there, it's available."

"Now, Ames, I wouldn't say it's a jig as much as a highly choreographed and nearly famous dance." He grinned, giving her a kiss on the cheek as she put down a delicious-looking croissant with a small pot of cream and jam in front of him. "Ms. Rowan, this is my daughter, Amulet Abernathy, the true brains of the business."

"Entirely true, Ms. Rowan." Ames flashed her a smile. "Although I wouldn't be anywhere without my spokesmodel here."

Sabine laughed and shook her hand. "Just Sabine is fine."

"You're interested in the lighthouse?"

"I am. If it's still for sale, I'd love to take a look at it, if possible."

Martin leaned back in his chair and grabbed the listing off the window. "I don't see why not, and we know the owner personally." He glanced at his daughter, who had slid into her chair at the other desk and opened her computer. "It's vacant, if I'm remembering right. Angus is very motivated to sell, so that may work in your favor."

"I can take you to see it, if you'd like?" Ames shut her computer and grabbed a set of keys from the cabinet behind her. "I have a showing later this afternoon, but nothing till then. It's a unique place with lots of features, but, fair warning. If you're looking to change any of them, it also has a lot of hoops to jump through with the HSC."

"That's the Historic Scottish Collective, love," Martin said, slicing into his pastry. "Or as we like to call it, the pain in our collective asses."

"Da, we try not to frighten the customers until *after* the sale, remember?" She leaned over and kissed his cheek, then stood and jingled the keys. "Ready?"

Ames walked Sabine out to her car, a gleaming black Vauxhall, and unlocked the doors from the sidewalk. Sabine got in and fastened her seat belt, smiling at the memory of Alden's truck with not a seat belt in sight. "I don't think I'll get used to driving on the wrong side of the road anytime soon."

"Aye. Americans drive on the opposite side, right?" Ames pulled out onto the street and took a quick left on St. Patrick Street, which led them out of town in the opposite direction of North Hill. The sea was calm and sparkled in the sunlight, with gentle, rolling waves that turned feisty as they collided with the boulders on the shore, throwing up white spray that turned to foam on the slick, stony beach.

"So, what do you know about this place?" Sabine said, "and how did you get the name Amulet, if you don't mind me asking?"

"Not at all, but call me Ames. All my friends do." She slowed to give an enormous red-headed cow with long, silky locks that completely covered her eyes time to cross the road. "You'll get acquainted with these bastards if you stay longer than five minutes. They're called Highland cows, but they grow on ye after a while."

"Are they dangerous?" Sabine wondered aloud as the cow swung her enormous head toward the car to greet them. Ames slowed to a reluctant stop and smiled while the cow continued ambling across the road as if it her name was on it.

"Not at all. Even the bulls are docile and downright friendly if ye stop and offer snacks. Highway robbery, I call it. Cheeky beggars." She paused as she accelerated slightly and passed the cow. "My da named me Amulet, to answer your previous question. It means 'to ward off evil.' He said he wanted to remind me every day that I'm a powerful force for good in the world."

"That's beautiful." Sabine caught sight of the lighthouse in the distance, and her heart seemed to stop, as if waiting for her next move. "He looks like he adores you."

"Aye, and let's hope it's not only because I do the lion's share of the work and bring him tea and biscuits all day." She smiled, clicking on her blinker as they turned into the lighthouse drive. "Honestly, I adore him right back. I got lucky in the family lottery. They're all annoying, but I love them to bits."

The gravel drive to the lighthouse wound itself into what felt like a knot, only to open at the edge of the sea and endless azure sky stretching out over the whitecapped horizon. Ames slowed as the drive narrowed into a beautiful red-brick driveway ending at the front door of the lighthouse. Her phone rang just as they were getting out of the car, and Sabine told her to take her time, that she was fine to look around.

The lighthouse that had seemed so tiny at a distance in the photo was much bigger than she had imagined. The outside was perfectly round, with iron-framed windows on three levels and a small landing surrounded by copper railing at the very top, oxidized to a pale green after years of being bathed in the mist rolling in off the sea. Bronze nautical lanterns with thick, reinforced glass were mounted at regular intervals around the outside, and the door was framed in scarred oak planks, nearly as thick as they were long, sanded and varnished to withstand the onslaught of the weather.

The rhythmic ebb and flow of the water created a wild backdrop that whispered she might be the only person left on earth, and the salt in the air stung her lips as she walked around to the front of the lighthouse and peered down over the railing. A sheer cliff dropped from the ends of her boots into the churning ocean below that swirled into and over itself in a kaleidoscope of color, sheer translucent green rolling into opaque steel grays before everything slipped away to reveal the deepest blue under the blanket of white foam.

"What do ye think, now that you've seen the lighthouse with the backdrop of the sea? This is one of the places that's always dramatically different in person."

Sabine turned to find Ames perched on the railing, the sea churning and crashing against the rock wall below. The wind was running its fingers through her pixie haircut, and she wore a down vest, with dark jeans and knee-length, brown-leather riding boots that suggested she didn't do most of her work behind a desk. Her eyes were brilliant in the sunlight and, not unlike her own, a tangle of greens and earthy brown, like a glimpse into the backdrop of a fairy tale.

"It's insanely beautiful." Sabine's hair slipped out of its twist as she spoke, unfurling like a flag in the wind. "It's savage, and ancient, and scary as hell. I love it."

Ames laughed, the surf stealing the sound and carrying it out to sea. She nodded toward the front, leading Sabine back around the north curve of the lighthouse to the front door.

Ames turned the key to unlock the door and gestured for her to go ahead. Sabine stepped gingerly over the threshold as the thick, black metal door swung open in a wide arc.

"So, the lighthouse has three levels. There's a woodstove on each and a main heating vent that goes through the center, serving as a chimney and a way to distribute heat throughout the house."

Sabine turned in a circle, taking in the spacious, perfectly round space, but she was drawn immediately to the cheery kitchen along the far side nearest to the windows, with butcher-block countertops and a long, green marble island with barstools. The main sitting area was to the left, with two cozy leather couches and a coffee table between, warmed by cable-knit pillows and tartan wool throws. To the right, bookshelves lined the entire wall, with a glossy, rolling teak ladder and a wide cherrywood desk and chair. A mica lamp warmed the space and brought an amber glow to the bookshelves behind, and a single book, bound in red leather with gold edging, sat beside it.

"This is the main level, and the largest, as you can see from the outside, and the staircase there—" Ames pointed to a staircase on the right side near the kitchen that looked as if it had been carved into the wall, with a bronze railing. It followed the curve of the wall and disappeared into a large round opening in the ceiling. Ames continued, glancing up to the second floor. "—circles around the inner wall of the lighthouse and connects all three floors."

"This is absolutely gorgeous." Sabine walked over to picture windows behind the kitchen area. The reinforced glass took up the top half of the back wall and looked directly out over the sea. One glance down tricked the eye and gave the sensation of being suspended above the churning waves. "And this is west, correct?"

"Exactly. The sun sets over the horizon and drops like a huge, gorgeous burning orb into the sea every evening." She glanced up. "That same window faces the ocean on all three levels."

"So, why is the owner selling this, if you don't mind my asking?" Sabine turned again to look out over the ocean. "I can't imagine ever wanting to leave here."

"I don't mind at all. The owner is my uncle Angus. He bought it ages ago, then remodeled it himself. He never lived in it, but I still didn't think he'd ever be keen on selling. However, about a month ago he called the office and asked me to list it." She dug in her bag and pulled out a sheet of paper. "Here are the specs, with a few more specific details, and at the bottom you'll see a QR code for the latest building inspection. And the asking price as well, although I'm sure ye saw that on the listing."

An hour later, Sabine had viewed all three levels, heard a flurry of confusing descriptions of nautical-weather reinforcements, made notes about the utilities, and received an earful about the SHC, which Ames seemed to like about as much as her father did.

"Any future changes ye make, whether structural or cosmetic, have to go through the Scottish Historical Collective, which is a bunch of right bastards, especially the current president. So, the less ye change the place, the more chance you have of not going crazy." She rolled her eyes and placed her bag on the countertop, taking a seat on one of the barstools. Sabine followed suit. "I suggest, if you do buy it, that you meet with one of their representatives immediately afterward and get a list of dos and don'ts. Then you don't spend time or money on things they'll just turn down."

"Any advice on who I should ask for?"

"They're all just as bad as each other, but usually the president makes the local call-outs, and, trust me, do what you can to avoid that." She rolled her eyes but smiled in a way that made Sabine think she didn't quite believe what she was saying. "How a prick like that got into an elected office is beyond me."

Sabine walked back over to the bay windows, mesmerized by the horizon. She looked down just as a dolphin and her calf broke the surface of the water and leapt into the air in a perfect arc, the sun sparkling off their slick gray bodies before they disappeared. Sabine's shoulder felt warm, suddenly, as if a hand had been there, and she looked in that direction but saw nothing, not even a beam of sunlight.

"Did you see that? The dolphins?" Sabine whispered to Ames, who was beside her now, looking out over the sea, smiling.

"It's a sign." They said it perfectly together, then laughed as the same pair of dolphins shot up from the water and spun together before splashing back into the Atlantic.

Sabine turned around, taking everything in. "I'll need to do a final check with my attorney in the States, of course, but I did most of the legwork last night over the phone, so I'm confident the transaction will be smooth." She took a deep breath, steadying her racing heart with her hand. "I'd like to make an offer."

"Brilliant," Ames said, pulling a notepad from her bag. "What's your starting price?"

Sabine turned back to the horizon. "Exactly what he's asking. It's a fair price. Plus one hundred pounds. I'll be a cash buyer, so if real estate works the same here as home, it should be a quick sale."

"That's excellent news." Ames jotted down the note on her pad. "But why the extra hundred quid?"

"Because this place was obviously loved." Sabine scanned the space, glancing up the stairs and remembering the thoughtful touches in every room. "If he's selling it after so many years, it's got to sting. So the extra hundred is to cover a night at the pub for him and whomever he loves." She smiled. "Just a gesture, I suppose."

Ames laughed, dropping the notepad back into her bag, and shook her head. "That's the most Scottish thing I've ever bloody heard from an American, I'll tell ya that fer free." They headed toward the door, and Ames pulled it carefully shut and locked it behind them. "I'll be sure to tell him exactly that. I have an idea why he might be selling, and that sweet gesture will be just what he needs."

CHAPTER FIFTEEN

The next day was a whirlwind with getting documents and details in line to buy the lighthouse, endless calls to and from Katherine, and updates from the estate agents. Fortunately, by the time evening rolled around, Sabine was waiting for final confirmation from Katherine, but she saw a glimmer of light at the end of the tunnel, and the closing had been scheduled for the following week. She'd bought the home she lived in before her parents' accident and handled the sale of Thea's home, and thankfully, real estate seemed to work much the same in Scotland, so that process was familiar at least.

Lavender evening light was sinking into darkness by the time Sabine was headed back from Ames's office to The Loch and Beadle. Sabine pulled her phone from her pocket and typed a quick message.

Feel like taking me to dinner tomorrow night? I've got news.

In only a few seconds Alden's reply flashed across the screen of her phone.

Then you've got news and a date. I'll pick you up at seven.

Sabine's heart skittered as she clicked her phone off and headed for the boardinghouse to give Rose a more accurate estimate of how long she'd be staying. A petite blond woman was at the front desk when she got there, leaning over the partition and searching for something on the desk. She straightened up when she saw Sabine and smiled. "Oh. Hi there. Are you the owner?"

"I'm not. I'm just staying here." Sabine dropped her phone back into her pocket and gave her a quick once-over, but she looked, in a word, perfect, with a sorority-girl quality to her American accent. "I think you're looking for Rose Haywood. Her apartment is behind that door, so she must have just stepped away for a moment."

"God." The stranger blew a stray lock of white-blond hair out of her face and rolled her eyes. "They could at least put a bell up here or something. Customer service sure didn't make it across the pond, did it?"

Sabine smiled and nodded toward a couple of chairs in the waiting area. "I'm looking for her too. She shouldn't be too long. She's usually front and center at the desk when I go by."

"I'm Ellie Murphy, by the way." Ellie offered her hand, and they sank into floral upholstered chairs with white doilies on the headrests. "Have you been in town long?"

"Just a few days." Sabine resisted the urge to roll her eyes as a loved-up couple passed them on the way to the stairs, holding hands and giggling. "It looks like I'm staying longer, though. How about you?"

Ellie turned to her, eyes sparkling. "Just for vacation. My fiancée and I are headed to Paris tomorrow. I got us tickets as a surprise."

"Oh, God." Sabine turned toward her and sat up straight. "I've always wanted to go to Paris. I had a trip planned once but never got to go." She pushed the memory of her parents' accident out of her head and gave Ellie an encouraging smile. "You're going to have a blast."

Just then, Rose opened the door behind the counter, peeling the violet wrapper from a family-sized Cadbury bar as she settled into her chair. Sabine pointed her out and stood to gather her things. "You go ahead. I'm coming back down later for dinner, so I'll stop at the front desk then. It's nothing urgent."

"Thank you so much!" Ellie's voice had a faint cheerleader lilt to it and just a twinge of a Texas accent. "Hopefully I'll see you again. I'd love to introduce you to my fiancée." She tucked a lock of hair behind her ear, and the light from the chandelier illuminated the solitaire diamond on her left hand. "Alden is from Muir Rothesay, actually. She'd love you."

❖

Alden pulled into town and parked by the pier just as the last slice of orange sun was visible on the horizon. She turned off the truck, listening to the clicks and pings of the engine cooling as she laid her head back against the headrest. The restoration on the abbey just outside of town was almost complete, so she planned to deal with the dreaded mountain of paperwork that came along with it tonight.

No harm in a wee dram before I start.

She dropped her keys into her pocket and headed past St. Patrick's Street, turned down the alley, and dodged the attack cat swiping at her ankles from the drain. Half the village was already in the Woolpack pub, so only her da noticed when she slid onto one of the barstools and held up a finger. Morgan poured her a dram and slid it down the bar to her.

"I was going to ask how your day was, love, but from the look of ye, I can guess."

Alden downed the whiskey in one go and plunked it down on the bar.

"You'd be right, but I'm nearly done whit the Abbey project, so I might survive it after all, saints be praised."

Morgan took the orders for a couple at the end of the bar and made their drinks, then filled her glass again and poured a dram for himself, pulling up a stool behind the bar across from where Alden was sitting.

"Want ta talk about it?"

Alden shook her head, this time only downing half. "No sir. I do not."

"Fair play to ya, but ye had the bad luck to have two professors of psychology for parents, so basically, yer fucked." Morgan smiled, clinking her glass to Alden's and taking a long sip.

"It's nothing." She looked up at her da, who was clearly not planning to let the subject drop, not that he ever did. "I just can't stop thinking—"

"Ya can't stop thinking about what? World peace? Cold fusion?" Morgan smiled, holding up his hand to another customer down the bar. "Or is it the beautiful little redhead you brought home and couldn't stop staring at all night?"

"We're going to dinner tomorrow night, apparently, and if history repeats itself, that will most certainly end in disaster." Alden smiled despite herself and picked up her phone for emphasis. "I blame you, obviously."

"As ye should." Morgan smiled and headed toward the new customers, with a wink at her over his shoulder. "She's terrible. Just shite. We all hated her, obviously. Can't believe I introduced ye."

Alden watched him pull a couple of pints for the newcomers down the bar, and Morgan gave her a look over his shoulder that said to wait for him to return.

He wasn't wrong about how it was to have psychology professors for parents. When Alden was a teenager, even if she didn't want to talk, they dragged whatever it was out of her. But at the same time, things that were hard for her friends, like coming out, were a walk in the park with those two, and she always had someone to go to when life flipped upside down, which, in the last couple of years, had happened more than once.

When Alden and her sister were growing up, their parents both taught psychology classes at Aberdeen University, just a few kilometers down the road, but when Covid hit and Declan came to live with them, they shifted to do what was best for him. Alden moved back home, Da retired altogether and bought the pub, and her mother switched to teaching online classes to stay home as Declan started with signing tutors. It all worked out. Da said he should have made the switch years ago, but Alden knew her mother secretly missed the university environment.

Glasgow had an award-winning boarding school for the deaf, which was a looming option for Declan's next school term, but he would have to live in the dorm four hours from home, which had seemed far too overwhelming the only time they'd broached the possibility with him. Gwen didn't push the subject, but Alden knew it would allow her to teach in person again, which was what she really loved.

"Yer away with the fairies. What are ye thinking about?" Morgan perched back on his stool, and his face dropped. "Oh, sweet Jesus. Did ye see her already?"

"What are ye talkin' about? I haven't seen Sabine since the morning she left, Da. That's kinda the point."

"Ah." Morgan slapped his hand on the bar like he was gearing up for something unpleasant. "Just as well. It's better ye hear it from me anyway."

Alden's stomach dropped, and she tossed back the rest of her dram. "You have that look I don't like. What happened? Is it Declan?"

"Na. He's been chuffed in general since your Sabine got him talking again. I've never seen him so happy. Well, not since…"

"…since Eileen."

Morgan nodded. "Listen. There's no good way to tell ye this, so I'm just goin' ta spill it."

"You know I don't like all the therapist double-talk, anyway, Da. Just tell me."

Morgan stood and looked around the pub, then again before he sat back down and leaned into Alden, dropping his voice. "Ellie's back. She came in today lookin' for ye."

Alden's head fell into her hands. She felt dazed, as if she'd been hit with a board out of nowhere, which would have made slightly more sense than Ellie being back in Scotland. Alden did a quick sweep of the crowd, suddenly feeling she might be lurking, waiting for the opportunity to fuck up her life again.

"Holy shit. Did she come into the pub?"

"Aye. She was lookin' fer ye, but I just told her you were out on a job." Morgan pulled Alden a pint and set it in front of her. "Has she not called ya? I figured she'd been blowin' yer phone up since she touched down from Florida or wherever the hell she fucked off to."

"California." Alden tried to wrap her head around the fact that her ex was back in town. Her town. "I blocked her number when she left, so I wouldn't know if she's been calling or not."

"Aye. Smart." Morgan looked around again. "If ya want my advice, ye keep it that way."

"Shit." Alden sat back and ran both hands through her hair. "Perfect feckin' timing, as usual."

"Listen." Morgan raised his finger to the lad at the other end of the bar trying to get his attention. "I know you don't want to talk about it, but I'm just goin' ta say this."

"Aye. Go on."

"Your sister died." He paused, probably to steady the emotion trembling in his words. "And while you were in Glasgow in hospital with your critically ill nephew…your girlfriend of three fuckin' years left you, Alden." The pub seemed to still suddenly, and the words landed hard and hollow. "She *left* you."

Morgan hesitated, then let her sit with that thought and moved down the bar to pull some pints for impatient customers. Alden sat there for a moment, gripping her glass hard enough to break it, until she got it together enough to shrug on her coat and head for the door, waving to her da behind the bar.

"What the fuck is Ellie doing back in Muir Rothesay?" Alden heard herself muttering and reminded herself to lower the volume, although thankfully, it was late enough that most of the locals were either at home or in the pub. The snow was mostly slush by now, and she kicked it off her boots as she walked, the streetlights illuminating the fog rolling in from the ocean.

Da was right. She left me because she was no longer the center of attention when everything went to shit. Alden scooped up a handful of snow and smoothed it into a ball, then tossed it at the nearest streetlight. She missed. *What is she expecting? That I'll just welcome her back with open arms now that she thinks it's over and things can go back to the way they were?*

Anger simmered low and hot as she headed for the truck. They'd never had a conversation about ending the relationship. Ellie had just become more and more distant over the phone until Alden came home after two weeks in Glasgow to find the home they shared empty and still around a single note on the table. *Sorry. This isn't working anymore. I'll call you.* Alden got the call the next day as she was walking into Eileen's wake.

She pulled the truck out onto North Road and headed toward home, driving too fast, the ocean eerily still under the hazy moonlight. She'd always wondered how she'd feel if Ellie showed back up, and now she knew. She was angry. She'd shoved those feelings down for so long in order to deal with the emotional chaos of losing her sister, that after a while it just seemed easier to avoid getting involved again rather than have to work through them. If she simply hated Ellie for what she'd done, it would have been easier, but a part of her still had feelings for Ellie. Reconciling those two sides of her heart had just never happened.

It was a relief to be driving out of town and away from the possibility of running into her. Alden forced herself to take deep, calm breaths. Mam and Declan had enough to deal with without bringing that drama back into the house. She climbed the hill and turned onto her street, dodging a stray red tricycle that had been abandoned in the center of it. The temperature had dropped dramatically without the sun, and ice had slicked the brick path to the house by the time Alden parked and unloaded everything.

She knocked the snow off her boots and hung her overcoat on the pegs by the door, locking the door behind her as she made her way down the hall to the kitchen. Her mam was sitting at the table with a steaming cup of tea, her face both tense and neutral. Sitting beside her was Ellie.

❖

Late the next afternoon, Sabine hopped off the Rothesay bus at the end of the lighthouse drive. The driver said it wasn't an official stop, so getting back to town after her meeting with the SHC president might be tricky, but worst-case scenario, she could take the taxi. If she got lucky and he wasn't six pints deep at the pub.

Swaying cedars lined both sides of the winding gravel drive, and the sea breeze lifted the edges of Sabine's hair as she walked toward the lighthouse. The sun warmed the shoulders of her wool sweater, and she rubbed the tight muscles at the back of her neck, the gravel crunching and shifting under her boots. She hadn't gotten much sleep the night before, after Ellie flashed her ring and dropped the bomb that Alden was engaged. She'd gone to her room, locked the door, then slid down the other side of it to the floor. The moon was rising and the wind whistling through the eaves when she finally brushed her teeth and got into bed, eyes wide open.

This was exactly why she didn't let herself get involved. Something about being with Alden made her feel like she was standing at the edge of a cliff, the wind whipping through her hair as the cliff crumbled and shifted under her feet, the rocks pinging off every ledge and boulder on the way to the bottom. She'd been right. It was dangerous. Too dangerous.

As she crested the hill the lighthouse came into view, blinding white in the sunshine, and she had the strange sensation of walking out of reality and into Thea's painting. Colette had finally texted her a picture of it around midnight and of course asked why, but Sabine hadn't answered. She didn't know how to explain to her sister she was buying the lighthouse, mostly because she didn't know how to explain it to herself. She had to live somewhere, but she hadn't quite been able to wrap words around something else yet. It felt like a memory that drifts across your mind until you look directly at it, and the image evaporates like vapor that was never really there.

Sabine dug in her bag for the giant key ring Ames had given her. It held seven old brass skeleton keys, each the length of her hand, so just dropping it in her pocket hadn't been an option. The wind was whipping up the cliff from the shore below and wrapped her hair around her face as she tried each of the keys in the front door. The last one finally turned in the lock, and as she let herself in, she heard tires crunch on the gravel drive, and one glance at her watch reminded her who it was. Ames had explained on the way back to town that first day that if you were buying a historic property in Scotland, the initial meeting with an HSC rep was a requirement for the sale to go through, though the actual point of it was still unclear.

She dropped her bag onto the desk chair and swept her hair up into a quick bun, listening as the sounds of the vehicle grew closer. What did one wear to this kind of thing, anyway? She sighed as she looked down. If snowy hiking boots, faded jeans, and a wool sweater were the secret dress code, she had this meeting in the bag. She glanced out the bay windows to the sea, barely suppressing an irrational urge to run down the stairs cut into the cliff and dash into the fresh, icy surf with the rush of the tide all around her.

An impatient knock at the door dragged her reluctantly from the window and back into reality. She wanted nothing more than to explore the nooks and crannies of the place without anyone peering over her shoulder, then crack open the bottle of scotch she'd brought and watch the sun set over the ocean.

"Fine," she muttered to herself as she started toward the door. "He doesn't know this yet, but this is going to the quickest meeting in the history of ridiculous real-estate requirements."

She smoothed her hand over the flyaway hairs already escaping from her bun and opened the door.

"What—" She steeled herself and went on. "—the *hell* are you doing here?"

"Me?" Alden smiled, stepping in and shutting the door behind her. She lifted the leather bag she was carrying and set it on the table beside the door. "What are *you* doing here? I'm here to meet the new owner of the lighthouse. I thought maybe I'd gotten the time wrong because I didn't see a car out there. How the hell did you even get here?"

Sabine took a step back and shoved her hands into the pockets of her jeans. She wanted to say a thousand things, but they were racing so quickly across her mind she couldn't even start to catch them. The burn of angry tears stung her eyes, and she looked down as she took another step back.

"Hey," Alden said, her voice low and soft. "Are you okay? Why are you upset?"

Sabine shook her head, then swiped at a tear with the heel of her hand and locked eyes with Alden. It was a long moment before she spoke. "Just tell me one thing."

"Of course." Alden reached out a hand, but Sabine didn't take it, and Alden let it drop, confusion flashing across her face. "Anything."

Sabine took a breath, steadying herself by looking out to the ocean before she turned back to Alden, who raked a hand through her hair and left it behind her neck.

"I need to know if you're going to Paris."

"What?" Alden shook her head and slowly replied. "How could you possibly know that?"

Sabine held her gaze. "Just tell me."

"Yes." Alden's voice was a low scrape, the words landing soft and heavy in the space between them. "I am."

CHAPTER SIXTEEN

Sabine shook her head, then turned around, walking toward the bookcase, letting her head sink into her hands. She couldn't look at Alden. She wanted not to care, but everything inside her had just wanted Alden to say no to her question. That was it. Just that one word. She wanted to be wrong about Ellie.

"Sabine."

Sabine shook her head, and Alden stopped, her name fading into the chilled silence of the room.

"I met Ellie." Sabine paused to steady her voice. "And she told me she was here to surprise her fiancée with a trip to Paris." Sabine couldn't go back now, so she straightened her shoulders and turned slowly around. "And don't tell me it's some kind of misunderstanding, unless two Aldens in Rothesay just happen to be engaged to ridiculously perfect American blondes."

"Sabine." Alden walked as near as she could before Sabine held up her hand and Alden stopped where she was. "It *is* a misunderstanding."

"How can you even say that?" Sabine wiped a rogue tear from her cheek with her fingertips and glared back at Alden. "I saw her ring, Alden."

"I believe that." Alden's tone was gentle. "She was wearing one last night when she showed up at my house. But it's not mine. I never gave her a ring. And I sure as fuck never proposed."

"What?" Sabine shook her head. "What are you talking about?"

"I'll tell you the details later, but I can see how hurt you are, and I don't want you to feel that way for a minute longer than you already have." She paused. "So, I'm going to just give you the short version right now so we're on the same page, okay? Then I'll answer any questions you have for as long as it takes."

Sabine nodded, and Alden handed her the folded linen handkerchief she pulled from her shirt pocket. It had a nautical compass embroidered on the right corner and her initials, A.W.

"Aye. You're right that Ellie was in town to surprise me with a trip to Paris. But I had no idea she was even here until Da gave me the heads-up at the pub last night." She took a deep breath and went on. "I left right away so I didn't run into her and drove back to the house, but she was sitting at the kitchen table when I got home."

Sabine dabbed at her cheek. "So, you didn't even know she was in Rothesay until then?"

"Nope. Not until Da told me she stopped by the pub looking for me. The first and only time I saw her was at my house with my mam."

Sabine folded the damp linen square carefully and thought about handing it back but didn't. "What did she say?"

"That she made a mistake, and she wanted me back." Alden took a slow step forward. "She told me she'd bought tickets to Paris and wanted us to get married. She'd even picked out her own ring, apparently." She stopped, shaking her head. "The Wallace clan has a three-hundred-year-old ring that's been handed down for generations, and my wife will be the next to wear it. Needless to say, that big fuck-off diamond was not it." Alden paused as she seemed to wrap words around her thoughts one at a time. "She wanted me to propose the entire three years we were together, and I never did."

"Why not?"

"Because she wasn't the one. She never was. Ironically, I've always wanted to fall in love, real love, and propose. In Scotland, and especially in the Wallace clan, family is everything. If she were the one, it would have happened a lot sooner."

"And what did you say? When you walked in and found her there?"

"I told her it was over and that I'd met someone." Alden took another step and smiled when Sabine hesitantly matched it. "And then I asked her to leave."

Sabine smiled as Alden took the last step that closed the distance between them. She drew in the warm, woodsmoke scent of her skin and tangled her fingers into Alden's. "And why did you do that?"

"Because I realized that I wanted to go to Paris," Alden whispered, tipping Sabine's face up to hers with a gentle thumb under her chin. "But only with the woman I love."

Alden's hand slid around the back of Sabine's neck, her touch light and strong as she kissed her, pulling the curves of Sabine's body into the angles of her own, the heat of Alden's body melding gentle into savage in the space of a breath. Her hands circled Sabine's waist as she slowly pulled away.

"Sabine?" Alden hands held Sabine's face, as light as air. "Will you go to Paris with me someday?"

Sabine leaned back and pretended to consider her options. "I'll have to check my schedule."

"Too late." Alden winked and lifted her, wrapping Sabine's legs around her waist. "I already have our tickets, and we can go anytime within a year."

Sabine leaned in and slid her hands under Alden's shirt to the bare skin of her back, brushing her reply across Alden's neck to her ear. "Aren't you here to apply your expertise to something, Wallace?"

"Shhh...Alden kissed her again before she slowly returned Sabine's feet to the floor. "Aye, so don't tempt me. I have a lighthouse to inspect first."

Sabine remembered suddenly what Ames had said about the inspection. "You're not the president of the HSC, are you?"

"Aye. How did you know that?"

"I'm not telling, but someone mentioned you might be a little tough with the inspections."

"Not hard to believe." Alden laughed and went to get her bag, then pulled up a stool for both of them at the kitchen island. "I bet Jolene out there that Ames said that and more, with a few illustrations and diagrams for good measure."

"Good guess." Sabine settled onto her stool and laughed. "How did you know it was her?"

"Ames and I have a decade-long professional rivalry, but don't let her fool ya. Her uncle Angus—"

"The previous owner of this place, right?"

"Exactly." Alden pulled a stack of papers out of her bag and handed the stapled form on top to Sabine. "He's been Da's mate since primary school, and Angus and Martin Abernathy are brothers. So, we've known each other all our lives. We battle it out at work, then go down the pub and forget all about it." Alden shook her head as she pulled a pen from her pocket. "And don't tell her I said this, but she drinks me under the table every damn time."

After dinner that night, Morgan poured them all whiskey from his secret stash while Gwen and Sabine cleared the table.

"Gwen, thank you for having me again tonight." Sabine took the stack of charmingly chipped dessert plates Gwen handed her and set them at the end of the counter by the pie. It was a cherry pie, the filling still hot and fragrant, bubbling under the etched surface of the crust. "Although I guess you didn't have much of a choice. Alden asked where I wanted to eat, and I kind of invited myself."

"Which was perfect." Gwen smiled warmly as she retrieved a small pot of cream from the fridge. "Ellie showing up out of the blue last night was a bloody shock to the system, so I was thrilled when she left five minutes later, and Alden called today to say you two were coming for dinner." She glanced toward the table where Alden was patiently hand-lettering to Declan that his hair was *a right mess.* "The first night you were here was blissful. It's the first time we've seen Declan seem like himself since… everything."

"Alden filled me in a bit on what happened." Sabine's voice softened. "I'm so sorry about Eileen. I can't imagine what that must have been like."

"Aye. It changed our world, to be sure. We had so much to process that I think all of us have just been working through it as we go. It has to be harder for our Declan, though." Gwen's voice caught, and she shook her head, untying her apron and folding it carefully onto the counter. "Sometimes I wish we could have just one afternoon back—one chance to talk like we used to. So I could understand more how he really feels."

Sabine picked up the stack of linen napkins Gwen had set out by the sink. "It's not easy for either one of you to have to learn a completely different language to communicate. My favorite aunt, the one I told you about when we met, was profoundly deaf." She paused, the familiar ache of grief settling onto her chest as she went on. "The whole family signed, of course, but when she moved out of the house and saw everyone less frequently, the habit of signing as we spoke at gatherings, or just talking to her one on one, sort of slipped away. She said she felt like the world had moved on without her."

"Aye. That must be how our Decs feels most of the time." Gwen glanced back at Declan, who was laughing at the table, peering over Alden's shoulder as she showed him something on her phone. "As much as I don't want to admit it, it's harder to communicate now, so I think sometimes we've avoided it."

"He probably has too. It's not just you."

"But now that we know better," Gwen said, her eyes sparkling as she pulled Sabine into a quick hug, "we can do better."

"I hate to point out the obvious, love." Morgan looked up with a wistful glance from the table. "But if that beautiful pie goes cold, it'll suck all the joy out of me life."

"Ah, the drama queen has spoken." Gwen rolled her eyes and winked in his direction. "You'll get it when we bring it to ye, ya cheeky beggar."

Gwen and Sabine joined them at the table, and everyone passed around the pie, pouring a rich pool of chilled cream on each slice. The plump, tart cherries were the perfect contrast to the cream and rich, flaky crust. After a few bites, Sabine got Declan's attention and set down her fork, signing and speaking at once.

"Show me everyone's sign just one more time. I want to be sure I remember them."

Declan broke into a smile and obliged, starting first with Gwen, making the shape of the letter G with both hands and touched them to the top of his head.

Gwen started to speak, then paused before she turned to Declan and signed *Why?*

Declan signed back and Sabine translated. *"It's a variation on the sign for crown because you're the queen of the family."*

"Mary, Joseph, and the wee donkey." Gwen grabbed her napkin. "I'm gan' ta cry for sure now."

Sabine smiled and helped translate as Declan went through each name sign again, as well as the story of how he came up with it. When he was done, everyone was laughing together, and the cherry pie was nearly gone. Morgan grabbed the last slice and said, with a perfectly straight face, that he needed it because cherries have antioxidants, and he was "looking after his heart."

"Declan?" Sabine signed and spoke. "If you could pick one thing, what do you wish your family knew about how to communicate better with you?"

Gwen squeezed Sabine's hand as Declan signed back to Sabine. *Will you translate?*

Sabine nodded and signed back. *Of course I will.*

Declan looked down at the table and picked at a thread on the edge of his napkin before he looked up to sign. *"When you talk to each other at the table without signing, it makes me feel like you wish I wasn't there."*

Morgan shook his head and started to speak. "Oh, Dec—"

Gwen put a finger over her lips, then fingerspelled slowly to Declan, *"Go on, love."*

"I know that's not true," Sabine translated as Declan signed, *"But it feels like that sometimes."* A tear dropped onto his cheek, and he wiped it away with the heel of his hand. *"I need you to include me."*

Morgan turned to Sabine to translate and started to reply, but Sabine gently turned him back toward Declan, signing as she explained why. *"When you're talking to him, look at him. Even if someone is translating or you think you're too slow."*

Declan nodded, signing *"What?"* to Morgan.

Morgan looked directly at him while he spoke. *"I'm so sorry we made you feel that way, son, and I can understand why you did. I know now, and it won't happen again. There's never been one minute we didn't want you here."*

Gwen wiped away a tear, and Sabine signed as she spoke. *"We love you. You're our family."* Gwen paused, glancing over at Morgan and Alden, who nodded in support, before she continued. *"I'm sorry we let you down, love. We've been a bit shit at learning to sign, but we'll dive back in and conquer it. I promise."*

Alden jumped in and haltingly signed for herself. *"Will you spend lots of time with us, though?"* She pointed back at Morgan. *"It may take some..."*

Alden looked at Sabine. "What's the sign for patience?"

She signed it and took over translating so Alden could say what she needed to say. *"It may take some patience. We all know that Da can be a little thick, but maybe if we spend lots of time together, we can pull him along and get him up to standard."*

Sabine signed to Declan. *"What does thick mean?"*

Declan laughed. *"It's Scottish for dumb."*

"Damn." Sabine laughed and sat back in her chair as she signed, awash in the warmth of the fire and the love so dense she felt it hovering over the table. *"Alden was right. Everything here is savage."*

By the time the dishes were done and Declan had polished off the pie Morgan gave up on, it was past nine. Everyone was starting to scatter when Sabine felt her pocket start to buzz. She pulled out her phone and asked Gwen if she could take her call in the greenhouse.

"Of course, love. Take all the time you need. We're all headed to bed in a minute anyway."

Sabine found the greenhouse door and stepped in, shutting the door behind her and picking up on the last ring.

"Katherine?"

"I won't keep you." She paused. "I just wanted to let you know the financial end of things has been taken care of. I wrapped it up this afternoon. Once I got in touch with Angus's lawyer, it was as simple as hammering out the details and completing the wire transfer."

Sabine ran her fingertips lightly over the silvery velvet leaves of a sage plant, rehomed into an antique metal lunchbox. The faint sounds of an owl outside the greenhouse glass faded into the brush of wind.

"If you don't mind my asking." The rhythmic tap of Katherine's pen on her desk filled the silence, and it was a long moment before she went on. "Have you met Angus yet?"

"No, but I'm sure I will at the closing next week." Sabine paused. "Why?"

Katherine started to answer, then redirected. "I'll let you go. I know it's late there. Don't hesitate to call if you need me."

The phone clicked off, and she was gone.

Sabine waited a moment before she went back, listening to the hypnotic hum of the warming lights glowing above the plants. When she finally stepped out of the humid warmth of the greenhouse, Alden was the only one left in the living room, and the only light came from a small lamp on the kitchen countertop and the crackling glow of the fireplace. She felt dazed and, strangely, closer to her aunt than she had been since she died, though she couldn't put her finger on why.

"Hey there." Alden threw a split pine log onto the coals with a handful of kindling and waited until it caught, the flames crackling and rising into the chimney. The fire threw copper light and flickering shadows onto the walls as the house warmed and settled around them. "Are you okay? You look pale."

Sabine sank back into the couch, Katherine's words still echoing in her ears. She rubbed the ache from her forehead and settled back into the wool throw and cozy pillows. "I think I need whiskey."

"Aye." A broad smile flashed across Alden's face, and she stood, opening the top of a roll top desk next to the hearth. "I see we're rubbing off on you already. Excellent."

Sabine watched her pour from the crystal decanter and took the glass Alden gave her as she settled back in on the couch. "I could do worse."

"You certainly could." Alden clinked her glass to Sabine's. "You could be in England."

"So, it's true, the divide between the Scots and the Brits?" Sabine smiled as she took her first sip and tucked her feet underneath her. "I've seen the BBC news once or twice at my aunt's house. I know things."

Alden leaned back and laughed, spinning the amber whiskey slowly in her glass. "Ye know things, huh?"

Sabine turned to the crackling fire and watched the sparks chase each other up the chimney. The rustic scent of burning cedar and pine hung in the air, and Sabine let the warmth start to unfold her muscles onto her bones, but the familiar push of grief was seeping in and settling over her heart. It was the only thing she couldn't control, this grief. It crept in and faded away on its own timetable, invisible yet crushingly heavy at the same time. After her dad died in the accident, people told her that time would heal everything, but that was a lie. You just grow accustomed to carrying the weight.

They sipped their whiskey and stared into the fire for a few minutes, and then Alden's voice steered her back to the present. "If you want to tell me." Her thumb traced the edge of the glass as she spoke. "I'd love to know more about your family."

Sabine nodded, sifting through where to start.

"My aunt died recently. She's the reason I'm here." Sabine pressed her fingertips into the etchings on the crystal. "When she died, she left me a choice in her will. I could stay in New Orleans and inherit nearly nothing, or I could take a chance and spend a year in Scotland and inherit a sizable chunk of her estate." She drew in a slow breath, trying to remember and not remember at the same time. "It wasn't about the money though. It's hard to explain."

"Why Scotland?"

"That's the thing. I literally have no idea, and the only clue she gave me was the name of this village." She thought for a moment, remembering Katherine's carefully chosen words. "I know her. She wanted me to find something. Now, I just have to figure out what that is."

Alden handed Sabine her glass to hold and pulled her wool turtleneck over her head, tugging down the slim black tee underneath. Sabine had had just enough whiskey to let herself notice the definition in Alden's biceps and the strong, muscular lines of her shoulders. Tattoos the color of drifting smoke wrapped her arms to her wrists, and her hands were square, scarred and strong.

Alden draped her sweater over the back of the sofa and smiled. "If I didn't know better, I'd think you were staring, Ms. Rowan."

"I'm just appreciating your tatts." Sabine sniffed and returned her attention to her glass, barely suppressing a smile. "I don't stare. I'm not that kind of girl."

"Sabine." Alden caught and held Sabine's gaze, then leaned forward slowly and took the whiskey glass out of her hand. "You're exactly that kind of girl."

She stood and refilled their whiskeys, then nodded toward the staircase. "Declan usually comes out and sleeps by the fire. "I'd love for you to stay the night. Do you mind if we take this upstairs?"

Sabine smiled and nodded. She followed Alden up the staircase, the wood slabs creaking under their feet in the silent house, the air somehow warming as they climbed, still as a church and heavy with dust and memories.

Alden handed her both glasses at the top of the stairs. "I'll be back. I'm just going to grab an extra duvet. The temperature is supposed to drop around midnight."

Sabine took off her jeans, folding them carefully by her boots, and pulled off her wool sweater, leaving her oversized white shirt buttoned to the center of her chest. She removed the pins from her hair, letting it fall to the small of her back as she heard the attic door open.

CHAPTER SEVENTEEN

Sabine sank down onto the couch, tucking her legs underneath her. A candle was flickering on the wooden table this time, with a box of matches beside it. "Last time I was here you'd almost given me frostbite."

Alden laughed, turning her hand over to look at her fingertips, then bringing them to her lips to kiss. "I think you're going to live. And thank God. My parents would have disowned me otherwise." She settled back on the couch, her eyes dark and sparkling.

Alden was magnetically confident: the way she moved, the way she slid her hand into the small of Sabine's back as they walked, even her gaze that was impossible to look away from. Sabine put down her glass and leaned over, her breath draped across Alden's neck as she pulled the leather lace wrapped around her hair. She ran her hands through it, letting the dark waves sift through her fingers and fall to Alden's shoulders. The scent of it, dark woodsmoke and dried rosemary, lingered between them as she sat back on the couch.

"The obvious question here is," Alden's eyes were dark and intense as she met her gaze, "are you trying to kill me with that shirt?"

"Certainly not. That's ridiculous." Sabine smiled. "I don't have anywhere to hide the body." She gazed at Alden's shoulders, then at her chest. She hesitated. She wanted to ask the question but didn't have the words.

"You can ask…" Alden's words were a low scrape in the attic stillness. "Or you can just give me your hand."

Sabine held her breath for a long moment before she leaned close and let Alden take her hand.

Alden placed it lightly over her heart, holding it warm and soft under her own. "You're shaking."

"I know." Sabine bit her lip, settling her other hand on Alden's thigh. "I don't know why."

Alden lifted her hand slowly and met her eyes. Sabine's voice was barely a whisper, her words shimmering like heat in the air between them. "May I touch you?"

Alden nodded and watched as Sabine ran her fingertips over her upper body, tracing the muscular lines of her chest.

"You've had top surgery?"

"Aye. In a way, yes." Alden said. "My mam had breast cancer five years ago, so I got tested for the BRACA gene to see if I was likely to get it as well."

Sabine reluctantly sat back and picked up her glass. "And you had the gene?"

"I did. And I spent a few weeks thinking about it before I decided." Alden ran her hand over her chest as she spoke. "I just didn't want the risk. For me, the chances were so high I didn't want to have to wonder when it would happen."

"I get that. I think I would feel that way too."

Alden raked a hand through her hair. "A lot of women get the double mastectomy, like Angelina Jolie, but afterward most opt for reconstruction with implants, and that just wasn't me." Alden ran her palm over her chest as she spoke. "Fortunately, I had an understanding surgeon, and she intentionally gave my chest a more masculine line with the nipple placement and hid the scars under my pecs." She smiled. "If you're not looking for them, you can't see them at all."

"That makes total sense," Sabine said, letting her gaze linger on Alden's shoulders. "I'm glad you didn't go for the reconstruction. This fits you perfectly."

The chandelier flickered above them, then sizzled, sparked, and went dark, and in the same moment, the candle blew itself out.

Sabine laughed, striking a match to relight the candle. "What was *that*?"

"I have no idea, but I'll be taking that fixture down soon to figure it out." Alden got up to inspect the switch, then tested the lights in the bathroom. "The lights in the water closet are fine, so for the time being I'll leave those on so you're not trying to find your way in the dark."

The moonlight cast a wide silver beam across the bed, and Sabine got up to transfer the brass candleholder to the nightstand. The quiet was intense as it settled across the attic, and from across the room, she watched Alden slide a hand around the back of her neck, eyes locked on hers. "Do you want me closer?"

Sabine's breath caught in her throat, but she nodded. Alden crossed the room, her gaze never leaving Sabine's. When she was so close Sabine felt the heat of her skin, Alden slid her hand around the back of her neck and pulled her close. The warmth of Alden's words melted across the curve of Sabine's neck. It was just a whisper, more breath than words, and Alden's voice was deep, resonant, and sexy as fuck. "Let's talk about consent."

Alden turned her around, words still dripping across Sabine's flushed skin, until her back was pressed into Alden's chest. Alden slid a hand under her shirt and around her waist, pulling Sabine against her. "I need you to know that we can stop, no matter what's happening." Alden waited for Sabine to nod before she ran her tongue across Sabine's shoulder, the shirt button at the center of Sabine's chest slipping like water through her fingers. "You don't need a reason."

Sabine turned in her arms. Alden's palm was warm and heavy between her breasts, her gaze intense. "Why are you telling me this?"

"Because it's the most important thing in the world." Alden brushed her thumb over Sabine's lower lip, as light as air. "I want you to always feel safe with me."

Sabine nodded, then caught Alden's hand. She brushed Alden's middle finger across her lips, swirling her tongue around it slowly, pulling it deeper into the heat of her mouth.

"Jesus Christ." Alden groaned and pulled Sabine's hips into hers. "You're killing me."

Alden picked her up with one arm, wrapped Sabine's legs around her waist, and backed her up to the wall beside the rafters. Sabine held on to one of the beams as Alden unbuttoned the rest of her shirt, slowly, the other hand pressed into the small of her back, tracing the curve of Sabine's breast with her tongue. A flush of sudden heat swept across Sabine's chest like a wide stroke of rose-tinted watercolor, and she arched her back, her fingers tangled in Alden's hair, pulling her closer.

Alden traced the edges of her nipple with her tongue, brushing it with the warmth of her breath, then looked slowly up at Sabine as she pulled it into her mouth. Sabine lost her breath and pulled her closer as Alden slipped the last button through her fingers and let the shirt drop off her shoulders.

"Take me to bed." Sabine whispered the words into Alden's neck. Alden wrapped Sabine's ass in her hands, walking them back to the bed as she pulled her own shirt over her head. A shoulder-to-shoulder tattoo of medieval armor covered Alden's chest in shades of dense black and sheer ash, the details shaded so beautifully it seemed to rise off her body. Sabine laid back on the bed, and Alden lowered herself onto her, brushing Sabine's hair out of her face as she spoke. She was still memorizing every detail of Alden's chest, tracing the outline of her armor with a gentle fingertip. Alden smiled, the candlelight casting gold light and shadows over the shaded angles of her chest and shoulders. "It's okay to tell me how you feel about it."

"It looks like courage." Sabine looked into her eyes and slowly spread her hands across Alden's chest. "And it's the sexiest thing I've ever seen."

Alden closed her eyes and took a deep breath, almost as if she were breathing Sabine's words into her chest. She kissed her, burying her hands in Sabine's hair as she traced her tongue across her chest. She moved slowly down to her waist, wrapping it in her hands as she slipped lower, as if worshipping the slope of her hip and delicate softness where the black silk met her skin.

Alden's breath felt warm and insistent as she lifted one of Sabine's thighs onto her shoulder and reached up to brush her fingertips across her tense nipples. Sabine arched into her touch, wrapping both legs around Alden's waist as she moved with aching slowness back up her body.

"Sabine." Alden whispered, her voice husky and raw. "I've got to stop before I can't stop."

"What do you mean?"

"I want you worse than I've ever wanted anyone, but I need you to sleep on it, to see how your heart feels, before we go further." Alden paused, tracing the line of her jaw with a gentle fingertip. "You've been through a lot recently, and I want to make sure I'm not taking advantage of that."

Sabine smiled and raised an eyebrow. "Worried you can't handle me?"

"Oh, that's cute." Alden laughed and slipped one thigh between hers. She leaned down and pulled Sabine's nipple into her mouth, swirling her tongue around it before she scraped it gently with her teeth. She wrapped Sabine's leg tightly around her waist and leaned into her until Sabine drew a sudden, sharp breath. Alden wrapped her hands around Sabine's hips and pressed slowly into her again, holding Sabine's center against her thigh, her body so close Sabine felt the rhythm of her heart.

"Oh, I can handle you, Sabine," she whispered, tracing the curves of her ear with her tongue. "I just need to make sure you're ready for me."

Alden slipped them under the covers and pulled Sabine into her, curving around her from behind. The moonlight bathed the roof and rafters in a translucent pewter glow as they drifted into sleep, Alden's hand resting warm and soft over Sabine's heart.

❖

Sabine opened her eyes slowly, adjusting to the dusky, predawn light. She turned to Alden, asleep beside her, her slow breath making her chest rise and fall, one arm draped over her eyes. She leaned up on her elbow and trailed a fingertip down Alden's abs, then slipped it under the waistband of her black boy shorts. Alden opened her eyes and turned Sabine underneath her before Sabine had a chance to react, then reached up to pull her own shirt over her head and drop it over the edge of the bed.

Sabine kissed her softly. "You said you wanted me to be sure."

Alden smiled, the kind crinkles around her eyes deepening as she watched Sabine's mouth. "And are you?" Her voice was a whisper, the only sound in the room.

"I was sure last night." Sabine leaned up and traced Alden's bottom lip with her tongue. "But I love that you waited."

Alden kissed her and got out of bed, reaching into the end table on her side for the matches. She struck one and lit the three ivory candles in the room, then locked the door before she got back into bed. Sabine put her hand in the center of Alden's chest. "I can feel your heart beating."

Alden held her eyes in the semi-darkness, her hand settling warm and soft over Sabine's. "And I've felt your heart beating in my chest since the moment I saw you."

She kissed her then, the candlelight throwing gold shadows over their bodies, and eased the shirt Sabine was still wearing down her shoulders and off. Alden dipped her head, taking Sabine's nipple deep into her mouth, stroking it with her tongue as her knee slipped between Sabine's thighs. She held the curves of her hips with both hands as Sabine wove her fingers into Alden's hair, lifting it to watch the strong line of her neck and shoulders as Alden moved down, grazing the inner slope of her hip with her tongue. She lowered the satin waistband of her shorts and followed them down, her mouth gentle but heated, the muscles in her arms tensing as she looked up.

"Take these off for me?"

Sabine slid them down her legs and handed them to Alden. Her eyes moved silently over Sabine's body, where now just a scrap of sheer black silk remained.

"Jesus. You're so beautiful." Alden ran her fingertip just under the edge of the silk, then followed the curve of Sabine's inner thigh with the slick heat of her tongue, grazing her clit before she looked up. Sabine held her eyes as Alden reached up, barely brushing Sabine's nipples with the flat of her palm, then capturing one between her fingertips hard enough to make Sabine arch her back and bury her hands in Alden's hair. She slid Sabine's panties down and off in a single second, then sank down between her thighs. She was wet before Alden touched her, before she parted Sabine's thighs with her shoulders, before she dragged her tongue across her clit, the touch as light as thought. Sabine tightened her fingers around Alden's shoulder as Alden traced just the edges of Sabine's clit with her tongue, her fingers everywhere, bare and slick with lust, until Sabine's hips grew restless, and her breath was as fast as her heartbeat.

"Alden," Sabine said, eyes closed, back arched. "I need you."

Alden crawled up her body to kiss her, her voice low and breathless against her ear. "What do you need, Sabine?"

"You." Sabine ran her nails up Alden's back, eyes locked on hers. "Just you."

Alden slid two fingers inside her before she'd even said the last word, turning them as she stroked them in and out, working her slowly until Sabine groaned, her voice heavy with lust and pleasure. She moved back down between her thighs, still deep inside her as she slicked the flat of her tongue across Sabine's clit. Sabine arched her back, moving her hips with the rhythm of Alden's tongue as it moved over her—slow, firm, and steady. Sabine felt her clit tensing against Alden's tongue, her thighs trembling, and then Alden added a third finger, achingly slowly. Sabine held her breath, and Alden stilled until she relaxed, then started again, her touch intense and rhythmic, as she stroked Sabine's clit, pulling it gently into her mouth and stroking the underside in the same rhythm as the fingers inside her.

"Oh my God." Sabine tangled her fingers into Alden's hair, meeting every thrust with her hips. Her damp breasts trembled as her breath shuddered through her chest. She bit her lip, lifting her hands to the headboard behind her, spreading her thighs wider for Alden. She started to come in that second, thighs shaking, lust flowing warm into Alden's hand as she rode out her orgasm, Alden meeting every pounding heartbeat with the steady rhythm of her tongue.

When Sabine finally stilled, Alden wrapped her in her arms, pulling the duvet over them, Sabine's breath slow and set.

"What did you do to me?" She snuggled deeper into Alden's arms. "My thighs are still shaking."

Alden smiled. "I'll take that as a compliment." She smoothed her hand over Sabine's hip, holding her close as she settled. "Are you falling asleep?"

Sabine tried and failed to open her eyes. "I'm totally not sleeping." She snuggled closer into Alden as she turned Sabine and spooned her from behind.

"Go to sleep," Alden whispered, warming Sabine's neck with her breath. "I'll still be here when we wake up."

❖

The next morning, they grabbed a late lunch at Avril's place, and a message from Ames pinged Sabine's phone just as they were getting back into Alden's truck.

Have time to meet me for a drink in a few? Going over a few details prior to closing may help us get this wrapped up in record time tomorrow.

Sabine texted a quick *yes* and made plans to meet her at The Woolpack, then rested her hand on Alden's thigh as she attempted to shift down to first to avoid the cows sauntering across the road.

"I'm meeting Ames later at your dad's pub. Want to keep me company?" Sabine assumed her most innocent face. "I mean, since you guys are secretly in love and all that."

Alden passed the last cow and made a show of almost driving off the road in response. "She's so straight not even I could turn her, and she'd most certainly put me off women forever." Alden rolled her eyes and put her hand on Sabine's thigh. "But Mam just texted when you were talking and said she needs to do an emergency counseling appointment. She'd promised Declan she'd make burgers tonight, though."

"So, you're playing grill master?"

"Exactly." Alden squeezed her thigh and dodged a slush pile in the road. "But you're welcome to come over after."

"I'd better stay and pack. If all goes well with the closing, I'll be moving into the lighthouse tomorrow." She leaned into Alden's shoulder. "But last night was magic. Every second of it."

"I loved it too." Alden smiled. "I definitely won't be thinking about burgers later, so you may never see our house again because I'll be burning it to the ground." She winked, looking quickly back to the road. "I'll keep you posted."

Alden pulled up to the boarding house and shifted into Park, waving at Rose, who was leaning out the door smoking a cigarette, gaze fixed on Alden's truck. "The closing is tomorrow morning, right?"

"First thing." Sabine nodded and dropped her phone into her pocket. "I'll call you when it's done."

"Do that." Alden leaned over and kissed her slowly, her hand resting warm and soft around the base of her neck, pulling away slowly only when she noticed someone trying to parallel park behind them. "I'll come load your things and give you a ride to your lighthouse. I don't start my new project until the next day." Alden held Sabine's face in her hands and looked into her eyes. "You know, you're getting to me pretty quickly for an ax murderer."

Sabine laughed, taking the rucksack Alden handed her. "You knew I was dangerous that first day in the pub. Should have seen it coming, Wallace. I don't know what to tell you."

She gave her a quick kiss before Alden pulled away, and Sabine glanced at her watch as she headed toward The Woolpack. It still seemed surreal, the fact that the lighthouse would be hers after closing the next day. As she rounded the corner in the alley, she found the knit cap Alden had given her deep down in one of her pockets. She pulled it on and smoothed her hair with her palms, trying to ignore the realization that even aside from meeting Alden, she'd been unexplainably happy in Scotland so far. She'd wanted to text Colette several times for details about Celestine, but the twisting in her gut every time she typed the text made her just as quickly delete it.

She dodged a group of teenaged boys careening down the sidewalk just in time and slowed her pace. She couldn't figure out what had made her happy here without thinking about how miserable she'd been in New Orleans. Just the thought of home upset her, and she couldn't very well meet Ames in the pub with tears in her eyes. She walked past The Woolpack and rounded the corner to duck into the next alley, leaning back into the cool stone wall and trying to stop her racing heart.

I'm halfway across the world. Why am I so angry about this now? Sabine noticed that her fists were clenched and tried to shake them out. *I never even have to see Celestine again if I don't want to. It makes no sense.* She shook her head as if to loosen the thoughts, but they dug deeper, expanding like bubbling lava until Sabine started walking back to The Woolpack just to shut them up.

I'm not thinking about her here. Sabine took a slow breath in and let it go, watching it freeze into icy fog in the semi-darkness. *I finally fucking got away. I can't let her steal this from me too.*

She reached the front door of the pub and wrapped her hand around the bronze handle, telling herself to leave those thoughts outside. It almost worked, but her stomach was still unsettled by the thought of her mother. At least she recognized what was happening now. It wasn't worry—it was anger—and that was worse. It was the only thing she'd never known what to do with.

She'd almost decided to just ignore it and hope it would disappear when Morgan pulled the door open and enveloped her in a huge hug. The comforting scent of peat smoke from the fire in the pub followed him in a rush, and the rough wool of his sweater scraped her cheek, the sensation just enough to pull her back into the present.

"What're ye doin' outside, lass? I stood inside and watched ye pass a wee bit ago, and now yer out here frozen to the door handle."

"I'm okay." Sabine drew in the scent of wool and whiskey, then smiled up at him as she let her go. "But that was excellent timing."

He laughed, then opened the door wider and motioned her in, taking her coat as she crossed the threshold. "Now it's not my Alden upsettin' ya, is it? I can straighten that out right quick." Morgan winked at her and rounded the corner of the bar.

"No. Alden is great. It's not that." Sabine settled onto a stool and slowly unwound her scarf. "It's just something from home." She paused, then downed the whiskey Morgan put in front of her in one gulp. Morgan nodded, then refilled her glass, pulling up his own stool behind the bar.

"Aye, well, I'd love to hear about it if ye feel like it might help to take it apart and look at it." He shook his head and poured his own dram. "I never get to flex my therapy muscles anymore, though I can't say I miss teaching. I've no idea why my Gwennie loves it so much. Most of them millennials were right bastards."

Sabine laughed, the whiskey starting to warm her from the inside out. The pub was still fairly empty, except for the cook she saw pass occasionally on the other side of the kitchen door, and a quick glance around told her that Ames hadn't arrived yet.

"I don't really know how to describe it, I guess. I have some thoughts that have moved into my mind and taken up space permanently. I should be charging them rent." Sabine placed her new dram on a pint coaster. "Although I don't mean to take advantage. You're a therapist. I bet people hit you up for free advice all the time."

Morgan laughed, a deep rumble that seemed to unfold into the room and warm it into the corners. "Are ye joking? Scots wouldn't talk about what's wrong with 'em even if it was the only thing that'd keep a bomb from going off, which is true in most cases." He sipped his dram and plunked it back down on the bar. "Hit me."

"I have a rocky relationship with my mom." She paused, trying to find words to wrap around their history. "She's an alcoholic, a bad one, and I didn't really know how awful she was to me until I left, you know? But it's not only the drinking. I just feel like…she never really liked me, and I guess I'm seeing it more clearly from a distance." She paused, tracing the side of the glass dram with her finger. "Like she resented me or something and being drunk was just an excuse to let that loose."

Morgan nodded. "And how do you feel now you're away?"

"That's the part I don't get." Sabine looked down, hating the tears suddenly burning her eyes. She tried to blink them away but gave up and took the folded handkerchief Morgan dug from his jacket pocket and handed her. "You'd think I'd be happy to be away from her, and I am. But now my mind keeps replaying all the things she said, all the ways she treated me, and I'm just—" She realized suddenly that she was gripping the edge of the bar so tight her fingertips were white and pulled her hands into her lap. "I'm really angry."

Morgan nodded, turning his dram on the bar. "If there was something you wish she understood better about you," he looked up at her, his eyes intensely kind, "what would that be?"

Sabine swiped at her cheek with the linen handkerchief. "That I tried so hard. My whole life." Her voice cracked. "I wanted her to love me, and I don't understand why she never did."

Morgan nodded. "It's not your job to make her love you, lass. It never was."

The knife in Sabine's stomach started to recede. Somehow just getting the words out of her head and into the air seemed to help. "But I have to do something to fix this, right? What can I do?"

"Nothing, except take the time away ye need to heal." Morgan turned to hold a finger up to a couple as they came through the door. They smiled instantly and nodded, seeming to understand pub sign language for "I'll be right with you," and went to warm up by the fire. "The only way out of this is to go through it. Let yerself feel all those feelings yer tryin' ta outrun. That anger is yer body's way of tellin' ya that someone trampled all over yer boundaries and something needs to change."

Sabine nodded. "The only way out is through it. I remember you saying something like that the first night I was here." She thought about that for a moment, then looked up, realizing suddenly that she felt lighter. "Thank you for listening, Morgan. It may seem like a small thing to you, but trust me, it's not."

"Lass, the difference you've made with our Declan in just the time we've known ye has meant the world to us. It's nice to be able to repay that debt a wee bit." The warmth between them shimmered in the air, and Morgan clinked his glass to hers just as Ames rushed through the door, her scarf flying behind her.

"I'm so sorry, Sabine! I know I was supposed to be here ages ago, but I lost my keys to the shop and then found them in my bag at the last minute but then that stupid cat got me—"

Morgan squeezed Sabine's hand before he went to collect the order for the previous couple. Ames chose a table closer to the fire and draped her coat over the back of the chair as Sabine sat down. "Don't worry. Your timing couldn't have been more perfect."

"Are ye all right?" Ames looked suddenly worried as she unwound her scarf and placed it over her coat. "You look like you've been crying."

"I'm better than I have been in a long time." Sabine let out a long breath, then one she'd been holding since she'd gotten on the plane. "They're good tears."

Ames nodded like that made perfect sense. "The Highlands will do that to ye. Everybody knows that Scotland will make everything right again if ya stay long enough."

Morgan took Ames's drink order on the way back to the bar, only to have her change her mind and call after him. "And a plate o' chips wouldn't go amiss."

"God. That sounds amazing." Sabine was suddenly starving. Ames nodded and leaned back in her chair to catch Morgan's eye. "Make that two plates of chips, handsome." She turned back to Sabine. "Ah, that's the life, innit? To own a pub and have beautiful women flirt with ya left, right, and center. Won't do ye a bit of good, mind. I've never seen him even glance at anyone but his wife." She shook her head, digging in her bag for a folder. "Proof that all the good ones are taken."

Morgan dropped off the drinks with a good-natured wink at Ames, then headed back to the bar.

"You're probably wondering why I asked to meet ya before the closing, and ye'd be right to ask. It's not how we usually do things." She took a slow, appreciative sip of her Guinness and licked the foam off her lip. "But for whatever reason, it's been hard for Angus to let this place go, so I thought I'd go over the paperwork beforehand with you, so if we have any last-minute changes, I can get those done before closing. I also have the info for you on how to switch the utilities over, etcetera, but everything is currently active, so you'll have a few weeks to get that sorted."

"Good idea." Sabine ran a hand through her hair and pulled it over her shoulder. "That way he doesn't have to do this twice."

"My thoughts exactly." Ames nodded. "His wife died about five years ago, and he retired from medicine—"

"He's a doctor?"

"One of the best. A pediatric specialist in Aberdeen." She set her pint down and pulled a pack of cigarettes out of her pocket, tamping the end of the box on the table. "Anyway, after my aunt Cherry died, he bought the lighthouse out of the blue and set about fixing it up. In fact, he worked with Alden pretty extensively to keep the exterior historically accurate."

Sabine glanced down at the pack of cigarettes in her hand. "Do you need to go smoke? I'll go out with you."

"Absolutely not." Ames dropped them back in her pocket. "I'm now a nonsmoker. As of yesterday. I'm just still carrying them around like some sort of freak."

"So, can I ask you something that's none of my business?" Sabine tried not to smile as Ames pulled a lighter out of the same pocket and turned it through her fingers. "Why is he selling as is, with all the interior furnishings included? All those books? There must be something sentimental that he wants to keep?"

"I asked him the same question. He didn't say much, and he never told me why he's selling. I'm sure my da knows. They've always been close. But that does me fuck-all good. He's never going to tell me either." She smiled as Morgan dropped their chips off with a bottle of something suspiciously dark he called "brown sauce." Ames slid the papers she'd taken from her bag across the table. "Anyway, take a look at these, yeah? Just make sure everything's the way ye want it." She bit into a steaming chip and burned her tongue, dramatically fanning her mouth with her hand as she went on. "This is a simple sale in the grand scheme of things, but if anything's amiss, I can straighten it out by tomorrow rather than making him wait."

Sabine leafed through the paperwork, but everything looked accurate, so it went quickly. She started on her pint, and by the time she was halfway through, she'd gotten to the last page.

"Everything's good. It should be quick and painless tomorrow."

"Brilliant." Ames nodded at the second plate of chips and handed Sabine her fork. "On a far more interesting note," she looked up, one eyebrow cocked, "I heard through the grapevine that you and Alden have been hanging out recently."

"Wow," Sabine said, popping a chip into her mouth. "Word travels fast."

"I had to call Alden before I got her to email me the HSC paperwork she signed off on. She gave me the highlights about how you gave her a black eye the first time you met."

"I did not!" Sabine laughed, pointing to the swinging kitchen doors. "Well, not on purpose." She sat back in her chair and smiled. "Anyway, something tells me she's over it now."

CHAPTER EIGHTEEN

The next morning, Sabine was just pulling on her coat to leave when she got a text from Alden.

Ames told me you're closing at the lighthouse in an hour. Your taxi awaits.

Sabine laughed and snapped up her coat, dropping the phone into her pocket. She was inexplicably nervous and had been up most of the night but couldn't put her finger on why.

Fuck it. She closed the door to her room and headed down the stairs to the front desk. *I'm doing it anyway.*

Sabine smiled as she got downstairs to see Alden standing at the front desk with two takeaway coffee cups.

"You have no idea how much I need this." Sabine took the coffee as Alden pulled her in for a hug. "I didn't sleep well at all. And I blame you."

"Me, huh?" Alden held the door open for her, then stopped when they reached the truck, pulling Sabine into her arms again. "Well, it can't be me. I couldn't sleep because I couldn't get the image of you, naked in my bed, out of my head. So clearly, all of this is your fault."

They were delayed on the way by an adorable Highland Bull that seemed dismayed he couldn't wedge his massive horns into the open window of the Land Rover to look for snacks. Alden fed him a bagel she had in the glove compartment and even persuaded

Sabine to reach over and scratch him between the eyes, which he seemed to adore.

Ames was there when they arrived and had the closing paperwork spread out on the kitchen island. Just as they were getting settled, someone knocked at the door. Ames answered it, and an older man with gray-streaked russet hair, a full, perfectly groomed beard, and a cream fisherman's sweater strode in, taking off his cap and hanging it on the hook by the door.

"Angus," Ames motioned him over to the kitchen island. "This is Alden Wallace, whom I believe you know from jumping through her ridiculous HSC hoops when you were renovating this place?"

Angus smiled with genuine warmth and shook Alden's hand, then turned to Sabine. His bright blue eyes sparkled, and the scent of winter air and pipe tobacco hovered in the air between them.

"And this is Sabine Rowan, the buyer for your lighthouse."

Angus offered his hand. "Thank you for agreeing to bring the closing date forward, Miss Rowan." Angus smiled at her as they took their seats on the stools. "Might as well get it done and over with."

"I heard you did all the renovations for this place." Sabine looked around the room, her gaze lingering on the bay windows looking out over the sea. "I fell in love the second I walked in."

"Ames didn't tell me you're an American." He hesitated. "Have we met? Ye almost look familiar."

"I was just thinking the same thing, but I don't believe we have. I would remember your beard."

"And I would remember your accent. It's lovely." Angus smiled warmly and turned to Ames. Sabine saw him take a deep breath before he continued. "Let's get this done, shall we?"

Signing the rest of the papers didn't take nearly as long as it had for the house she'd bought in New Orleans, and after the second the last set was finished, Angus stood. "I'm sorry to run off on you, but I need to get back home." He pulled two brass skeleton keys out of his jacket pocket and handed them slowly to Sabine. "Take good care of her for me, will ye?"

"Of course, I will, and you're always welcome to visit." Sabine stood and walked him to the door. "Thank you for creating such a beautiful space." She paused, looking toward the desk and bookcases. "Are you sure there's nothing you want to take with you? Nothing you'll miss?"

Angus picked up his cap and placed it back on his head, looking slowly around the room as if he were alone before he shook his head. His eyes were rimmed with red, and his voice caught as he turned back to her. "It's the memory I'll miss. Not the things." He tipped his cap to Sabine and slipped out the door, closing it carefully behind him.

❖

The only thing the lighthouse didn't have was bedding, so Sabine and Alden spent the day in town picking out everything she'd need for her bedroom, then chose area rugs for the second and third floors, just to warm the space a bit. Alden reminded her she might want to get something for her empty pantry, so they stopped by the grocery store on their way back to stock up on the basics she'd need for dinner.

By the time they returned to the lighthouse, the sun was setting, and the wind was starting to rush in off the ocean, bringing a wall of cold, salted mist sweeping up the cliffs to the lighthouse. Alden brought in the rugs and shopping bags before the worst of it hit, and Sabine grabbed the groceries as the sun set in a vivid, coppery pink wash across the water.

"Okay. I'm only asking this because you didn't seem to see the value in a proper overcoat before you met me," Alden said, opening the stove door and tucking her windblown hair behind her ears. "But how much do you know about fireplaces?"

"Um," Sabine said, pulling a package of polenta out of the shopping bags and holding it aloft as she thought. "I'm familiar. My aunt had one in her living room, although I never saw her use it. It's always sweltering in New Orleans." She pulled out a carton of milk and turned to put it in the refrigerator. "You can just show me where the gas switch is. As long as there's a dial or whatever, I can figure it out."

Alden smiled, then motioned her over to the cast-iron woodstove with the glass door. "Babe, ye do know it's a woodstove, right?" Sabine's mouth fell open, and Alden looked as if she was struggling not to laugh. "You're going to have to actually build fires in here all winter and get them to stay lit on all three levels, which is no easy task."

"Oh, shit." Sabine gingerly pulled on the bronze door handle and peered inside. "How do I do that?" She picked up one of the pieces of split wood piled beside the stove with her thumb and forefinger and set it carefully in the center. "I think I built a fire once at summer camp."

"When was that?"

Sabine closed the door with a sigh. "I was eight." She let her head fall into her hands and sat slowly down by the stove. "Holy shit. I'm in way over my head, aren't I?"

Alden went to get the grocery bags and returned, twisting each paper bag into a loose log before she stacked all of them on the grate, adding some split pine kindling she found in the brass bucket by the stove. "The next time you start thinking like that, I want you to remember that you packed up your life in three hours and moved across the feckin' globe where you knew no one." She leaned over and lifted Sabine's face, kissing her softly before she let her go. "Everyone knows that only badasses come to the Highlands in paper shoes."

Sabine rolled her eyes, and Alden laughed, pulling her into her arms. "I'm kidding. But if you can do that, you can do anything. The rest is just trial and error."

"Actually, you may have a point there." Sabine took the hand that Alden offered her and stood up. "If I make you dinner, will you spend the night and teach me how to build a damn fire that stays lit?"

Alden's hand slipped from Sabine's back to her ass, and she pulled her tight against her hips. "Aye." Her words felt like a slow melt over Sabine's neck. "And then I'm going to fuck you in front of it."

A shiver ran through Sabine as Alden kissed her and slipped a thigh between hers. She ran her hands under Alden's black wool sweater to the strong lines of her bare chest. "Or, we can just go upstairs right now?"

Alden bit Sabine's shoulder lightly and stepped back, running both hands through the windblown waves of her hair. "Hold that thought. Unless you have a lighter hidden somewhere, I'm going to have to run home for one, and I'll pick up some stuff for overnight while I'm there." She kissed her again, slipping her warm hand around the back of Sabine's neck. "I'll be back in about twenty minutes, tops."

Sabine headed back to the kitchen as she heard the Land Rover crunch down the gravel drive back out to the road. She hadn't cooked since New Orleans, and truthfully, she'd missed it, but the more her mother drank the less she bothered eating real food, and cooking for one just didn't hold the same appeal.

Sabine found a colander in the cupboard and rinsed the fresh shrimp she'd picked up at the market, then cleaned and trimmed them, setting them aside in soak in a marinade she put together with oil and a few spices. The polenta thickened and took on a creamy texture as she mixed it with warm water, shaped it, and sliced it into thick rounds.

She'd leaned down to dig around in the lower cabinet for the cast-iron pan she'd seen earlier when her phone rang from the counter above. It seemed ridiculously loud from the inside of the cabinet, and she banged her head against the top as she grabbed for her phone.

"Hey, Colette." Sabine rubbed the lump rising on the back of her head and headed for one of the kitchen island stools. "Did you get the photos I sent?"

Sabine heard a rush of noise, a faint, persistent beep, and the hollow sounds of people talking in the background. She waited a moment, but Colette didn't reply. "Colette?"

"Hi." Her voice was muted, and Sabine heard the tears in her voice. "Do you have time to talk?"

"Of course." Sabine's stomach twisted, and she felt nauseous as she traced a line in the wood-plank countertop with her thumbnail. "Tell me what's wrong."

"Mom had an accident. This morning when I went to check on her after I got the boys off to preschool, I found her unconscious on the bathroom floor." She cleared her throat, then seemed to walk into a quieter area with less noise. "I thought she was just drunk, but it was different this time, so I called an ambulance. James was already taking the boys to preschool by that time."

Sabine reminded herself to breathe. "What happened?"

"They took her to the emergency room and pumped her stomach. I found an empty prescription bottle for Xanax next to her."

"Xanax? I don't remember her having that prescription. Where did she get it?"

"It's dated back three years, like maybe someone prescribed it when she and Daddy had the accident?" Colette's voice was tired and thin. "I guess it's really dangerous to mix with alcohol, and the doctor said if I hadn't found her, she would have died."

"How is she now?"

"She's okay. She's awake and trying to check herself out, but they have her on a twenty-four-hour psych hold apparently, because they think she tried to commit suicide, which she swears she didn't. But maybe the hold is a blessing in disguise."

Sabine's shoulders slumped, and she had to bite back the urge to tell her sister she'd catch the next flight home. "What did the doctor say?"

"That she'll be sore for a few days, but she's fine for now. He's sending her home this afternoon, but if she keeps drinking, she's going to die. They ran some tests, and she has scarring on her liver." Colette took a deep breath. "It's cirrhosis. She's got to stop."

"Thea left money for rehab." Sabine closed her eyes against the headache starting behind her eyes. "Is she open to going?"

"Yes. In fact, she can leave from here and go straight there. The hospital said it would organize everything, and I called Katherine to let her know what's going on. Mom says she'll go... if you come home. Like, now."

Silence echoed on the line. Sabine rehearsed the words in her mind before she spoke. They still sounded wrong when she heard herself say them. "Why do I have to be there for her to go to rehab?"

"I shouldn't even be telling you this." Sabine recognized the exhaustion in her sister's voice because it was exactly how she used to sound. "But she made me promise I would."

"Are you at the hospital now?"

"Yeah. I've been here all day, but they just transferred her to the psych floor, and now they won't let me go in with her."

Sabine stood, straightened her shoulders, and walked around the kitchen island to the bay windows overlooking the darkening sea. "Collette, you can't do anything there. You need to go home."

"But I can't just leave her—"

"Go home." Sabine stared at the last crimson sliver of the sun at the horizon, sinking slowly into the water. "She's assuming you'll step into my shoes, and you can't let that happen. Go home, take a shower, and hug your boys when they get home this afternoon. Tell Mom if she wants you to take her to rehab, you'll arrange transportation, but other than that, she's on her own."

"I thought about it." The line fell into a dense silence. "But you haven't seen her. She's just pitiful, and she swears she's ready to get help. I just feel like she needs me."

"Colette, I get it. But what she wants is someone to enable her." Sabine paused, softening her tone. "I was there waiting on her hand and foot for three years. If she wanted to get help, she would have gotten it then. I brought it up about a million times."

"Do you think it's just that easy? To simply walk out and go home?" A desperate edge sharpened Colette's voice. "I can't just leave her here."

"I don't for a second think it's easy." She paused. "In fact, without Thea, we both know I'd still be there, right where you are. But you saw me waste three years of my life cleaning up after her. Don't make the same mistake." Sabine steadied her voice. "Start right now by walking out the goddamn door."

CHAPTER NINETEEN

A lden knocked, then opened the door with her shoulder, carrying a canvas bag of kindling and pinecones, weighed down with a bottle of chilled white wine. Sabine was standing at the hob, frying something that smelled like heaven, wearing black jeans and an oversized green hoodie that read *Central Grocers World Famous Muffuletta* on the back, whatever that was. She unloaded the pinecones and stacked the kindling, Sabine still at the edge of her eyesight. Something about Sabine was always intensely sensual. No matter what she was wearing, or doing, she always reminded Alden of a French charcoal sketch, on antique paper, aged and curled at the edges.

"Mam wanted to send some wine for us, so I told her white was a good guess?" Sabine turned around and smiled as she nodded, spatula in hand. "I saw you buying shrimp today, so I just guessed."

"That's just like her." Sabine turned the heat off, scooped strips of crispy bacon out to drain on paper towels, then put a cover on the pan. "I'll have to call her tomorrow and thank her."

Alden dropped the kindling at the stove, then walked to the windows and wrapped Sabine in her arms. "You looked beautiful when I walked in. I wanted to just freeze that moment in time." She dipped her head to kiss Sabine, holding her cheek gently in her hand. "How does it feel to be cooking dinner in the lighthouse you never knew you wanted?"

"Amazing." Sabine kissed her, then took the corkscrew out of the drawer and handed it to Alden, sliding two wineglasses out of the wooden undercabinet rack and turning them right-side-up on the counter. "It's so strange that the place is already set up like someone lives here. I have literally everything I need."

"Aye." Alden twisted the corkscrew into the bottle and pulled out the cork with a hollow pop. "And I've been to his home here in Rothesay, which is nothing like this place. His taste is masculine and spare, like a retired philosophy professor or something." She looked around at the plush cushions, buttery leather couches, and thoughtful touches. "I always got the feeling he was making a home for someone other than himself, but he never said a word about any of it, and after the first time, I knew better than to ask."

Sabine started to raise her glass for a toast, then jumped at a loud noise that sounded like something flat hitting the floor. "What the hell was that?"

Alden shook her head and set her glass down on the counter, holding out her hand to stop Sabine when she started to come with her to investigate. Alden peered out the window nearest the door, then went to the bookshelves, where she picked up a red book with a leather cover and gold-edged pages.

Sabine leaned onto the kitchen island and pushed up the sleeves of her hoodie. "Where did that come from?"

"No idea." Alden slid it back into the only empty slot in the stacks. "I guess it just fell off the shelf."

"Anyway." Alden checked that the door was locked and picked up her glass from the counter, clinking it to Sabine's. "I think we were just about to toast to your first night in the lighthouse."

"Almost." Sabine smiled. "But it's *our* first night in the lighthouse."

They took the first sip, and then Alden set her glass on the counter and went to build the fire. "I'll teach you more about how to do this next time, including all the ins and outs of the flue and airflow, but it's getting chilly, so I'll just get this first one going. With wood heat you have to catch the cold while you still have time to get ahead of it."

"So." Sabine turned around with a colander of rinsed shrimp in her hand. "We build a fire down here, and the heat rises to the two upper floors?"

"That's right. It flows through the heat vents as it rises, but when it's really cold, you'll want to keep a fire burning on all three floors. They share the same chimney, so one helps the other stay lit and so forth." Alden stacked logs on top of the tinder pile she'd made earlier. "Once you know how to really get it going, you can tamp down the air flow. You'll find they burn for hours at a low smolder, which heats all three open levels." Alden coaxed the logs into catching fire and adjusted the flue, closing the door to the stove. The flames licked the glass, turning and twisting from a pale yellow to brilliant orange. "What are you making over there, by the way?"

Sabine tipped the raw shrimp into the sizzling cast-iron pan and smiled over her shoulder. "I wanted to make you a classic Southern dish that screams New Orleans. We call it shrimp and grits. But I couldn't find any grits."

Alden slid onto one of the island stools and took a sip of her wine, which was perfectly chilled, condensation slipping smoothly down the side. "What's a grit?"

Sabine tipped her head back and laughed, which melded with the heat radiating from the woodstove and warmed the house instantly. She turned around with her glass in her hand, still stirring the shrimp as she spoke. "I'm not going to answer that question, because if we ever go to New Orleans together, you have to ask my sister." Her eyes sparkled under the lights. "And you have to say it exactly like that too." She pressed the shrimp lightly under the spatula to brown them to a golden crisp and added a generous splash of wine from her glass. "I actually got a call from Colette while you were at home."

"Really?" Alden shifted her face into neutral. "Is that good or bad?"

"It's the kind of call that probably would've given me an ulcer a few weeks ago, but tonight…something clicked into place for me."

Alden watched her turn down the heat under the pan and settled in on her stool. Whatever she had in that pan smelled like creamy browned butter, seawater, and the sharp tang of white wine, and she had to remind herself to stay focused. "Tell me about how that went."

Sabine's answer was slow, thoughtful, as if she were talking to herself in an empty room. "She took it too far with the booze this time, I guess. She piled some pills on top last night and landed in the hospital."

"Jaysus. What did the doctor say?" Alden leaned forward on the counter. "Is she okay?"

"She'll be fine, but the doctor said she had to stop drinking, that she was damaging her liver." She stopped, then turned to face Alden. "She told my sister to tell me to come home, and that if I did, she'd go to rehab."

"But not if you didn't?"

"Exactly."

Alden forced herself not to comment. She just nodded, allowing space for Sabine to go on, but it was a long, tense moment before she spoke.

"And I told her no."

"Aye. That's my girl." Alden smiled. "How did it feel to lay down a boundary?"

"Honestly?" Sabine paused. "It felt foreign, and selfish…" Her voice trailed off. "And it also felt like freedom. I could tell my sister thought I was being cold, but it's hard to understand when you're in it, and now she's the one looking from the inside out. This is her first time really being in the trenches of what it's like to live with Celestine." She stopped talking, giving the shrimp another toss and topping them with a lid she found in the drawer. She took a baking sheet out of the oven, topped with rounds of Spanish polenta, and set it on the counter to settle as she listened to Alden.

"I think people don't understand that we put boundaries in place not to shut people out, but to try to keep them in our lives." Alden hesitated, trying to think of how her mother would explain the concept. "It's you saying you want to keep them in your life and giving them a clear guideline of how to do that."

"But then it's up to them to respect that boundary if they value you and the relationship, right? That's the crux of the problem with my mother." Sabine looked up, meeting Alden's gaze. "But finally setting some boundaries feels right somehow, no matter what she chooses to do about it. It finally takes the pressure off me."

Sabine served the crisped polenta onto the plates, then tipped the shrimp and buttery wine sauce over the top. She topped each with torn fresh green parsley and set the plates on the table, fragrant steam rising between them as she handed Alden a knife and fork, carefully arranging her own beside her plate.

"It's nice to just get to live my life for change without constantly worrying about what Celestine may do to throw a wrench in it."

"Was she always like that? Alden inhaled the savory steam rising from her plate and picked up her fork. "When you two were growing up?"

"Somewhat, but a toned-down version. Dad was responsible for her then, so we saw much less of it. She considered herself the grande dame of the theater world in New Orleans, and I suppose that was true. Daddy was gone all the time and just gave her whatever she wanted. You had to know her only five minutes to guess she was a pampered former actress."

Alden speared a shrimp with her fork and made room for a piece of polenta to go with it, swiping up some of the fragrant, garlicky sauce in the process. "More importantly, how was she as a mother?"

"I don't know." Sabine put her fork down and met Alden's gaze. It was a long moment before she spoke. "She never was one. Not to me, anyway."

Alden nodded, then took the first bite before she sank back on her stool and closed her eyes. "This is fucking fantastic. What's in it?"

Sabine was laughing, wineglass dangling from her fingers, when Alden looked back up at her as she went for another bite. "It's just shrimp sauteed in shallot butter, herbs, and chilies over a grit or two, and fresh parsley. It's actually pretty simple."

"When are you going to tell me what the hell a grit is? Or do I have to look it up?"

"Well, in this case I had to substitute polenta, which is considerably different." She smiled. "You still haven't tried grits, so that just doesn't concern you, Wallace."

❖

Days spent listening to the waves crash into the cliffs at the lighthouse turned to peaceful weeks, and by the time the village started to glow with Christmas decorations, Sabine had started to think about not going back to New Orleans at all. She was in love with the lighthouse, which was looking even homier since she'd bought a beat-up truck to haul her antique finds back and forth from town, and she and Alden were growing closer every day. She'd started to feel like part of the family at the Wallaces' house, and Declan had even asked her and Alden to take him to visit the boarding school for the deaf in Glasgow.

She'd planned to visit her sister and her nephews as soon as the year was up, but her mother still refused to go to rehab, despite Colette stepping back and making it a condition of seeing the boys. Sabine decided not to engage until Celestine made an effort toward change. She still had to remind herself every day that it was okay to put herself first, but it was getting easier.

She'd finally told Colette about Alden and buying the lighthouse, and without her mother's constant drama whirling around them, they'd gotten closer than they'd ever been. Sabine had always felt like an outsider because Celestine had made it clear in a thousand ways that she preferred Colette, so she'd learned to disappear into the background. But after several late-night conversations, she'd started to realize that if her sister had been Celestine's favorite, Colette had never known it. Her mother had always aggressively pushed Colette to follow in her footsteps as an actor, and when she didn't, she'd only felt like a disappointment. Once they'd started to create their own relationship as sisters, without having to try to catch a glimpse of each other around the tornado that had been their mother, they felt like they'd been gifted a second chance to get close, this time as their authentic selves.

The time at the lighthouse had also given her time to grieve. She'd barely had time to think after Thea died, but somehow being where Thea apparently wanted her be, in Muir Rothesay, gave her comfort. It had been difficult, shedding her former life like a skin, but in a way, everything had fallen into place in Scotland. Well, almost everything. Something was missing, although Sabine couldn't start to identify what it was. She just knew she felt like her life was a painting hanging on a museum wall with a blank square in the center.

Thea never did anything without a reason. To Sabine, the fact that she'd written Muir Rothesay on that Post-it note in her own handwriting was significant. It was her last contact, the last thing she did. But the mystery of *why* had lived in the back of her mind, along with an odd a sense of déjà vu, since that day she'd stepped off the train and into the blizzard in Rothesay. Over time, she'd come to realize that Katherine knew everything and of course refused to say a word about it, which made it even worse. But now the icy December sun was setting over the ocean, and Sabine reached into the refrigerator for a bottle of French chardonnay she'd fallen in love with after a dinner in Glasgow with Alden. She'd asked the local wine shop for it so regularly that they'd finally given up and just started stocking it for her. The cork lifted easily with a satisfying pop and poured into the chilled glass like winter sunlight. She left the bottle on the empty counter and balanced the glass in her fingers as she walked over to the bay window. The pale expanse of blue sky had started to melt into layers of translucent pink and brilliant orange, shifting like fire until the color sank silently into the white-capped ocean.

Sabine sifted through everything Katherine had said in the past few months, turning it over in her mind, searching for anything to fill in that blank square on the canvas. She watched a seagull swoop low over the water and glide out toward the warmth of the sunset, joined by another, and then a single dolphin that swam beneath them. Its pewter fin sliced through the dark water, keeping perfect pace with the gulls, until all three disappeared over the edge of the earth.

She finally turned to start dinner, then stopped abruptly. The bottle of chardonnay she'd left on the empty counter was now perched atop a book. Specifically, it was the red leather book that had fallen out of the bookshelves her first night in the lighthouse. *But Alden picked that up and put it back on the shelf.* Sabine took a step forward. *I watched her do it.*

Slowly, she lifted the bottle and picked up the book, turning it over in her hand. The leather was cool and smooth against her palm, and the edges gleamed with aged gold. It was the same book she'd seen by the desk lamp the day she'd toured the lighthouse with Ames.

The air warmed around her, and she held her breath as she cradled it in her hand. It had no title on the outside, but someone had obviously loved it over the years; the pages looked worn, and the edges of the cover were scuffed, revealing the leather beneath the shiny red lacquer. The green-Scottish-pine fire in the woodstove crackled and sparked against the glass as Sabine walked slowly from the kitchen to the desk and sat in the cherrywood chair.

She opened the front cover of the book. The title page read *The Unbearable Lightness of Being*, and just below was a faded pencil inscription in small, cursive letters. *August 17th, 1989*. She found an envelope inside, postmarked August 2022, with the same handwriting on the front, addressed to Angus Abernathy.

Sabine's fingers shook as she took the single page of writing out of the envelope and smoothed it open on the desk.

My love,

I've never forgotten it. Our last day together at the lighthouse. That delicious afternoon that went on forever, when we were convinced the sun would never set and I'd never have to leave to go back to America.

I remember everything. The dust motes floating in the air, those awful ham sandwiches I brought from the dorm for lunch, and how we watched those two dolphins jumping in a perfect arc over the waves as we lay on the bed by the window upstairs. I was pregnant that day, though I didn't know it at the time. I sent a letter to your family's estate when she was born, but it came back marked Return to Sender. *The handwriting wasn't yours, so I know you never received it. None of that matters now.*

We have a daughter, Angus. A brilliant, beautiful-beyond-words daughter. She's the best of both of us and the embodiment of your promise to me on our last day together, at the lighthouse. The sun was setting in the window behind you, and your eyes

were shining when you told me that love is the only thing that
never dies. It simply changes form.
   You were right. My only regret is that I didn't fight harder for
us, but I loved you every day of this life, Angus.
   I'll see you soon in the next, my darling.
   Your Thea

"Holy shit." Sabine only mouthed the words, but they still hung heavy and silent in the air. She carefully folded the letter back into the envelope and laid it gently on the desk, turning Thea's ring on her finger. "Holy shit."

An hour later, Sabine shut the door to her truck and walked up the steps to the door. Her heart was beating out of her chest, but she had to do this, and for some reason, she knew she had to do it exactly this way. She lifted the brass doorknocker and knocked three times. Hurried footsteps preceded the door flying open and blowing back her hair.

"Sabine, love?" Morgan stood in the doorway, holding one half of a split baguette. "This is an unexpected surprise. Are ye looking for Alden? I think she's in town with our Declan. She went with him to get a burger."

Sabine took a breath and willed her voice to stay even. "No. I'm here to see you."

"Aye. Of course, lass. Come inside an' I'll pour ye a dram. Ya must be parched."

He looked slightly confused when she didn't step inside, but then he seemed to sense the tension in the air and simply waited for her to speak.

"Morgan." Sabine heard her voice falter. She shifted on the straw welcome mat and took a breath to center herself. "I'm coming to you because I trust you."

"Aye." He nodded, his smile warm and calming. "The feeling's mutual. Ya know we all think the world of ye."

She cleared her throat, not needing to contemplate the best way to say what she needed to say. Because there wasn't one.

"Could you help me with something?" Sabine took a slow breath and met Morgan's gaze. "You can't ask me about it. I have no idea what's going on or how this will go down, and it may not end well."

Morgan listened, nodded, and then tossed the baguette onto the entry table without looking behind him. He grabbed his keys off a hook by the door and stepped out, locking up as he went. "Let's take my truck." He shot her a smile as he led the way back down the path to the vehicles. "I dunno what the hell yer drivin' there, and I've got more room for a body in the back. That's what ya call an undeniable advantage in Scotland."

Sabine laughed despite herself, suddenly weak with relief as she followed him out and slid into his vehicle after he opened the door for her. He jumped in the other side and fired it up like a jet engine, and she half-expected to see flames coming out the back as she turned and looked for the seat belt. Morgan glanced at her and laughed as he backed out of the drive.

"I hate to dash yer dreams of safety, lass, but I'm the one that taught me daughter how to yank those belts out and do somethin' useful wit' 'em." He straightened the wheel and headed to the end of the street, turning left onto the hill down into town. "Where to, love?"

"You know Angus Abernathy, right?"

"Aye, since primary school. He's me best mate."

"I need to go to his house." Sabine pulled her hair into a quick bun and glanced in Morgan's direction. "And I can't tell you why."

"Excellent!" Morgan flipped his lights on and leaned into the gas. "This is already more fun than I've had in ages. Does he know you're comin'?"

"God no." Sabine laughed into the open window, letting the wind whip her words around the cab of the truck. "In fact, that might be the understatement of the year."

Morgan drove in clearly delighted silence for the few minutes it took them to get into town and slightly beyond it, where he turned onto a country road, trees lined up on both sides that filtered the light from the moon just starting to rise. As the trees thinned, a huge stone mansion came into view, just below the glowing crescent. Gothic, dark-gray arches rose into the sky, and a circle drive shaped itself around carefully groomed hedges and endless patterns of thick green ivy climbing up the sides of the place.

"Holy shit." Sabine shook her head as Morgan pulled in front of the towering oak doors with hammered, black iron hinges. A massive iron lantern, lit with a tall gas flame, cast imposing gold and shadows across the entrance. "I don't know what I was expecting, but *this* was not it."

"Aye, it's gorgeous, isn't it? Your Alden has done quite a bit of work on this place over the years, and Angus's family has owned Carthington Manor since the early 1700s." Morgan cut the engine, and the truck shuddered into sudden silence. "It's just him rattling around in this place with a few servants now though, since his wife died. They never had children, ye know." Morgan lowered his voice as he opened his door. "He's always said it's his biggest regret."

Sabine opened her door and slowly stepped out of the truck, the gravel crunching under her feet. An owl flew out from under the eaves and dipped close enough to stir her hair before it hovered for just a second and flew straight up into the darkening sky.

One of the servants, wearing a tidy gray uniform dress and white apron, answered the door. She led them into what she called the "library," where Angus greeted them, getting up from his leather-trimmed desk with a wide, genuine smile and gesturing for them to sit on the couches facing the crackling fire in the fireplace. He was wearing a navy-blue wool fisherman's sweater and olive corduroys, which made him look like more of a literature professor than a doctor.

"Morgan, it's about time we visited outside the pub. And it's Sabine wit' ye, is it?" His face lit up and he extended his hand. "How's the lighthouse treatin' ye?"

Sabine sat beside Morgan on the couch, clutching her bag to her chest, suddenly unable to speak. She saw Angus glance in Morgan's direction, and Morgan waited for a long moment before he stepped in.

"Mate, I know you're wonderin' what we're doing in your study, and I'm here to support Sabine, but I can truthfully tell you I don't have a feckin' clue what else is going on."

"Excellent!" Angus laughed, which seemed to break the tension, and Sabine finally took a breath.

"Angus." She raised her eyes to his, slowly taking her hair out of the bun she normally wore and letting it fall around her shoulders. She knew from Thea's pictures that she'd had waist-length hair the year she went to Scotland. "Do I remind you of anyone?"

Angus's smile slowly faded as he looked at her, memories seeming to flash across his eyes like a silent movie. He shook his head, slow and silent, as if to convince himself. "We've only met that one time at the lighthouse. At the closing."

His gaze didn't waver from hers, though, and the truth began to take shape between them like a ghostly apparition stepping into the present. He finally crumbled and covered his mouth, his eyes glistening with emotion.

Are you sure? Sabine only signed her words and did nothing to stop the tears warming her face. *You don't see my mother in me?*

Angus tried to answer, but his voice cracked. He and Sabine stood at the same moment, and then Angus stepped into the gap between them and held out his arms. Sabine fell into them, her arms around his neck. His broad shoulders and beard smelled of fresh air and tobacco, and she breathed it in, imprinting the scent memory deep into her mind. Angus held her, shoulders shaking in silent sobs, for a long moment, then stepped back, her damp face still in his hands.

"Forgive me, Sabine." He shook his head, his gaze never leaving her face, as if he were afraid she might disappear if he even blinked. "I never knew you existed until the letter from Thea this summer, and I chased down every lead I could think of to find you, but all I discovered was that I was too late. Thea had passed away, and I couldn't find one bloody person in America that even knew she had a child."

Morgan cleared his throat, and both turned, as if remembering suddenly that someone else was in the room. He was now standing at the gorgeous mahogany bar, built into the floor-to-ceiling bookshelves, leaning casually on the rolling ladder, one hand poised over the whiskey decanter.

"Forgive me for stating the obvious here, but if this doesn't look like an occasion for Angus's finest whiskey, I'm not sure what is." His broad smile lightened the air, and he winked. "Now, before you tell me what the hell is goin' on, can I interest anyone in a wee dram?"

"For the love of God, yes." Angus clapped his hand over his heart. "A double."

Morgan laughed as he poured the drinks, and by the time Angus had stoked the fire, the tightness in Sabine's chest started to unravel. All three of them sank back into the couches in front of the fire and toasted with their whiskeys, which seemed to contain very fancy square, rough-cut ice cubes.

"Morgan," Angus's voice cracked with joy as he looked at Sabine. "I'd like to introduce you to my daughter, Sabine."

Morgan's mouth fell open and stayed that way for so long Angus and Sabine burst into laughter, which seemed to finally break the spell.

"Jesus, Mary, and the blessed wee donkey." Morgan looked slowly from one to the other. "Can someone get me up to speed on how the hell *that* happened?"

Angus smiled. "Do ye remember that American lass I met and fell in love wit' after my engagement to Cherry?"

"I do. You introduced me down the pub one night after classes, but ye were both signing, so I didn't have a feckin' clue what was goin' on."

Sabine turned to Angus. "How did you know sign language, by the way?"

"I was in medical school in Aberdeen when I met your mother, and training to be an ear, nose, and throat specialist in Pediatrics. I'd already been studying it for nearly two years when I met her."

"So." Morgan tipped his crystal tumbler to his lips. "You already spoke her language?"

"Exactly. She knew I was engaged, and back then, we both realized there was no way my family would accept an American into the family, so she left at the end of the year, even though I begged her not to." His voice trailed off. "I never knew she was pregnant. If I had, I would have left Scotland to be with her that instant, family be damned. I even swore to her I'd buy the lighthouse and make it a home someday, in case she ever changed her mind." He paused, his gaze falling on the diamond and sapphire ring on Sabine's hand. "And I gave her that ring in the lighthouse on our last day. I told her I wanted to replace it someday with a wedding band."

Sabine looked into her glass, her words soft. "It makes sense now. Her parents must have convinced Thea to let her sister Celestine raise me. They were always image-conscious, and Celestine was already married with one child by the time I was born." She paused. "I know them. It wouldn't do to have their unmarried, deaf daughter turn up pregnant."

Morgan nodded. "So, you grew up thinking Thea was your aunt?"

"I did, but I always felt that Celestine resented me, and now I know why. It all truly does make sense." She smiled, relishing the feeling of a lifetime of weight levitating off her shoulders. "I'm so glad you left the letter behind. I can't believe I almost didn't know you existed."

"What now?" Angus looked baffled. "The letter from Thea?"

"That's the only reason I found you. You left it in the book she gave you." Sabine paused. "*The Unbearable Lightness of Being?*"

"How in the world do ye know that?"

"It was on the desk, by the lamp. It's why I asked you at the closing if you wanted to take it with you. I hadn't seen the letter yet, but the book seemed like it might be special." She met Angus's gaze, tilting her head in confusion. "I brought it with me. It's yours. The letter from Thea was inside it when I opened it, and the inscription was in her handwriting, dated 1989. She talked about your last day at the lighthouse together and told you had a daughter."

Morgan handed Sabine her bag as Angus got up and walked over to the bookcase. He pushed a button, and a panel of false books slid silently to the right, revealing a black iron safe. He punched in a code and the door clicked open. Inside was only one item: a red leather book with gold-edged pages.

Sabine watched, then shook her head in confusion as she pulled a second, almost identical red book out of her bag. She turned it over in her hand. It seemed different now, in a way she couldn't put her finger on, but it had to be the same. She'd placed it in her bag herself, and it hadn't been out of her sight since she'd found it.

Angus returned to his seat. He opened the book he'd taken from the safe, and the creak of the aged leather and the rustle of pages were the only sounds in the room. He held up the envelope. "Is this the letter you're talking about?"

WINDSWEPT

Sabine's mouth dropped open. "No. It can't be. The one I saw was here."

Sabine hurriedly opened the book she'd brought from home to reveal...nothing. There was no letter, and all the pages were blank now. The book itself looked identical to the one Angus was holding, but hers was newer, somehow, the pages bright white, as if it had never been cracked open.

Angus handed her the letter. Sabine's fingers were shaking, and it slipped through them to land on the floor. Morgan picked it up and looked to her for permission to open it. She nodded, then took it hesitantly when he held it out to her.

It was the exact same letter, in Thea's handwriting, that she'd just read in the lighthouse. Even the paper felt the same in her hands. She turned it over, then slowly handed it back to Angus. "That's the letter, but why is it not still in mine? And how do we both have the same book?"

Angus handed her his red book that he'd taken from the safe, and Sabine handed him the one she'd pulled from her bag. She instantly recognized the slightly yellowed edges on the paper, the scuffed gold finish on the outside, and the penciled inscription, yet the one she'd brought from the lighthouse was suddenly unblemished, with new, blank pages. She shook her head slowly as she looked up at Angus. "This just doesn't make sense."

Angus held up a wrinkled Post-it note that he'd pulled from the center of the book Sabine had handed him. "What's this?"

Sabine reached out to take it. It was the note that'd been in the folder Katherine had given her in New Orleans. On the front of the note was *Muir Rothesay*. Then, for the first time, she remembered what Katherine had said about it later, when they were on the phone. She'd forgotten about it, but now she held the note Katherine had suggested that she turn over.

"This is a note Thea left me. I'll have to tell you how everything came about later, but Thea wrote *Muir Rothesay* on the front, which is the reason I'm here." She slowly turned the note over and smiled. She looked up at her father and handed it to him.

He read it silently as Sabine felt the same slow warmth settle onto her shoulder that she'd felt the day she saw the lighthouse. She reached up to touch her shoulder again and this time felt the warmth settle under her fingertips.

"So." Morgan sat on the edge of his seat, glass in hand. "What does it say?"

"It says," Angus looked up at her, his daughter, and smiled, "Follow the lighthouse home."

CHAPTER TWENTY

S o, that was it?" Alden signed and spoke at the same time, as did everyone at the table. "That was all it said?"

"I can't believe you just said that." Gwen flicked her handkerchief at Alden and rolled her eyes. "That has to be the most romantic thing I've ever heard. Thea did all of this just to reunite Sabine and her father." She sniffed and dabbed at her cheeks as Declan tried to hide a smile. He signed discreetly to Morgan and asked to be excused. Morgan smiled and signed back to not forget to take a brownie. Declan wrapped one up from the still-warm, dented tin pan on the kitchen counter. He was halfway down the hall with it when he turned around and waved to get Sabine's attention. *Does this mean you're staying in Scotland?*

Sabine smiled as she signed. *I'm in love with your aunt, so I was never going back to America anyway. Guess you're stuck with me.*

Declan's smile lit up the hall as he signed back. *Best news ever.* Then he took a massive bite of his brownie, dropped a shower of crumbs on the hardwood floor, and disappeared up the stairs with a clatter of footfalls.

Alden leaned over to whisper in Sabine's ear as Morgan told Gwen the story of the sliding library safe one more time. "Did you just tell my nephew you're in love with me?"

"Of course, I did." Sabine nodded, leaning against Alden's shoulder. "Everything about us has always felt like home."

Alden whispered something in her ear, then got up to cut the rest of the brownies, which she stacked on a plate and brought back to the table just in time for her mother to dab away the last of her tears and lean over the table to squeeze Sabine's hand.

"Yer one of us now, dear, although there was never any doubt about that. Ye look more Scottish than the lot of us put together. Those freckles alone are like a road map to the Highlands."

Sabine laughed and passed around the dessert plates Alden handed her.

"Da," Alden said, laying her hand on Gwen's shoulder. "It's time for the Scotch from Islay."

"The Islay? That's the—"

"While I have a little chat in the other room wit' Mam."

Gwen burst into a wide smile and grabbed her handkerchief. Morgan winked at her as she left with Alden, hugging her as they walked down the hall to the study.

"What was that all about?" Sabine reached for her brownie and admired the decadent chocolate steam that rose into the air as she broke it in half.

"Who knows when it comes to those two. They've always been thick as thieves. I gave up trying to figure them out a long time ago."

"I think I might stay here tonight with Alden, if that's okay." Sabine caught a stray crumb on its way to the plate and popped it back into her mouth. "I'm getting the hang of the woodstove, but I've also been at it long enough to know that if you start too late, you'll never catch up to the cold."

"Aye." Morgan nodded. "That's in the bible, ye know."

"The lighthouse bible?"

"Of course." Morgan winked at her as he brought the decanter of scotch over to the table with three glasses. "What else would I be talking about?"

Morgan and Sabine chatted about putting Christmas lights on the lighthouse until Gwen and Alden came back down the hall and Alden tossed out a halfhearted comment about historical guidelines, but even she couldn't keep a straight face after Gwen rolled her eyes. They all toasted with the remarkably buttery scotch that went down like spring water before Gwen sat back in her chair and shooed them upstairs.

"All right, you two. Out of my way. How am I going to get Morgan to clean the dishes if you two are hanging about looking handy?"

"Excellent point, Mam." Alden picked up their glasses. "I don't ever want to stand in the way of Da doing the washing up. I hear it's good for his character."

Sabine followed upstairs and sank into the couch with the port Alden poured her. She unlaced her boots and settled into the cozy wool throw as Alden dimmed the lights and lit some candles, including the beeswax taper in the patinaed holder she'd lit the first night Sabine stayed with her in the attic.

"You must be exhausted, baby." Alden sat down as she set her port on the table. "It's almost ten. How did it get to be so late?"

"Time flies." Sabine smiled. "Finding out your parents are completely different people than you thought will do that to you."

"That still blows my mind. I can't imagine how you must feel." Alden took off her shoes and settled in, pulling Sabine's legs into her lap. "But you know what hit me when Da was retelling everything for Mam and Declan at dinner?"

"God, tell me. I was so shocked in the moment it all seems like a blur."

"The letter was switched so you'd find it. The real book and letter were in Angus's safe, right?" Sabine nodded. "So, it was either Thea in some capacity—"

"Which feels amazing and surreal at the same time."

"—or the faeries, which in Scotland is the catchall term for magical happenings we can't explain."

"Well, whatever it was, we can just call it straight-up magic." Sabine spoke softly. "I left Angus's book with him, of course, and as we were leaving, I looked at mine again. I just couldn't get over how it was a novel when I saw it in the lighthouse, then suddenly we both had one, but all the pages in mine were blank. I felt like it had to mean something."

Alden nodded, pulling Sabine's feet closer and warming them under her sweater.

"Well, I thought all the pages were blank. But I was wrong." Sabine smiled. "When I looked again, I saw an inscription in the front of mine as well."

"In Thea's handwriting?" Alden arched an eyebrow. "What did it say?"

"It said, *It's time to write your own story.*" Sabine looked up and smiled. "And everything has kind of made sense then. The first book was their story. She's always wanted me to live my own life, to do as much with it as I can, so it makes sense."

Alden sipped her port, then leaned forward and kissed her, holding Sabine's face in her hand as she pulled away. "If you were completely overwhelmed that would be understandable, but you actually seem really calm." She kissed her softly again. "If you had to describe how you feel now with one word, what would it be?"

Sabine paused, but it took her only a handful of seconds to reply. "I feel peaceful. Like everything is exactly the way it should be."

"You know what this means, right?" Alden smiled at the very earnest look on Sabine's face as she seemed to sift through all the possibilities in just a few seconds. "You're a Scottish citizen. Or you will be when you file the paperwork. You can live and work here as long as you like and not have to worry about all the visas and red tape. There's actually an official term for it."

"And what would that be?"

"That I might have an outside chance at keeping you here."

"It's a possibility." Sabine unbuttoned her shirt, slowly letting the buttons slip through her fingers. "If you play your cards right."

"Well then." Alden's gaze was fixed on the soft curve of Sabine's breasts as the buttons fell open. "In that case I'm going to require a foolproof instruction manual on how one exactly plays those cards right."

Sabine dropped her shirt off her shoulders, laughing as Alden picked her up from the couch and set her down on the bed. "Trust me. I've been with you long enough to know you don't need an instruction manual on anything."

"Is that right?" Alden laughed, pulling her sweater over her head. "Well, I'm going to take that as a compliment." She slid out of her jeans and confiscated Sabine's as well, then stood at the foot of the bed for just a moment, taking her in. Nearly naked and beyond beautiful, Sabine's ivory skin was luminous, like an antique painting in the golden glow of candlelight. The deep curve of her waist giving way to her hips made Alden instantly wet and reminded her of something.

She excused herself, then closed the door to the water closet and looked at herself in the mirror over the sink, shaking her hair out to fall around her shoulders. She hadn't thought about this for a while, but she'd bought a new leather harness a few weeks after they met. It had just never seemed to be the right time to bring it out, and it hadn't helped that they'd ended up spending most of their nights at the lighthouse.

She found it in the dresser by the cast-iron tub and strapped it on, then chose some black boy shorts to go over it. She tried to imagine how Sabine saw her as she looked in the mirror, but the image that stuck in her mind was Sabine's initial reaction to seeing her chest for the first time. Alden had played if off well, but she'd been so nervous in the moment that she couldn't draw a breath. Sabine had made her feel like her chest made her more attractive, not less, which was a possibility she'd never even considered.

Before she'd met Sabine, worrying about having the gene that increased her risk of breast cancer was rough, and she was aware that the decision to not opt for reconstruction wasn't the norm, to say the least. The reaction she'd gotten from her ex had been warily neutral at best, but the entire concept had never seemed to faze Sabine. In fact, it had the opposite effect, which felt like a huge boulder that Alden never knew she was carrying had just rolled off her shoulders. They'd talked one night about the process of how she'd made the decision, and Sabine had said that maybe by choosing the tattooed armor and no reconstruction she'd simply "found a way to bring her body in line with her soul." Alden would never forget how she'd felt in that moment. It was like being seen, really seen for who she was, for the very first time.

Alden smiled as Sabine knocked hesitantly on the door.

"Alden?"

"Yes?"

Sabine cleared her throat. "I just want you to know that I think it might be illegal to look as hot as you do and leave me waiting for more than five seconds."

Alden opened the door and scooped Sabine up in her arms, carrying her back across the attic and dropping her playfully onto the bed.

"Do you remember the first night we met?" Alden settled in on the bed beside her. "I was so glad you asked me to stay on the attic couch with you. I'd been having a hard time leaving. I didn't want you to be scared after what happened earlier."

Sabine nodded. "You saved me that night."

"Do you ever have bad memories?" Alden held her closer, pulling the warm duvet over them. "About what happened in the train station?"

"Sometimes." Sabine wrapped her arms around her and rested her head on Alden's chest. "But then I always think about how you knocked that guy into Sunday, and it just makes it go away." She smiled up at Alden. "Like magic."

"Like magic, huh?"

Sabine slipped her thigh between Alden's and stopped still. "Is this what I think it is?"

"It is," Alden said, sliding off the shorts and dropping them over the edge of the bed. She found Sabine's hand and wrapped it slowly around the shaft. "It's yours if you want it, but it can be gone in two seconds if you don't."

Sabine locked eyes with Alden and sat up slowly, letting the duvet fall off her naked shoulders. She sat between Alden's knees, the candlelight falling over her intensely feminine curves and shadows as she reached out and trailed her fingertips over the length of it. Alden watched as she memorized it by touch and reached inside her panties, stroking her clit as she moved her other hand up and down the shaft.

"Fucking hell, Sabine."

Sabine held her gaze as she leaned into Alden, hesitating for a moment, then tracing the tip lightly with her tongue. She circled it slowly, then started to take it deeper as she reached up with the wet fingers that had been stroking her clit and slid them into Alden's mouth. She pulled the cock into her own mouth, taking her hand back and working the shaft at the same time, creating a rhythm with the heel of her hand that pushed the smooth back side of the harness against Alden's wet clit in a steady, perfect rhythm. Alden watched Sabine's nipples tighten as she worked her cock, glancing up several times and holding Alden's gaze until Alden thought she might explode.

"I have to touch you." Alden started to sit up until Sabine put one hand in the center of her chest and pushed her back down into the pillows.

"I think you'll find," she said, her lips slick and flushed, "that the only thing you *have* to do is lie there and try to behave."

Alden laced her fingers behind her head and groaned as Sabine slid off her panties and straddled Alden's bare thigh. "Holy hell. You're killing me."

Sabine leaned back, stroking her own clit as she rocked back on Alden's thigh slowly with the wet heat of her body, then rode it slowly, one hand still wrapped around Alden's cock. Alden closed her eyes, memorizing the heat of Sabine against her until she felt her take the tip of her cock into her mouth again. She swirled her tongue around the tip, her gaze locked on Alden, then sucked it into her mouth and slid her thumb under the harness, slicking the tip of it across Alden's clit. Alden watched Sabine take her cock deeper into her mouth as her thumb stroked her clit, then steadily built the pressure as she took every hard inch of it deep inside.

As Sabine worked her and slicked her thumb over Alden's hardened clit beneath the harness, Alden was conscious only of the woman she loved taking her cock and letting her watch every second as she careened toward a rock-hard orgasm.

"Fuck." Alden finally leaned back into the pillows and raked both hands through her hair. "Fuck, baby. Don't stop. Just don't stop."

That's when Sabine sank all the way down on Alden's cock with her mouth and stroked her clit with a more intense touch, her hair falling in wild waves around her shoulders. She held the base with one hand and slid her lips all the way down to her fingers, shifting to a lighter touch below when she obviously sensed Alden getting closer to the edge.

"Baby." Alden heard her own voice like it was someone else's, breathless and pleading. "Please."

Sabine lifted her head, brushing Alden's nipples with the fingers of one hand while she continued stroking Alden's stiff clit under the harness. "Are you ready to come for me?" Alden groaned and Sabine stilled, her eyes locked on Alden's. "Come in my mouth, baby."

Alden arched her hips as Sabine took every inch of her cock down her throat, stroking Alden's clit in a hard, slick rhythm until Alden shuddered into the most explosive orgasm of her life. Endless waves of it shook her long and hard, and when she finally opened her eyes, Sabine was straddling her hips, stroking her clit with the tip of the cock.

"Sit back on me, baby." Alden's voice was a low scrape in the still attic. "Brace yourself on my thighs and let me have your clit."

Sabine guided Alden's wet cock past her flushed, trembling inner thighs, and then inside her. She closed her eyes and leaned back, hands braced behind her on Alden's thighs. Alden stroked her thumb over Sabine's clit as she watched her cock slide in and out of the woman she loved. A slow wash of pink wrapped itself around Sabine's breasts and hips as her breath grew shallow and she gripped Alden's thighs.

"Just ride me, baby," Alden whispered, feeling the heavy brush of Sabine's hair fall back against her legs, watching her clit as it stiffened under her touch. "I want to watch you come all over my cock."

Sabine lost the rhythm as she fell forward, her orgasm shaking the breath from her lungs as her entire body trembled. Alden held her, one hand braced gently in the center of her chest, until Sabine slowly found her breath. She watched her open her eyes, Sabine still contracting around her cock, still pulling it deeper inside her.

She relaxed into Alden's arms, her breath already slowing and deepening as Alden unbuckled her harness, dropped it over the side of the bed, and wrapped Sabine in her arms.

"Sabine?" Alden smiled as Sabine stirred and snuggled in closer. Alden dropped her voice to a whisper. "I love you too."

Chapter Twenty-one

The next morning was Sunday, and Alden left a note on her pillow that she'd gone downstairs to do some paperwork for the next day. Sabine stretched in the lazy patch of sunlight coming through the window above her head. She was deliciously sore and completely relaxed, scenes from the previous night playing on a sensual loop in her mind.

She took a hot bath and dressed, already breathing in the delicious wafts of pancakes coming up from the kitchen. She and Alden came over for brunch most Sundays. It was Gwen's favorite excuse to cook, and watching her in the kitchen as she enthusiastically talked back to the public-radio shows never failed to make her laugh.

She pulled a cream wool turtleneck sweater over her head, paired it with black winter leggings, and sat back on the bed to lace up her tall brown boots. Winter was definitely here to stay in Scotland, but after the first freak snowstorm when she'd arrived in Rothesay, she'd also been able to enjoy fall. It had lasted about three days before the next snowfall, but it was an undeniably gorgeous three days, and she'd blanketed her Instagram with photos.

She pulled the door to the attic shut, dropping her phone into the pocket of her leggings as an afterthought, then wandered downstairs, where Gwen was holding a mason jar aloft next to the window, eyeing her cranberries.

"Good morning." She flashed Gwen a concerned smile. "Are the cranberries talking back again?"

"Aye. They might as well be. They baked up like shite on the first try, so I'm on ta the second batch now." She held the jar a bit higher to catch the sunlight. "I'm not goin' fer juicy here, ye wee bastards. It's chewy I'm after."

Alden looked up from her work folders and motioned Sabine over, pulling her down for a kiss. "Morning, gorgeous."

"Sorry I slept so late." Sabine tried not to laugh as Gwen unscrewed the lid and continued talking to the cranberries, in case they hadn't been paying attention the first time. "Have you almost finished your reports?"

"I was on the right track until you came down here in leggings," Alden whispered, with a wink in her direction. "But I can't think of fuck-all else at this point."

Sabine whispered into her ear about the previous night and smiled when it only seemed to make things worse for Alden. She pulled out the chair next to her and put her hand on Alden's knee under the table.

"Gwen, I've been thinking about something, and I was wondering if I could ask you for a favor."

Gwen set the jar of cranberries down and turned around, drying her hands on her apron. "Perfect timing, love. I was about ta say some things to those berries I'd regret at me next confession." She poured a cup of coffee and set it on the table for Sabine, along with the sugar and cream pot. "And I'd love ta do anything for ye. Ya know that."

Sabine cleared her throat, suddenly a bit nervous. "You know I was a set dresser for the theaters in New Orleans—"

"Aye!" Gwen came over with her own coffee cup and scooped in a few teaspoons of sugar. "Alden showed me a few of them you'd won awards for. Some of those before and after pictures showing how ye built and decorated those sets. Well, they were just gorgeous. I had no idea that could even be done."

Sabine smiled and thanked her, secretly basking in the praise. "I've been following a job listing on the Aberdeen City Council website, and now that I'll be an actual citizen, I could apply as a council housing officer, but in a specialized position. I'd be responsible for fund-raising to enable the city to improve the interiors of the council houses for people on housing assistance in the city." She paused to take a sip of coffee and smiled at Alden. "I'd have a budget already in place I could start with, of course, and I'd love to use it to improve the flats, much like a theater set, and make them as nice as possible, so the people that live there have better spaces to raise their kids." She paused, taking a sip of her coffee. "I know Alden mentioned that you've worked with the city in the past, so I was wondering if I could use you as a reference?"

Alden put down her pen and smiled as her mam nodded. "I literally can't think of a more perfect person for the position." She leaned forward as if she was spilling classified information. "And I happen to know the hiring chairwoman. Go ahead and complete the online application, and I'll call her personally tomorrow."

"I was hoping you'd say that." Sabine smiled. "The position doesn't start until February, but I submitted the application yesterday."

Alden nodded in the direction of the door. "The chairwoman she just mentioned has been mam's best mate since I was a kid. In fact, she still lives one street above us, and mam goes up there for tea and a catch-up most afternoons." Alden stacked her papers and slipped them back into her folder with a wink in Sabine's direction. "I'd say your chances are excellent."

A phone started ringing, and all three of them looked around, but there wasn't one in sight. It wasn't until Sabine noticed her leg was vibrating that she realized it was hers. She looked at the caller ID and excused herself to go to the greenhouse, her stomach twisting in a now-familiar knot.

"Hey, Colette." She made a spot to sit on a bench between a flowering chamomile vine and a violet proudly overflowing an empty glass milk jug. The air was damp and humid, and smelled like sweet summer soil. Sabine brought the phone back to her ear. "What's going on? How are the kids?"

There was a pause, then Colette's voice, barely audible above the noise in the background. "You're in Muir Rothesay, right?

"Yep. In the Highlands. Are you trying to send me something? You know I said not to bother with Christmas presents."

"Christmas is the last thing on my mind," Colette said. "But I'll tell you all about what is when you get here. I'm at the Muir Rothesay train station with the boys."

❖

"Babe, are you okay?" Alden threw the truck into reverse and backed out of the drive. "You look like you might pass out."

Sabine just stared straight ahead. Whatever the reason her sister was here out of the blue, especially with the boys in tow, it wasn't going to be good.

"I knew life was going a little too smoothly." She reached out and braced herself on the dash. "I mean, I'm super happy to see them, but I just have a knife in the pit of my stomach." Sabine felt her mouth drop open as Alden turned to go down the hill toward town and clapped her hand over it. "And what the hell am I going to say about the fact that our mother isn't my mother?"

Alden pulled the truck over and pulled both of Sabine's cold hands into hers. Suddenly, Sabine felt fragile, overwhelmed, like she was clinging to a rock on the shore with the sea wind blowing her in all directions.

"Look at me." Alden's voice was honey-coated, soft and soothing. She waited until Sabine looked up. "All you have to do is hug your sister. Everything else we'll do together, okay? I'm going to drive us to the train station, and you'll walk in and hug Colette. And we'll take it from there together."

"Okay." Sabine's cheeks warmed with just a bit of heat, and she almost smiled. "I can do that."

"I mean it." Alden veered back onto the road, slowing for a pack of schoolkids on bicycles. "There really is nothing to worry about except the one obvious thing."

"Oh, shit." Sabine glanced at her phone and then over to Alden. "What else could there be?"

"Does your sister know I haven't had seat belts since 2002?"

Sabine dropped her head into her hands. "Fucking hell. Unless you brought a flask, Colette the Supermom is going to drop dead of a heart attack."

Alden turned into the train-station parking lot and popped the glove box with the heel of her hand. A stainless-steel flask dropped unceremoniously onto Sabine's lap, and Alden winked. "At your service, ma'am."

As they approached the open front of the train station, Sabine spotted her sister, sitting in one of the plastic row chairs with Fletcher, her two-year-old. He was playing contentedly with a bag of crisps while his mother slowly rubbed her temples with her fingertips. A crumbling tower of bags threatened to topple over beside her.

"Colette?" Sabine watched as she raised her head, then ran the short distance to hug her. Sabine clung to her for a long moment before it occurred to her to finally pick up her nephew, who looked delighted to see his favorite "Annie Sabby" again. He clapped his chubby hands together and enthusiastically thrust his packet of crisps toward her.

"Where's Thomas?" Sabine looked around for her other nephew and realized at the same time that she'd forgotten to introduce Alden.

"Hi, there." Alden offered her hand to Colette. "I'm Alden Wallace. Delighted to meet ye, finally."

"I'm so sorry!" Sabine shook her head and sighed. "My brain's scrambled at the minute."

Alden put her arm around Sabine's shoulder and pulled her into a hug as Colette looked Alden up and down.

"Wow." Subtlety had never been a part of Colette's social toolbox, and Sabine knew today would be no different. "You look like one of those sexy Scottish pirates. Think you can give my husband some pointers?"

Sabine covered her face with her hands as Alden threw back her head and laughed, the sound instantly warming the chill in the air. "That is officially the best compliment I've ever received."

A lanky ten-year-old walked up beside them and gave Sabine a half-hearted side hug. "What's with Scotland that none of the vending machines work? I haven't eaten since Atlanta. I may starve standing right here."

"Alden." Sabine wrapped an arm around him. "This is my other nephew, Thomas. He's ten."

"Hey, man," Alden said to Thomas, pointing to a little café in the corner of the train station with warm light spilling out onto the bistro tables. "That place over there is Butler's Chocolate, and they have the best hot chocolate in the world, plus tons of pastries. Some of 'em even have ham and stuff."

Fletcher reached out for Alden as if on cue, and Alden laughed as she took him and settled him on her hip. "If it's okay with yer mom, I can take you guys over there and get ye all sugared up with some snacks." Thomas looked instantly thrilled and nodded. "We'll sit outside at those tables so you can keep your eye on her."

"Finally. Proof of a benevolent god." Collette sighed with relief and reached for her purse.

"Don't be silly." Alden waved her gesture away and headed toward the café with the boys. "Take your time. They've got enough amazing food to keep us busy for ages."

"I don't have a clue what the hell she just said, but…damn." Colette settled back into the chairs beside her and watched Alden walk away. "She's a keeper."

"That's the truth." A weight settled onto Sabine's chest, and she turned to look at her sister. Colette, who already had tears in her eyes, reached for her hand.

When they were little girls, Colette would wake Sabine up to crawl out her bedroom window and lie on the roof where the stars were the brightest. Mostly it was when their mother was drunk and screaming about something downstairs. The second they crawled out there and shut the window, everything fell silent, and the scary things just floated away with the noise. Sabine never forgot how it felt to be able to breathe again the second the silence settled.

"Just tell me," Sabine said, focusing on the chrome railroad clock hung on the wall across the waiting room. The second hand jerked slightly every time it ticked forward, and an incoming train's brakes screamed against the iron rails in the background. "I can take it."

Sabine looked across at her sister. Colette's cheeks were already wet. Colette swiped at them with her sweater sleeve but didn't look back at her.

"She's gone."

Sabine nodded and turned back to the clock. "When?"

"Three days ago." Colette's voice caught in her throat. "I didn't want to tell you over the phone." She straightened her shoulders as people streamed past them, hurrying to board the next train to Aberdeen.

Sabine nodded and squeezed Colette's hand.

They both caught sight of Thomas at the same moment, walking toward them in Alden's waxed jacket, which reached almost to his knees, and carrying two takeaway mugs. He stared intently at the cups in his hands as he walked and seemed relieved when he finally reached them, glancing back over his shoulder at Alden.

"Hey, buddy." Sabine smiled, taking both cups from him and handing one to her sister. "What are these?"

"They're both hot chocolate with extra whipped cream." He smiled. "And extra sprinkles."

Thomas started to turn around, then pulled a neat, folded handkerchief out of the pocket of the jacket and handed it to his mother. "Alden also said to give you this."

Colette took it, and they both looked over to Alden, who was laughing at Fletcher as he sat on her lap waving a croissant around like a victory flag.

"I like him," Thomas said. "He's cool."

"I'm so glad," Sabine said, taking the lid off her hot chocolate and blowing on it. "But Alden is actually my girlfriend."

"Yeah. I guess I should ask what pronouns they like. But either way, they're cool." Thomas took off to run across the station and back to the café.

"Kids are so amazing." Colette said. "Any adult would have gotten all awkward, and he handled that like a pro."

"I need to know how it happened." Sabine felt a wave of guilt that she wasn't crying, yet she didn't feel anything except the twenty-pound weight on her chest. "But I understand if it's too much right now."

"No. It's okay. I'd feel the same way." Colette sat up straighter and crumpled Alden's handkerchief in her hand. "She got drunk, took an overdose, and wrapped her car around a light post at sixty miles an hour."

"Holy shit." Sabine shook her head, glancing toward the ceiling. "I'm sorry I asked."

"The power lines went down, and half of the ninth ward didn't have power or heat for six hours." Colette's voice was soaked with anger. "In December."

Sabine nodded, then looked down at the haphazard pile of luggage. "Where's James?"

"God. If I ever doubted that I married the right man, this whole fucking situation is proof I did." She sniffed, staring at Alden's initials embroidered on the hanky in her hand. "He came home from a business trip the second I called, bought me and the kids tickets to Glasgow, and told me to pack. He said the least he could do was clean up the mess she left in New Orleans without me having to be there." She looked over at Sabine. "He just said he wanted us to be together and not have to deal with it."

Sabine smiled. "I love James almost as much as Thea did. I have a feeling he and Alden would like each other."

"Well, if it's okay with you, he's taking charge of settling her affairs and overseeing the funeral arrangements. Then he's taking some time off work and joining us. He should be here in a few days."

"Tell me there's not an actual funeral?" Sabine shook her head, trying to stave off the headache lurking like a storm cloud behind her eyes. "All of New Orleans must hate us after what she did. We're just lucky no one else was killed."

"I wouldn't blame them, but at least when I left, her name hadn't come out in the papers yet." She paused. "Sometimes I want to do what you did. Just get the hell out of New Orleans." She dropped her head back to look at the ceiling. "She didn't leave a will. Can you believe that?"

"Are you kidding? Of course I can." Sabine hesitated. Her sister already looked close to the edge. "Is James arranging for cremation?"

"Yeah. He says he'll make sure her ashes go beside Daddy. He bought that plot for them ages ago, so at least that part is easy."

Sabine nodded, the weight of her secret bearing down on her shoulders. But now was not the time.

They sat there for a few minutes in silence, watching Thomas and Fletcher chattering to Alden across the station. Trains came and went, and dozens of people walked past with bags, magazines, and steaming cups of coffee to go wherever people go. When Thea died, Sabine had looked down at the street from her window and wanted to scream at everyone for going about their daily lives like the world hadn't changed forever. Now it was actually comforting that they were.

"Excuse me."

Sabine and Colette looked up together, snapped back to reality by the same voice.

"I'm Morgan Wallace, Alden's father." Morgan's wavy silver hair fell around his shoulders as he squatted to eye level with them and went on, his voice low and soothing. "Ye must be Sabine's sister. I don't want to bother you two, but Alden called me and told me what happened. She thought ye might want me to start the fires on a slow burn in the lighthouse, so it feels like home when ya get there."

"Oh, God. I didn't even think about that. I'm sure it's freezing in there." Sabine dug her keys out of her jacket pocket and handed them over. "Thank you, Morgan. That's incredibly thoughtful."

"Nonsense. Ye shouldn't have to think about things like that right now. I'll take whatever luggage you think ya might not need to get into as well, just so it's out of yer way. It'll be in the lighthouse when you get there."

"Thank you." Colette dried her eyes and stuck out her hand. "I'm Colette, Sabine's sister, and those are my two boys over there with Alden." She pointed at the three of them across the station.

"Oh, sweet Jesus." Morgan shook his head, a wide smile lighting up his face like sudden sunlight. "Ye just wait until I tell my wife, Gwen. No one loves having wee ones around more than her. She'll be absolutely thrilled." He stood up and waved to Alden and the boys, then turned back to Colette. "Now, Gwen is making cranberry-cordial pancakes with rosemary syrup and bacon butties for brunch. No pressure, of course, but we'd love to have everyone over to our house. Just ta warm ye up a little. It takes a good few hours for those woodstoves to catch up in Sabine's lighthouse, and she stayed with us last night."

"That's so kind. We'd love to, actually, if you're sure it's not a bother."

"Are ye jokin'?" Morgan waved Alden and the boys over and picked up the two biggest suitcases with a wink in Colette's direction. "I'm afraid fer me life if I come home without ye. Alden told her what happened, and Gwen can't stand the thought of you up here when you should be relaxin' wit' her pancakes."

Colette smiled, and the color rushed back to her face for the first time. Alden and the boys came back, and Fletcher reached for his mom, chattering about the croissant, while Morgan introduced himself to Thomas.

"Thomas, if it's okay wit' you, Alden's mam is making a big brunch at our house, and I thought ye might want to join us wit' yer mother and yer brother?" Morgan smiled as Thomas nodded enthusiastically, and the two of them joined Alden in getting the suitcases organized and carried out of the station.

"God, you know I was dying to see you, of course." Colette dried the last of her tears and picked up her purse from the chair. "But I was dreading getting here because everything seemed so overwhelming. Those two have made everything better already, and I literally just met them."

"Oh, you have no idea." Sabine smiled. "Remember when I almost froze to death my first night here?"

"How could I forget? It took you long enough to tell me. That was horrifying, thank you very much."

"Well, I spent the night at their house that night and felt instantly at home. I can't explain it, although it doesn't hurt that Alden's parents are both psychologists. Morgan is retired now and runs a pub in town." They walked through the arches and out of the station, and Morgan opened the door to Gwen's comfortable car, already heated up and ready to go.

"Make yourself comfortable, ladies. Gwen insisted I bring her car with seat belts so ye didn't have to ride home like savages in my rig." He laughed. "And that's a quote."

He went with Alden to put all the luggage in in her truck and took off in it, leaving tire tracks woven into the snow. Alden slid in the driver's seat of Gwen's car and pulled a cap over her hair, winding the length of it around some leather at the base of her neck. "Ready? I've got an extra seat belt here if anyone needs one."

CHAPTER TWENTY-TWO

Twenty minutes later, everyone was sitting around the table at the Wallace house, and Gwen was dishing up her pancakes with a stack of toasted bacon sandwiches and a beautiful winter fruit salad with clotted cream to pour over the top. A crackling fire danced in the wide stone fireplace to the right, and there was even an old bassett hound in the corner, snoring. Apparently, according to a phone call to Gwen from the neighbor, she had a houseful of guests, and Betsy the dog was less than thrilled at the noise. She'd wandered over for some peace and quiet, which turned out to be perfect for Fletcher; they'd bonded instantly, like they'd known each other all their lives.

Sabine noticed the empty chair at the end and looked down the table to Gwen. "Where's Declan?"

"He'll be another five minutes or so. He had an online quiz with his tutor, but the time is nearly up."

Thomas looked up from admiring his pancakes. "Who's Declan?"

Gwen pulled a rubber-coated baby spoon out of the drawer and handed it to Colette. "He's my grandson, but he lives here with us. Something tells me you two are just what the doctor ordered for each other."

"He's the one I was telling you about," Colette said, pointing to the napkin still beside his plate. "Alden's nephew." She raised an eyebrow, and he gave in, picking it up and smoothing it over his lap.

Once everything was dished up, Alden settled in beside her dad and Thomas, and Gwen squeezed in at the other end beside Sabine and Colette. She didn't bat an eye when Fletcher reached over to sit in her lap.

"I'm sorry," Colette said, putting down her fork with a worried expression. "He just loves you. I'll take him so you can eat."

"Nonsense." Gwen gave Fletcher a beaming smile and a slice of strawberry from her plate. "I couldn't be happier." She nodded in the direction of Thomas, who was happily chatting with Alden. "Fletcher's so young, bless him." She lowered her voice to a whisper. "But how's your Thomas doing with all of this? He's had a lot of loss in a short amount of time."

"Honestly, it's been hard for him because he's so worried about me. Living with our mom next door to us has been hell the last few months. She just went off the rails. My husband has been wonderful, but I wish life would calm down for a while so the boys could just be kids."

"There he is!" Morgan's booming voice announced Declan coming down the stairs before he even rounded the corner. "I'd know that clatter anywhere."

Declan stopped short as he caught sight of everyone around the table, and he looked back up the stairs as if contemplating a hasty exit. Thomas waved to get his attention and signed. *Hi. I'm Thomas, Sabine's nephew. Are you Declan?*

"Thomas, that's wonderful," Colette said, her fork poised in the air, "but please remember to speak as you sign."

A slow smile spread across Declan's face as he nodded to Thomas and pushed up the sleeves of his rugby shirt. *You sign?*

Yup. Thomas spoke and signed. *Sabine and Thea taught me. She was deaf and lived across the street from me my whole life.*

Declan plunked himself down in the empty chair beside Thomas, signing happily at a breakneck pace while Morgan filled his plate. Morgan smiled down the table at Gwen, who was obviously trying her best not to get emotional watching Declan make a friend he could actually talk to.

"Of course, it makes sense that he would, but it hadn't occurred to me that your Thomas knew sign language." Gwen smiled, laying a hand over her heart as she watched them, so busy talking they'd forgotten to even touch their food. "Look at that smile on our Declan. I haven't seen him like that since the first day Sabine started signing to him at this very table."

"It's just as good for Thomas." Colette smiled down the table at him. "He's been pretty withdrawn lately. He's had school, of course, but he hasn't been able to have friends over for a long time because of Celestine. She was pretty out of control at the end, and it didn't seem like a good idea."

"Mom." Thomas turned to her, remembering to speak as he signed. *"Declan wants to show me his computer. He has that sign-translation program on it. Can I go see?"*

Colette put down her fork to free up her hands to sign. *"Why don't you both eat your food, and then if it's okay with Gwen, you guys can go play."*

Fletcher patted Gwen's arm with his chubby little hand and made the "eat" sign, putting his fingers to his mouth with a pointed glance at the pancakes on her plate, which Gwen promptly declared was the cutest thing she'd ever seen. Declan and Thomas somehow managed to talk and eat at the same time, each looking animated and happy as they dug into their bacon butties.

Gwen fed him another bite of pancake and looked over to Colette. "How are you coping with everything, Colette? I can't imagine what this has been like for you."

"I feel so guilty." Sabine cut in with a sigh. "I should've been there to make it easier. I can't believe all this happened without me there to help."

"Are you kidding?" Colette turned in her chair to look her in the eyes as she reached for her hands. "When you left, I finally realized I didn't want my kids to grow up watching her self-destruct like we had to."

"Really?"

"Yes. You did exactly the right thing." She pulled Sabine in for a hug. "At exactly the right time."

Betsy the basset let loose with a loud groan and turned over in her sleep. Everyone laughed, including Declan, because Thomas signed to him what was happening.

The rest of the day flew by, and by the time she'd finally gotten to show her sister the lighthouse, late afternoon was fading into twilight and the sunset was putting on a vibrant, cranberry-tinted display for Colette. Fletcher was napping on the sofa, wrapped up in one of the wool throws, and Thomas had convinced his mother to let him stay overnight with Declan, so he was still at the Wallace house.

When they'd walked in, the entire house was toasty warm, and Morgan had even delivered a couple of kids' camping cots piled with extra blankets. Colette wandered over to the window and stared at the waves breaking on the rocks below. "I can see why this place has been so good for you." She turned around, accepting the glass of sauvignon blanc Sabine offered her. "Did I tell you there was a shooting at the high school in Metairie last week?"

"What?" Sabine put her glass down and leaned against the counter. "That's like ten miles from your house."

"Exactly." She turned back to the window. "And I've been thinking that the memories there are just too heavy. I look across the street and see Thea's house, and having Mom and Dad's house right next door, empty..." She sighed. "Is it crazy to think I might be done with New Orleans too?"

"Hell, no. You've got way more reasons than I did to get the hell out of there, and James is from Manhattan, so he's always hated it. Are you worried about having the kids in school there?"

"Yeah, of course. It keeps James and me both up at night. Thomas will be in high school in three years, and we could put him in private school, but there's no guarantee that a shooting wouldn't happen there either."

Colette's phone pinged, and she pulled it out of her pocket. She read the text and started rubbing her forehead, a dead giveaway when she was feeling overwhelmed.

"Everything okay?" Sabine pulled two of the kitchen stools over to the window so Colette could watch the last of the sunset. "What's going on?

"James said he's sending some presents here for the boys just in case, but he wants to know what to do with all the Christmas presents we already have hidden in the house for the boys. Mom started really going off the rails in December, so we told the boys if they could wait just a couple of months, we'd do an extra special Christmas anywhere they wanted to go." Colette looked up, her eyes red. "I haven't even thought about it since all this happened."

Sabine took the phone out of her hand. "Why don't all of you have Christmas here with us? Gwen will be thrilled, and I know she'd love to help us make it special for the boys."

"I don't want to impose. It's not fair to just dump our entire family on you."

Sabine rolled her eyes. "First of all, have the boys ever even had a white Christmas?"

"No, but..."

"And when James gets here, you guys can have the whole place to yourselves. I'll just stay with Alden at her house. I'm over there every day anyway." Raising one eyebrow, she looked at her sister. It took a few seconds, but Colette finally smiled and nodded.

"Fine. It's settled. Let me see what your handsome hubby thinks." Sabine let her fingers fly over the keyboard of her sister's phone. "Then he can just have the presents shipped and get his ass over here."

Both of them jumped when Colette's phone rang. Sabine handed it over, and Colette put it on speakerphone.

"Hey, gorgeous," James said. "How are the kids?"

Colette brightened. "Baby, they're so happy here. Thomas and Declan had an instant bromance, of course, and the baby is just in heaven with all the food and cuddles." She smiled up at Sabine. "And I'm doing better. Just being out of New Orleans helps. You're on speakerphone, by the way."

"Hi, Sabine," James said, a smile in his voice. "Are you serious about having our late catch-up Christmas at your house? I'm only asking to be polite, 'cause we're all staying whether you like it or not."

"I'd love nothing more." Sabine said, squeezing her sister's hand. "Now get your ass over here."

"Really, James?" Colette said excitedly, leaning forward on her stool and holding the phone between them. "Are you being serious? Because that would make the boys so happy."

"My love, anything that makes the three of you happy is *exactly* what we're going to do. I'll get my secretary to ship all the gifts, and I fly out to Glasgow tomorrow morning. Goldman Sachs has a branch office in Glasgow, so I can just arrange to use one of their company cars." He paused. "And Sabine, start working on getting your sister to let me transfer to the Glasgow office. I can have that done in a heartbeat. Anything to get the hell out of New Orleans."

Colette laughed, then clicked off the speakerphone and finished tying up the details with her husband. She turned around to Sabine, who was topping off both their glasses and paused, studying her face.

"Uh-oh," Colette said, taking a sip of her wine. "You look worried. I see that little wrinkle in your forehead that you get when you're stressed."

"Colette," Sabine said, pointing down to a dolphin showing off near the shore. "You might want to drink that wine. I need to tell you something."

CHAPTER TWENTY-THREE

M organ?"
Sabine pushed open the door to the Wallace house and stepped inside, listening to the strangely silent home as she walked down the hall. It was late afternoon, and Morgan had called to get her help with something, but everyone else seemed to be MIA. With her sister and the boys still in town, usually her phone was buzzing with texts, but today Colette and even Alden had been strangely quiet. She'd grown close to her father as well over the last few months, and she'd texted him earlier to see if he wanted to go out to lunch, but he'd never responded.

She took a cookie off a saucer on the kitchen counter and bit into it, muttering to herself. "Where the heck is everybody?"

"Right on time, I see." Morgan strode into the kitchen, already shrugging on his coat as he picked his keys up off the counter. "Ready?"

They were about five minutes out of town and headed toward the countryside before Sabine remembered to ask where they were going. "You're being awfully mysterious about what you wanted help with. I'm starting to think you have something up your sleeve."

"I certainly do have something up my sleeve, and frankly, I'm offended that ye ever thought otherwise." Morgan shot her a smile as he veered off the main road to follow what was little more than a worn path straight up an imposing hill. One glance to the right told her that the hill became a sheer cliff that plunged to the ocean, as if lightning had split it in two and half had perished in the sea. The snow was patchy, thank God, but she still felt like careening backward and landing in the ocean was a distinct possibility. The hill turned out to be not quite as tall as it looked from the bottom, and they reached the top mercifully quickly, coming to a stop just under a plateau she imagined must look down over the sea. A small footpath led up to the flat area above, which looked grassy and windswept from where they were parked.

Morgan looked over to her and tapped the steering wheel with his thumb. "This is where I leave you, love."

Sabine looked around them and saw nothing but Scottish grasses swaying above patchy snow, the wide, deeply blue sky and the ocean below that was crashing into the cliff they'd just climbed. "You're leaving me here alone?"

"You're not alone." Morgan smiled and pointed to the plateau. "Just crest the top there, and you'll see."

"You're lucky I trust you," Sabine said with a smile as she got out of Morgan's truck, reluctantly waving good-bye as she watched him make his way back down the hill.

The wind whipped up the cliff from the ocean, a cold rush of seawater freshness. Snow tufts clung to the grass as she followed a narrow, worn path up to the plateau, turning to glance back down the mountain at the red glow of Morgan's disappearing taillights. She pulled her overcoat around her more tightly, suddenly glad she'd decided on the thick, emerald turtleneck underneath.

She reached the edge of the plateau and walked across it, turning slowly to look around her, but saw nothing. Just one massive flat stone near the edge, topped by another larger and rather precarious-looking stone circle with a wide opening in the center. She traced the edge of the circle with her hand, searching for an inscription or a brass plaque to tell her what it was and why it was placed here, by itself, overlooking the sea.

Sudden footsteps made her turn around to see Alden walking up from the opposite side of the plateau, her dark hair loose and wild, the wind tossing it around her face. She was wearing a kilt of vibrant scarlet, yellow, and black tartan plaid, with a black wool sweater edged in leather. Her shoulders were broad and gorgeous, and she looked like a medieval Scottish hero striding across the plateau. Sabine wanted to freeze the moment in time, memorizing every detail as Alden grew closer, so she could have it forever.

Alden ran the last few steps to reach her, then swept her up in her arms and lifted her off the ground, kissing her slowly while the wind whipped around them, and the seagulls swooped overhead and called to each other as they made their way to the ocean. They were the only two people in the world as Alden let her slip slowly back down to the ground, then walked around to the other side of the circular stone.

She took a knife out of the small black leather pouch around her hips, then pulled up a scrap of fabric, about five inches square, from inside the waistband of the kilt. Sabine watched her as a peregrine glided over the cliff's edge, then swooped straight up and over their heads.

Sabine smiled. "Is this the Wallace tartan I've heard so much about?"

"Yes, ma'am." Alden sliced the top of the tartan fabric square and pulled it away from her kilt. "Do you remember when you saw that diamond ring and thought I was engaged?"

Sabine nodded, pulling her coat tighter against the wind and holding her hair over one shoulder with her hand. "Yes, and you told me you never would have proposed with a ring like that—"

Her words faded away as Alden pulled a solid-gold, etched band out of the leather pouch. Suddenly it dawned on her what it was, and the wind stole her breath as she covered her mouth

• 253 •

with her hand. She looked up, tears already shimmering in her eyes.

Alden smiled, reaching through the stone circle between them to hold Sabine's face in her hand. "That's because our family has proposed with this ring for the last three hundred years." She turned it in her fingers. "The Wallace Clan crest is etched around it, and it's been reworked and strengthened several times over the centuries, but no one who has ever worn it has ever been divorced."

She smiled, brushing her thumb over Sabine's cheek before she pulled her hand back through the circle. "It's offered from one side of this marriage stone and accepted from the other for the tradition to be complete, and if you say yes, this piece of my kilt will be sewn into your wedding dress." She placed the ring on the tartan square and held it in the center of the stone circle, her dark eyes soft and intense. "Sabine, I've been in love with you from the day we met, and I promise to love you with every breath of this life and beyond." She paused, her voice cracking with emotion. "Will you marry me?"

Sabine extended her left hand through the circle, and a tear dropped down Alden's cheek as she slid the ring onto her finger. It was a perfect fit.

Alden ran around the stone and kissed her, the waves crashing beneath them at the bottom of the sheer cliff that dropped off the plateau. They stood there, wrapped in each other's arms, for what seemed like forever, until Sabine pulled back with a slightly worried look.

"Oh, no." She looked around at the empty plateau. "We don't have to walk back, do we?"

Alden laughed, the sound weaving itself into the wind as if it had always been there. "No, and it's a good thing since both our families, and literally half the town, is waiting with your da at Carthington Manor to celebrate with us. I was there yesterday to go over the details, and I've literally never seen so many cases of French champagne. He's been so anxious about getting everything just right for his daughter's engagement party." She smiled and pointed to the other side of the hill. "Jolene is parked on the other side just out of sight."

Alden took Sabine's hand and kissed it as they walked toward the opposite side of the plateau. "I know you must wish you could tell your mother you're engaged, but I have a feeling"—Alden paused and looked slowly around the windswept landscape— "that she was here with us."

"She was here." Sabine leaned into Alden's arms and closed her eyes, relaxing into the warmth she felt all around them. "And she knew here was exactly where I needed to be."

About the Author

Patricia Evans is currently writing your new favorite novel in her hand-built tiny house, nestled deep in the forest, where she's surrounded by a bevy of raccoons and a sleepy brown bear named Waddles.

She travels to Ireland and Scotland several times a year in search of the perfect whiskey and cigar combination and spends most of her time trying to ignore the characters from her books that boss her around as she writes by the fire.

Follow her adventures on Instagram: @tomboyinkslinger and at her website: www.tomboyinkslinger.com.

Books Available from Bold Strokes Books

Hands of the Morri by Heather K O'Malley. Discovering she is a Lost Sister and growing acquainted with her new body, Asche learns how to be a warrior and commune with the Goddess the Hands serve, the Morri. (978-1-63679-465-5)

I Know About You by Erin Kaste. With her stalker inching closer to the truth, Cary Smith is forced to face the past she's tried desperately to forget. (978-1-63679-513-3)

Mate of Her Own by Elena Abbott. When Heather McKenna finally confronts the family who cursed her, her werewolf is shocked to discover her one true mate, and that's only the beginning. (978-1-63679-481-5)

Pumpkin Spice by Tagan Shepard. For Nicki, new love is making this pumpkin spice season sweeter than expected. (978-1-63679-388-7)

Rivals for Love by Ali Vali. Brooks Boseman's brother Curtis is getting married, and Brooks needs to be at the engagement party. Only she can't possibly go, not with Curtis set to marry the secret love of her youth, Fallon Goodwin. (978-1-63679-384-9)

Sweat Equity by Aurora Rey. When cheesemaker Sy Travino takes a job in rural Vermont and hires contractor Maddie Barrow to rehab a house she buys sight unseen, they both wind up with a lot more than they bargained for. (978-1-63679-487-7)

Taking the Plunge by Amanda Radley. When Regina Avery meets model Grace Holland—the most beautiful woman she's ever seen—she doesn't have a clue how to flirt, date, or hold on to a relationship. But Regina must take the plunge with Grace and hope she manages to swim. (978-1-63679-400-6)

We Met in a Bar by Claire Forsythe. Wealthy nightclub owner Erica turns undercover bartender on a mission to catch a thief where she meets no-strings, no-commitments Charlie, who couldn't be further from Erica's type. Right? (978-1-63679-521-8)

Western Blue by Suzie Clarke. Step back in time to this historic western filled with heroism, loyalty, friendship, and love. The odds are against this unlikely group—but never underestimate women who have nothing to lose. (978-1-63679-095-4)

Windswept by Patricia Evans. The windswept shores of the Scottish Highlands weave magic for two people convinced they'd never fall in love again. (978-1-63679-382-5)

An Independent Woman by Kit Meredith. Alex and Rebecca's attraction won't stop smoldering, despite their reluctance to act on it and incompatible poly relationship styles. (978-1-63679-553-9)

Cherish by Kris Bryant. Josie and Olivia cherish the time spent together, but when the summer ends and their temporary romance melts into the real deal, reality gets complicated. (978-1-63679-567-6)

Cold Case Heat by Mary P. Burns. Sydney Hansen receives a threat in a very cold murder case that sends her to the police for help where she finds more than justice with Detective Gale Sterling. (978-1-63679-374-0)

Proximity by Jordan Meadows. Joan really likes Ellie, but being alone with her could turn deadly unless she can keep her dangerous powers under control. (978-1-63679-476-1)

Sweet Spot by Kimberly Cooper Griffin. Pro surfer Shia Turning will have to take a chance if she wants to find the sweet spot. (978-1-63679-418-1)

The Haunting of Oak Springs by Crin Claxton. Ghosts and the past haunt the supernatural detective in a race to save the lesbians of Oak Springs farm. (978-1-63679-432-7)

Transitory by J.M. Redmann. The cops blow it off as a customer surprised by what was under the dress, but PI Micky Knight knows they're wrong—she either makes it her case or lets a murderer go free to kill again. (978-1-63679-251-4)

Unexpectedly Yours by Toni Logan. A private resort on a tropical island, a feisty old chief, and a kleptomaniac pet pig bring Suzanne and Allie together for unexpected love. (978-1-63679-160-9)

Bones of Boothbay Harbor by Michelle Larkin. Small-town police chief Frankie Stone and FBI Special Agent Eve Huxley must set aside their differences and combine their skills to find a killer after a burial site is discovered in Boothbay Harbor, Maine. (978-1-63679-267-5)

Crush by Ana Hartnett Reichardt. Josie Sanchez worked for years for the opportunity to create her own wine label, and nothing will stand in her way. Not even Mac, the owner's annoyingly beautiful niece Josie's forced to hire as her harvest intern. (978-1-63679-330-6)

Decadence by Ronica Black, Renee Roman, and Piper Jordan. You are cordially invited to Decadence, Las Vegas's most talked about invitation-only Masquerade Ball. Come for the entertainment and stay for the erotic indulgence. We guarantee it'll be a party that lives up to its name. (978-1-63679-361-0)

Gimmicks and Glamour by Lauren Melissa Ellzey. Ashly has learned to hide her Sight, but as she speeds toward high school graduation she must protect the classmates she claims to hate from an evil that no one else sees. (978-1-63679-401-3)

Heart of Stone by Sam Ledel. Princess Keeva Glantor meets Maeve, a gorgon forced to live alone thanks to a decades-old lie, and together the two women battle forces they formerly thought to be good in the hopes of leading lives they can finally call their own. (978-1-63679-407-5)

Murder at the Oasis by David S. Pederson. Palm trees, sunshine, and murder await Mason Adler and his friend Walter as they travel from Phoenix to Palm Springs for what was supposed to be a relaxing vacation but ends up being a trip of mystery and intrigue. (978-1-63679-416-7)

Peaches and Cream by Georgia Beers. Adley Purcell is living her dreams owning Get the Scoop ice cream shop until national dessert chain Sweet Heaven opens less than two blocks away and Adley has to compete with the far too heavenly Sabrina James. (978-1-63679-412-9)

The Only Fish in the Sea by Angie Williams. Will love overcome years of bitter rivalry for the daughters of two crab fishing families in this queer modern-day spin on Romeo and Juliet? (978-1-63679-444-0)

Wildflower by Cathleen Collins. When a plane crash leaves eleven-year-old Lily Andrews stranded in the vast wilderness of Arkansas, will she be able to overcome the odds and make it back to civilization and the one person who holds the key to her future? (978-1-63679-621-5)

Witch Finder by Sheri Lewis Wohl. Tamsin, the Keeper of the Book of Darkness, is in terrible danger, and as a Witch Finder, Morrigan must protect her and the secrets she guards even if it costs Morrigan her life. (978-1-63679-335-1)

A Second Chance at Life by Genevieve McCluer. Vampires Dinah and Rachel reconnect, but a string of vampire killings begin and evidence seems to be pointing at Dinah. They must prove her innocence while finding out if the two of them are still compatible after all these years. (978-1-63679-459-4)

Digging for Heaven by Jenna Jarvis. Litz lives for dragons. Kella lives to kill them. The last thing they expect is to find each other attractive. (978-1-63679-453-2)

Forever's Promise by Missouri Vaun. Wesley Holden migrated west disguised as a man for the hope of a better life and with no designs to take a wife, but Charlotte Rose has other ideas. (978-1-63679-221-7)

Here For You by D. Jackson Leigh. A horse trainer must make a difficult business decision that could save her father's ranch from foreclosure but destroy her chance to win the heart of a feisty barrel racer vying for a spot in the National Rodeo Finals. (978-1-63679-299-6)

I Do, I Don't by Joy Argento. Creator of the romance algorithm, Nicole Hart doesn't expect to be starring in her own reality TV dating show, and falling for the show's executive producer Annie Jackson could ruin everything. (978-1-63679-420-4)

It's All in the Details by Dena Blake. Makeup artist Lane Donnelly and wedding planner Helen Trent can't stand each other, but they must set aside their differences to ensure Darcy gets the wedding of her dreams, and make a few of their own dreams come true. (978-1-63679-430-3)

Marigold by Melissa Brayden. Marigold Lavender vows to take down Alexis Wakefield, the harsh food critic who blasts her younger sister's restaurant. If only she wasn't as sexy as she is mean. (978-1-63679-436-5)

The Town that Built Us by Jesse J. Thoma. When her father dies, Grace Cook returns to her hometown and tries to avoid Bonnie Whitlock, the woman who pulverized her heart, only to discover her father's estate has been left to them jointly. (978-1-63679-439-6)